Magnuscarter

A Bill Reyner Mystery Adventure

Wentworth M. Johnson

Published by New Generation Publishing in 2013

Copyright © Wentworth M. Johnson 2013

First Edition

www.newgeneration-publishing.com

 New Generation Publishing

This book is dedicated to
Andrew Clive Johnson

Chapter 1

The Legend

Some say that King John of England, Duke Normandy and Aquitaine, known as Lackland, was a bad king. Like most things in ancient history it is only a matter of opinion and of course who wrote the history. Either way, the Magna Carta and the unusual death of the king are well-documented facts.

To stir up trade and keep an eye on his magistrates, King John spent most of his life on the move, stopping only to throw huge parties. The wine, and beer consumed at these parties and the utensils used, created work and helped to maintain a busy commerce for the local inhabitants. A large entourage of troops, camp followers and even governing officials travelled with the king and partook of his generosity.

In October of the year 1216, the king's entourage moved from Yarmouth in Norfolk England and eventually finished up in what was then called Bishop's Lynn, where another slap-up shindig was held. Bishop's Lynn stood on the edge of a tidal swamp known as the Great Lavar; today it is called the Wash and to reach Lincoln the often dangerous Wash had to be crossed. The night before the intended crossing King John overindulged – as was usually his way, but this time on peaches and new cider. Needless to say he became very sick.

In the thirteenth century both medicine and hygiene were unheard of. The local practitioner of doctoring and the king's advisor could do nothing for the king, whose health rapidly deteriorated. The decision was made to move the ailing monarch by boat up the swampy river to Wisbech and then by land to Newark near present-day Peterborough. A day or so after King John had left for higher ground, the leading military officer made the decision to move the entourage across the tidal Wash swamp to be close to His Majesty. This proved to be a fatal error in judgement, for the tide came in and the swamp opened up, swallowing all but a handful of survivors, who barely reached the other side. The king's Treasury, Crown Jewels and private possessions sank into the murky depths. On 18 October 1216, King John of England was informed of the disaster and shortly thereafter succumbed to his illness and died of dysentery.

That's all very interesting and I do love a good treasure mystery, but I had never given King John a second thought until now. Though I remember that when I worked on the Houdini Heist, someone mentioned the story – but who cares about long-dead kings and their mythical treasure? I would expect that after 800 years there wouldn't be much to find, even if you knew where to dig.

Our new house, donated by my wife's father, is larger than some hotels. In fact, I think it's larger than the hotel I own just the other side of Hamilton. We all live together in the same building ... in different apartments, of course. The servants are a pain in the rear end, but I do like the fact that they do all the work, leaving my grandmother to do her own thing in her own way.

Newf, the old retrograde, had at last come home from the hospital. The dumb twit had given his bulletproof jacket to his girlfriend, Morag, and then promptly took a bullet in the chest. We almost lost him, but a small fortune and some excellent doctors managed to pull him through. His spine had been injured and now the twit goes most places in an electric wheelchair thing. We have a therapist come in every day and poor old Newf gets tortured for a good hour at a stretch – the theory being that they will eventually teach him how to walk again.

It is amazing how resilient Newf is. Even after being in a coma for just over a week and suffering several operations, he is as chipper as ever. You would think he had spent his entire life in a wheelchair. He would make a joke of zooming around the house in his thunder buggy, as he calls it.

We sat in the indoor swimming pool room and watched Morag and Deloris exercise in the water. Quite often Newf would partake as it relieved the stress on his bones.

'I had a queer phone call yesterday,' I said.

He gave me one of those sideways glances and said in a hushed voice, 'You ain't fell for another lesbo, 'ave yous?'

'Not that kind of queer, you twit. This geezer asked me if I was interested in the Magna Carta.'

'And?'

'So, don't you think that's a bit off the cuff? Like some dink calls and asks a dim-witted question like that. I mean, like, well … the Magna Carta.'

'So what was he sellin'?'

'Ah, you see that's it, nothing. He just wanted my opinion on the Magna Carta.'

'So what is it?'

I sighed. Poor Newf's education leaves something to be desired. Now history is not my strong point, but even I know what the Magna Carta is.

'You ignorant twit. The Magna Carta contains sixty-three clauses, which is the basis of all modern human rights. Without it you'd probably be someone's slave.'

'Huh, I am someone's slave; 'ave bin since I met you.'

7

'Ingrate. The great charter was signed by King John in England around 1215, I think.'

'Like quarter after noon?'

'Pillock. The year 1215.'

'So what did this telephone geezer want?'

'Don't know. He seemed extremely knowledgeable on the subject of King John, but he never actually came to the point. I thought, or at least got the impression that he wanted something but was too timid to ask for it.'

A huge smile slowly crept across Newf's face and after a few seconds he said, 'I gotta brill' scheme.'

'Go on, then. Don't keep me in suspense; let's hear this brilliant idea of yours.'

'Why don't we look for King John's treasure? Just fink of it! There ain't gonna be any gun-totin' madmen, no nicked paintings or lost submarines. The worst that could 'appen is some ancient dead geezer comes after us wiv a bow and arrah.'

'You know, Newf, if you had a brain you'd be dangerous.'

'I take that is a no, then.'

Although Newf is an idiot, occasionally he comes up with a reasonable idea. Not being an expert on history I cornered Gran later that same day. She was sitting minding her own business in the lounge. Oh! my mistake, it's called the drawing room, even though no one ever does any drawing in it.

'What's up, Gran?'

'Oh, William, dear. Young William Tan is having his lessons; I thought I would come and sit in here in silence with my book.'

'So what you reading?' I walked over and sat beside her. Poor old girl, she looked rather tired these last few days.

'Oh, just a book I found in our library. You know,

William, we should collect useful books, or old books. Why don't you invite your friend Young Harvey over here for a holiday? I would imagine he could stock us up with books of higher interest.'

'What do you know about King John, Gran?'

She looked at me with some surprise on her face. 'King John? Which King John would that be?'

'Oh, like there's more than one?'

'Oh! lots, dear. There were several King Johns of Poland, Casimir and Sobieski. There was at least one King John of Portugal and one or two of France.'

'So how many did England have?'

'Only one, dear.'

'So my question concerns him – the one in England.'

'King John, Duke of Aquitaine – a very unfortunate king, indeed. Most of his troubles were because he opposed the Pope. Poor man should never have been king in the first place.'

'Is that all you know about him?'

'Good heavens, no. Other than Henry the VIII, I would say he is the most interesting monarch of ancient times; though, strictly speaking, he falls into the medieval category. Did you know he signed the Magna Carta? I believe it was 15 June 1215. Poor man had very little choice; a sort of national mutiny, you see.'

I sighed. 'Gran, for heaven's sake, I don't want a history lesson. I merely asked if you knew anything about him.'

'Which I suppose leads us to your second question, William, which is?'

'I wanted to know if you'd heard of King John's treasure.'

'Yes, dear, I would say every schoolchild has heard the legend of King John's treasure.'

'Did it really exist, Gran?'

'Why?'

'North wants to go look for it.'

She smiled sweetly. 'Dear William, many people have looked for the lost treasure, but none have ever come close.'

'I found Fiend's gold – no one had ever got close to that, either.'

'This is different, William, dear. In the sixties they spent a great deal of time, money and labour on the project. I do believe it was supported by several universities. Absolutely nothing was ever found. You would need a great deal of geological knowledge. Plus you'd have to study the tides, silt movement and the changing landscape.'

'What do you mean, changing landscape?'

'The Wash used to extend all the way to Wisbech but the monks built ditches, drains and canals, which eventually led to the draining of the entire area. Now Wisbech is miles inland.'

'Kilometres inland, Gran.'

'Yes, dear.'

'So to put it in a nutshell, you don't think it would be a good idea.'

'I didn't say that. I implied it would be very difficult. I surely would not want you to build up too much hope and finally be disappointed by finding absolutely nothing.'

'Newf, I mean North wants to do it. What d'you think?'

'It just might be the project to get him walking again. The lad needs an interest other than Morag. That reminds me, is he ever going to marry that young lady?'

'I'll ask him, Gran.'

'So what brought up this King John idea, William?'

'I guess it all started with a phone call.'

'I see. Does that mean that someone else is interested in the same project?'

'No, Gran, just a discussion.'

'Have you read the newspapers lately, dear?'

'Why?'

'I thought you might be interested in that strange case up north.'

'Gran, I told you, North and I have finished with detective work. Too many people carry guns these days.'

'Yes, dear, I know, dear, but this is a simple case that I am sure you could amuse yourselves whilst solving it. You see, a young lady was found dead in the middle of the road wearing only a nightdress.'

'So what's so peculiar about that? She probably walked out of her house and had a heart attack or something.'

'No, dear. It said in the paper that she had recently given birth and was found on a lonely road up north more than 20 miles from the nearest house.'

'You mean 30 kilometres, Gran.'

'You don't find that intriguing?'

'Not in the least. The cops will do a fine job. I'd rather look for King John's treasure; less likelihood of getting shot at.'

Boy! Talk about the third degree. You ask a simple question and receive the Spanish Inquisition. I made my exit as quickly as possible. However, the thought of another project did interest me a little. Newf could do with the distraction and so could I, as long as there's no gun-slinging. Deloris, my wife, is pregnant and showing it. If I'm clever I can arrange for the birth to occur when yours truly is unable to attend. All I have to do is get a project going, and then come up with the perfect excuse and then the birth can proceed without me. After Newf's torture session I asked him if he'd like to go to Hamilton with me.

'What for, Bill?'

'Just some time away from the girls. I'd like to take a look at the library.'

'The library? Like, you think it might not be there any more?'

'No, you twit. I want to know more about King John and his treasure and all that.'

He stroked his chin thoughtfully for a moment as a smile slowly spread across his face.

'You know, it's there in the library that I first saw you. You was workin' on the TOD murders.'

'Yeah, I know. So what yah say?'

'You'll 'ave to do the drivin'. I can't drive until I takes a test again.'

'Newf, I love you like a brother, would I ever make you do anything you don't want to?'

'Yeah, all the time.'

'Shut up and let's go.'

Although he can sort of walk, we took his electric wheelchair thingy. I didn't want him falling down and me having to carry him like a baby. Actually, he was doing extremely well. The therapist said if he keeps going the way he is he'll be walking before next year.

I ran round to the back of the house and collected the SUV, while Newf motored to the front door. I didn't want to be chauffeured; I wanted it to be a boy's day out without nosey servants. The wheelchair thingy can fit in the back while Newf sits up front with me – just like old times.

The main branch of the Hamilton Library is huge and well suited for wheelchair traffic. All floors are accessible by elevator and the aisles are wide and smooth. Our quest would begin on my favourite floor – that being the third. We moseyed along directly to the lady at the enquiries desk.

'Excuse me,' I began. 'We'd like to see something on the subject of English history.'

She smiled sweetly. 'What exactly, sir?'

'We's interested in King John,' Newf blurted out.

Again she smiled sweetly and punched a few keys on her keyboard.

'Hmm. It's quite a popular subject; looks like we have several dozen books on the subject. Is there anything in particular that you are interested in?'

'Yes,' I said. 'We're interested in the legend of King John's lost treasure.'

'Oh yes. There are several books on that particular angle.' She hit another key and her printer spat out a list with brief descriptions. She handed the list to me and said, 'Select the ones you want and I'll have them brought up for you. Do you wish to take them out?'

'No, we'll read them here, thanks.'

'Very good.'

Newf and I moved over to the reading area where we could examine the list.

'So what we looking for?' Newf growled.

'You see after that strange phone call, I thought it might just be a decent quest, say our next summer project.'

'What, the phone call?'

'No, you berk. The treasure. No one has ever managed to find even the slightest trace of it.'

'So you figured we can find it.'

'Yeah, exactly. Now which books shall we read?'

We selected four, one of which was appropriately entitled *The Lost Treasure of King John*. The lady quickly located the volumes for us and we sat in a secluded area to brush-up on our history. Newf took to it like a fish to water. In moments he was nose deep in the project.

After about fifteen minutes' study he said, 'Yah

know, Bill, I reckon we could find this treasure, what wiv you're nose fer gold. Shouldn't be too 'ard, should it?'

'Why the sudden confidence?'

'Well, it says 'ere a Roman bank runs roughly from Clenchwarton to Tilney All Saints.'

'So what's a Roman bank when it's at home?'

'The Romans tried to keep the sea out and built a earf bank. King John's men would 'ave started their last trip on the swamp side o' the bank. So all we 'as to do is look between there and a place called Sutton Bridge.'

'Yes, you nit, but it's like hundreds of metres below the surface. It's not going to be sitting there for someone to go and pick it up, just like that.'

'I reckon you can do it, Bill.'

Carefully, I closed my book and looked at Newf.

'You know, your trust and belief in me is what keeps me going. Tell you what; I'll make a bargain with you.'

'Yeah, like what?'

'You get back on your feet and promise never to let anyone else wear your bulletproof vest, and I'll take you on this trip to find King John's treasure. All at my expense.'

'What about Morag?'

'Now that is an excellent question. I'll add one more proviso to my original deal. You have to marry that girl and stop kissing her in public – it's quite sickening.'

'That's two.'

'Alright, one and a subclause.'

It's difficult to explain the relationship that Newf and I share. He's like a brother, but somehow I love to tease him and call him names. He's actually very smart when he wants to be. He never had the chance of a good education like me, but his father seems to have taught him some very unusual skills. Newf can navigate in almost total darkness and never seems to get lost. There are very few locks he can't open and would you believe, he not only can but does eat anything.

Gran would be the whizz on this case. She solved our first mystery, Fiend's gold. Gran's a darling, but these last few years she seems to have slowed down a lot. In the old days she did all the cooking and man, can she cook! Now, though, she leaves menial tasks like that to the household staff.

Deloris and I got married last year and now that she's expecting her first baby I have to watch what I say or do. I already have a son by my first wife, little William Tan. I have supposedly given up detective work, mainly because it's too dangerous. Would you believe, in almost every case we had I was the one who got shot, but last time poor old Newf caught the lead and it almost killed him. With my money and Deloris', we certainly are set up for life. We all live in the same huge house and there are no monetary problems. Detective work is off my list of things to do but, and that's a big but, why not look for treasure? That's not really detective work, is it?

Deloris does these annoying breathing exercises every night before she sleeps. She lays there with only her silk trousers on grunting and groaning, and then excitedly counting. Looks like a grounded albatross trying to take flight. I can't take all the bouncing around, so I sit on the chair waiting for the demonstration to end. I have to pretend I'm enjoying it all so as not to upset her. Eventually, all the activity comes to an end and we can settle down for the night.

'Why do you do this every night?' I once asked, climbing onto the bed beside her.

'For our child. I need the oxygen for his brain. Healthy mom, healthy child.'

'Okay. So what you think about the legend of King John?'

'Then I won't be drinking any apple cider, if that's what you mean.'

'No, and it was peaches and apple cider. No, what I mean is, well … Newf needs an interest. I thought looking for the long-lost royal treasure might just help him recover.'

She smiled, rolled over and kissed me. 'I love you, Mr Reyner. You truly are a thoughtful man. I think it would be a fabulous interest; it's educational, geographical and not dangerous. There is one thing, though.'

'Which is?'

'No overseas travel until junior is born.'

I pushed her flat and then put my ear to her tummy. Man, talk about industry. The noises going on in there would put any factory to shame. Whilst I was listening to the bubbling, gurgling and rushing sounds he or she kicked me right in the ear.

'You sure it's not twins, then,' I said jokingly.

It was settled, for in my mind I could see Newf and myself enjoying the Norfolk warmth and searching for the legendary treasure of King John. It really didn't matter if we found it or not. What the hey! It's a holiday we could all enjoy. I decided we would all go: Deloris, Gran, Newf, Morag, William Tan and the newborn. The sea air would do us all good.

Chapter 2

Three Musketeers

There were several things to get neatly tucked under my belt before I launched a massive treasure hunt. There were birthdays, including an actual birth, a wedding anniversary and of course Gran wanted me to arrange for Newf to marry Morag. Gran also had a bee in her bonnet about that dead woman found on a road somewhere up north. After Newf shook hands with the Grim Reaper I put my foot down – there'd be no detective work at all for him or me. If Gran wanted to know how a dead, near-naked woman got in the middle of a road up north, then she could find out on her own.

When a physiotherapist wasn't torturing Newf he would spend a lot of time in the swimming pool just to ease the weight off his aching muscles. He also liked to play that disgusting game, snooker; of course Miss Suck-my-face-off Morag would be there glued to him. This particular time I wandered into the pool area to see what they were up to and a few moments later Griffin, our butler, came into the room.

'Sir,' he said in his usual non-committal way. 'Mr Barker, the gatekeeper, reports that there are three gentlemen to see you who wish to enter the grounds.'

'So who are they?'

He handed me the cordless phone. 'Mr Barker is on the phone, sir.'

'Thanks. This is Reyner. So who wants to come up to the house?'

'Three gentlemen, sir, claiming you would like to see them.'

'Really, what kind of car are they driving?'

'It's an old banger, sir. A Ford, I think.'

'No, tell them to clear off. Give them any excuse you like – no appointment, no entry.'

'Yes, sir, very good, sir.'

I handed the phone back to Griffin. 'I don't want anyone coming up to the house unless I know who they are and what they want. If they call again, tell them to make an appointment in the normal fashion.'

'Indeed, sir.'

'Getting picky,' Newf shouted as he tried to climb from the water.

'No, just careful. Remember, there is a motorcycle gang out there still nursing a grudge as someone I know in this pool destroyed their bikes.' I leaned down and helped him to his feet. 'Can you walk?'

'Not very well. You and Morag 'old us an' I'll get to the seat.'

'So how's your physio coming along?'

'I walked five steps today all on me own wiv no 'elp.'

I sat on one side of Newf and Morag sat on the other. 'Newf,' I said in my most officious voice. 'I've been thinking and have decided we will look into the lost treasure of King John, but there are a couple of provisos.'

'What, more?'

'No, just listen; give me space.'

'Go on, then.'

'First, you have to learn to walk, and second, you have to marry that girl who's always stuck to your face.'

'Sound's good to me, so what's the prob?'

'Great. I figure we'll start work planning today. There's a load to get done. Gran can help. I've got to organise my birthday, Gran's birthday, my wedding anniversary, Christmas, William Tan's birthday and your birthday. And on top of all that I have to organise an expedition to Norfolk, England.'

'What about Deloris?'

'What about her?'

'Like, first she 'as a birfday just like everyone else. Then you's gotta 'old 'er 'and when she pops the sprog.'

'Newf, you have a knack of saying things in a way that would put a priest off religion. She's going to have a baby, not pop a sprog.'

Griffin walked back into the swimming pool room. 'Excuse me, sir,' he said.

'Yes, Griffin?'

'It's the three gentlemen again, sir.'

'I thought we had got rid of them?'

'They seem to have made an appointment through Mrs Hubert, sir.'

'And?'

'I have asked them to wait in the lobby, sir. Mr Evans, our chauffeur, is watching them.'

I sighed. 'Very well, have them conducted into the den; I'll be there in a short while.'

'Very good, sir.'

I scooted off to the den so that I could pretend to have been working on secret documents when they arrived. Quickly, I slipped in behind the desk and opened a blank folder from the top drawer. After a few moments Griffin knocked.

'Come in.'

The men were ushered into the den as I closed the folder and carefully placed it back in the drawer, then I rose to greet them.

'So what can I do for you, gentlemen?' I said, shaking hands with the first.

'John Magnus,' he said and grinned from ear to ear.

'So?' I asked and calmly sat before offering a hand

to the others.

Magnus was tall and slender, about 40 years old with thick dark hair well-greased down. The man was at least clean-shaven and neatly dressed in a business suit.

'Mr Reyner, sir,' he said and eased himself down on a chair opposite me. 'Have you ever heard of King John's treasure?'

'Yeah, what's more I've been in the area where it was lost.'

The other two stood behind him looking like bodyguards. Magnus continued, 'Actually, sir, we came to you because of your fame in the field of finding things, such as treasure.'

'So?'

Poor chap looked as nervous as a virgin on her first date. 'Sir, we can help you find it.'

'Who said I'm looking for it?'

'That's true, sir, nobody, but, well … I … that is, we have a device that can locate such a treasure.'

'And?' I encouraged.

'Well, sir. I … well, that is we ... Well … would you be interested in finding a king's treasure if we did all the work, sir?' The poor fellow turned quite pink and perspiration trickled down his brow.

'Maybe. What's your proposal?'

'Oh, that, right. You see, I'm John Magnus, MA, BA. My thing is history.'

'I'm not interested in academic qualifications. What's your proposal?'

'Oh, right. I, er … that is we … well, we're looking for a backer.'

I smiled. 'And you want me to cough up the cash so you can take a holiday looking for the impossible?'

He looked terribly disappointed. For a moment I thought he was going to burst into tears.

The medium-height geezer with the heavy bottle-glass spectacles spoke up. He looked about 25 years old but was almost totally bald and he seemed rather animated like a drug addict about to throw a conniption.

'I'm David H. Carter. P.Eng. My expertise is computer programming, you know.'

'So?'

'We've devised the perfect algorithm of Doppler soil analysis. We can find anything. It's not a con or a joke. We can do it, I promise you that.'

'So who's the third musketeer in your team?'

The last member of the trio, a man in his fifties with a large moustache and a heavy build said, 'I'm Paul Manningham, MA. Geology's my field.'

I thought for a moment or two then said, 'I'm sorry, gentlemen. I can understand how you feel, but I have all the money I need so why would I bother to risk capital on a venture that is doomed from the very beginning?'

Paul Manningham took up the challenge.

'Sir, the system we have developed will work for oil, gold or any other mineral. It would prove invaluable for anyone prospecting for a tunnel. The system gives an X-ray view of the subsoil. Even without King John's treasure, the system is invaluable.'

I decided to string them along for a while just for amusement.

'I thought you were looking for the Magna Carta?'

'Oh no, sir,' said Magnus. 'We have the Magnuscarter – that's how we'll find the treasure.'

'Magnuscarter?' I queried.

'Yes, sir. It's a system we have developed. You see, I'm Magnus and he's Carter … get it? Like Magnuscarter.'

I nodded without saying anything. These guys were

either absolutely stupid or suffered from overdeveloped brains or maybe both.

Magnus looked at me with imploring eyes. 'You see, sir, we would like to field test it.'

'So go ahead and field test it.'

He shook his head sadly. 'We can't. You see, the logistics – we just can't.'

I sighed. 'Listen, why don't you get your presentation together and present it in a reasonable fashion. This smattering of info crap is getting on my tits. Now either you have something to offer or you don't, which is it?'

The older guy, Paul Manningham, tried to bolster their failing request. 'You see, sir, the system works on paper and even in uni tests, but the entire system can't be tested because of the magnitude of the exercise. We hoped you would be interested – help us complete our development and share in the profits. Simple investment in a going concern, so to speak.'

I looked at him and frowned for a few moments then said, 'So, where exactly is it going? Like, I mean what exactly do you want from me?'

He smiled warmly. 'Sir, for a full-scale test we need an open area of at least 10 kilometres in diameter and we need to build thirty GPS controlled geo-echo recorders. Oh, yeah, and we'll probably need an aeroplane or a helicopter.'

'You gotta be kidding me,' I said and chuckled.

Manningham looked most serious. 'Not at all, sir. We have one echo recorder and a geophone, which we have tested. The system works; we've used a computer simulation and it surely works, sir. But most of it is theory and simulation. We need to do a full-scale field test just to iron out the bugs.'

'Alright,' I said, grinning. 'You present me with a working plan, a list of what is needed and an itinerary of operation and I'll consider bankrolling the operation.'

Griffin led the men to their car and saw them off the property. I had some serious thinking to do. My lawyers up in Parry Sound would perform their usual duty and take their usual cut. There was no way I would enter into a money pit without some legal documentation setting out the rules. I had decided even without consultation with the three musketeers that there would be five partners of equal share – Newf would be the fifth. The only reason I didn't include Gran was simply that she seemed more interested in that near-naked dead woman.

A whole week drifted by before I heard from the three musketeers again. This time only Mr Manningham turned up, driving an old, beat-up car. As the gatekeeper recognised him, he was allowed to drive up to the house. Griffin informed me that I had a visitor.

'In the den, please, Griffin.'

'Indeed, sir.'

Not wishing to be thought of as a layabout, I performed my usual trick of pretending to be very busy. Manningham entered carrying a briefcase; he looked most businesslike. You could easily see the man had been round the block a few times – well experienced, I mean. When he spoke his moustache wobbled from side to side in an unusual way.

'Take a seat,' I ordered. 'So what have you got for me this time?'

He eased himself down onto a chair and placed his case on his knees.

'Actually, sir, I have a proposal for a field study.'

'Okay, and please call me William, or even Bill, but definitely not sir. If we're going to be partners in this venture, we should at least be on a first-name basis,

23

don't you think?'

'Yes, sir. My name is Paul.'

'Okay, Paul, let's see what you have.'

'Yes, a full field test would cost too much. I thought it would be better to do a small-scale demonstration first.'

A knock came to the door and Griffin put his head round.

'I'm sorry, sir, but there is a rather excited gentleman on the phone for you.'

'Okay, I'll take it.'

Griffin entered, handed me the cordless and then retired from the room, closing the door behind him.

'Hello,' I growled into the phone.

'Oh, sir, this is Harold Stilton. I desperately need your help. It's a matter of … well, it's very important.'

'I'm kind of busy at the moment. Would you like to call me later?'

'No, and I can't discuss it on the phone. May I come to see you?'

'Alright, call my gateman for an appointment.' I switched off the phone and turned to Paul. 'Sorry about that. Some people think I have nothing to do all day except listen to tales of woe. Now, where were we before the interruption?'

'You should get yourself a mobile; you know, a cell phone.'

'I have one but I never remember to carry it around the house. So what were we discussing?'

'A test.'

'Ah! yes, a demonstration or a test?'

'Erm! both, actually. A full-scale test would cost something in the region of half a million dollars. I figure we can perform a small field experiment for less than $50,000.'

'Without getting too technical, explain what you

mean.'

'Sure. A full test would require thirty wells, each with a G. E. R. A. Each one would cost around a grand to sink and each gera would cost about ten grand a piece.'

'I said not too technical, I didn't say anything about codes. What the hell is a gera?'

'Oh, it's a geological echo recording array.'

'So be it. So what's the low-cost test? Explain that to me.'

'Oh! that. Well, I figure that using only three geras, we'd be looking at a field cost of only around thirty grand, then there's the drilling gear and getting to the site.'

'Okay,' I said, trying to be friendly. 'So what's with the briefcase?'

'Oh, yeah, that. Well, I've brought survey maps of the proposed test site and if you are interested, all the technical details of the gera.'

'No, I'll leave all that crap up to you. One thing, though. Where is the proposed test site?'

'Oh, yeah, that. maybe, I thought we wouldn't want to attract any attention, so we should go where no one lives. I've chosen a site up by Lake Muswabik. I've written the coordinates down.'

'Never heard of it. I suppose it is in Canada?'

'Yes. It's inaccessible; that's why I chose it.'

'If it's inaccessible, how you gonna get there?'

'Oh, yeah, um! It's not that inaccessible. It's about 280 kilometres due north of the Soo.'

'North of the Soo? Where's that?'

'Oh, well, I mean Sault Ste Marie.'

'Oh! that Soo. So how do you propose we're gonna get there?'

'I thought we could use a Beaver floatplane and land on Lake Muswabik. We'll need transportable drilling gear.'

'Alright. I've decided that North, that's Mr East, will also be a partner. That makes five of us, at exactly 20 per cent share each. You guys will share in the cost, by coughing up if and when we hit pay dirt. My lawyer's working on the details at this very moment. When the paperwork is complete we can all sign it and the work can begin, providing you are all in agreement.'

Somehow it felt good; at last I was in charge of things again. We certainly wouldn't want Gran on this expedition and there was no likelihood of motorcycle gangs, irate Italians or art thieves on this gig. Newf would love it. I found him in the billiard room playing snooker. He claims it's good therapy because he has to stand to make his shot.

'Newf, you old retrograde,' I jibed on entering.

He sank gracefully to his electric wheelchair. 'You ruined my shot, Bill. I 'ope this is gonna be worf it.'

'O' course it is.' I plonked my backside down on the billiard table almost directly in front of him. 'How'd you like to go on a mock treasure hunt somewhere up north?'

'What's mock treasure?'

'He means the hunt is a mockery,' Morag said and cuddled up close behind Newf before leaning over and giving him kiss.

'What for, Bill?'

'I've bought a partnership in a mining exploration company for you and me. We're each 20 per cent shareholders.'

'And?'

'And, we'll be doing a test on a brand new treasure-hunting device at a place called … er, Mus-something. Anyhow, it's a lake several hundred K north of Sault Ste Marie.'

26

Newf looked at me with a puzzled expression on his face and then said, 'I fort we was going to Norfolk to 'unt fer King John's booty.'

'That, too. This is only a preliminary. I thought you might just like the trip and if this gadget works it might just be the answer we're looking for.'

'So you can crash in the wilderness an' leave me to drown in the bogs.'

'Not exactly. I just thought it might be a good place to hide the body, so when I dump you there'll be nothing to find and no incriminating evidence.'

Newf laughed. 'Roger that, Bill. You can count me in. Will there be any bad geezers wiv guns?'

'No.'

''ow about polar bears or dead Italian sailors?'

'None of them, either.'

'Great, when do we leave?'

'As soon as our new partners can sort out the details.'

Griffin entered the room. 'I'm terribly sorry, sir, but it's that excited gentleman again.' He handed me the cordless then stepped back awaiting me to finish and give further orders.

'Hello,' I barked in a stern fashion.

'It's Harold Stilton again, sir. I'm at your gatehouse and the gatekeeper won't allow me to pass.'

'What are you doing at my gate?'

'I have to see you, sir. It's vital. A matter of life … moreover, it's imperative that I speak with you alone.'

'Listen, I'm a very busy man; that's why I have a gatekeeper. I can't see you at this time. Phone my butler and make an appointment. I can't see you today.' With that I switched the phone off and handed it back to Griffin. 'Griffin, if he calls back, tell him I'll see him … let's say tomorrow. Maybe that'll get him off my back; he's becoming rather a nuisance.'

'Very good, sir.'

The following day Paul Manningham turned up in a Land Rover. Again the gateman allowed him in and then phoned the house to report the entry. While he was calling me another car slipped in behind Paul's.

The day had turned out cold with a little drizzle. I stood in the doorway waiting for him to park his vehicle. The other car drove directly to the porch and this scruffy little man jumped out without bothering to close his car door.

'Mr Reyner, sir,' he called breathlessly. 'I have to see you; it's imperative.'

I stood my ground. 'So what's so important that you have to break into my estate?'

He stood before me wild-eyed and panting. 'It's my daughter, sir. She's been murdered.'

Chapter 3

Hit-and-Run

Harold Stilton looked terrible, like some second-rate hobo. His clothes were dirty and worn and his car looked like it had narrowly escaped the scrap dealer. I just hate it when people beg, but in this case I felt more annoyed than anything else – the audacity of the fellow.

'So you're Stilton?'

'Yes, sir. Please, please just hear me out.'

I sighed and called over to Paul Manningham. 'Paul, I'll be with you shortly. Ask Griffin to show you into the drawing room.' I then turned my attention to Harold. 'You, sir, are beginning to be a pain in my backside. I hope this is the last time you'll be dogging me. Come, we'll talk in the den. You can tell me all your woes in private.'

Griffin was just inside the main entrance, I told him to see to Paul Manningham while I took care of Stilton. We entered the den and I closed the door.

'So why all the cloak-and-dagger shit?' I asked and sat at my desk.

I thought he was going to start crying, as he pulled a face and his eyes looked watery.

'You have to help me, Mr Reyner, you have to.'

'I don't have to do anything. Take a seat and start from the top then I'll be the judge as to who gets my help.'

'Yes, sir.' He eased himself down onto the chair opposite me and leaned on the desk in an anxious pose. 'Sir, my daughter was murdered and I need you to help me put the culprits in jail.'

'Culprits? Why don't you tell me the whole story?'

'Yes, sir.' He took a deep breath and began. 'When Jenny was fourteen she ran away from home. You see, her mother had died and I took up with another woman. It's just that the two of them didn't get along. One morning after a real flaming row, she upped and left. Never took a thing with her, just upped and left.' He paused and looked into his opens palms.

'Go on. Then what happened?'

'Oh, she did contact us once … yeah, it was just the once. Anyhow, she had gotten herself a secretarial job in Toronto. Seemed that the poor kid was at last doing something right. I wanted her to go to university but, well, she said she wouldn't come home until I got rid of Darlene – that's my new, er … new lady.'

'So you never married this new wife replacement?'

'No. Anyway, we never heard no more of Jenny. It was as if she'd dropped off the map entirely. Then I gets this peculiar note. It said she'd escaped and was coming home.'

'Peculiar in what way and escaped from where?'

He sniffled a bit and wiped a tear from his eye. 'Well, we hadn't seen or heard neither hide nor hair of her for five years. Would you believe, five years? Then we gets this second note: Daddy, I love you. I'm coming home.' He stopped talking as his throat closed up for a moment. When at last he controlled himself he said, 'She said she couldn't bring her babies as them lot at the Cormorant Institute wouldn't let her.'

'I think you have left me somewhere out in the left field. What's a Cormorant Institute and what do babies have to do with anything?'

'The point is she's dead.'

'Who, Jenny?'

'Yeah.'

'So why don't you tell me what happened and forget the history lesson.'

'That's her they found. She were dead in the street.'

'Okay, I understand most things, but would you like to elucidate?'

'Jenny was coming home, but they stopped her. They killed her and left her in the street.'

'Where?'

'She escaped from them Cormorant lot and they killed her to stop her talking. Don't you see?'

'No, where?'

'Oh, she were killed just a little north of Arthur.'

'And that's where the institute is?'

'No, the Cormorant is up at Opinnagau.'

Now I've never thought of myself as thick, but this guy made as much sense as chocolate snow tyres.

'Alright,' I said, trying to calm the man down. 'So if she was supposed to be at the Cormorant Institute why, or how, did she die at Arthur? You do mean Arthur just north of here?'

'Yes. She escaped but they must have caught up with her at Arthur and killed her there on the spot.'

'Okay, so what exactly do you think I can do about anything?'

'Get them arrested. They are bad people.'

I sighed. This guy was obviously suffering from grief and not thinking too well.

'Alright, so why don't the police do something? I would hazard they might just be better at it than I am?'

'The Cormorant lot have perfect alibis, but they are to blame, I know they are. You need to prove it to protect all the others.'

'Others, what others?'

'It's what they do.'

I shook my head in amazement. 'So how do you know all this and why don't you tell the police and let them do their thing?'

'I know because she smuggled a note out to me a

couple of years ago. The cops won't do anything because the Cormorant lot are supposed to be all legal and upfront, like.'

The best way to get rid of this guy was obviously just to get rid of him.

'Alright, I'll look into this thing for you, but first you have to tell me why you think I should.'

He wiped the tears from his face and after a couple of short coughs he said, 'You solved the TOD murders. This is just another one like it, but these guys are scientific instead of religious. You have to do it to protect all the other girls they have in their grip. That's why I came to you. I knew you would not only want to do it, but you would also be the only person in the world who *could* do it.'

I hadn't the heart to tell him that I no longer did detective work; my only interest being treasure hunting. Maybe I could get Mr Spadafora, an associate of mine, working on it. I convinced Harold that I would look into the Cormorant Institute for him and that he shouldn't worry any more – everything was in good hands.

After the poor fellow left I had to see to Paul Manningham. As if I didn't have enough to do, now I had a murder to solve as well – assuming it to be murder. Gran was the one interested in this case, I should talk to her.

Paul had brought the weirdest-looking gismo with him. I found him taking it easy on one of the sofas in the drawing room, with a glass of beer in his hand.

'Enjoying your day?' I asked sarcastically.

He leapt to his feet. 'Oh, sure, sorry.'

'Nothing to be sorry for. So what's the purpose of this visit?' I made myself comfortable on a chair facing him.

'Ah, oh, well, yes. You see, I brought a gera to show

32

you. And, well, a … well, a sort of bill.'

'Bill?'

He laughed. 'Oh, yeah, it's a bill for Bill. I've ordered two new GPS controllers so we can build two more geras.'

I nodded as if I really understood. 'I see. So how much is the bill?'

He coughed in a form of mock embarrassment. ' You see, we have to have them for the test.'

'And how much?'

'They're $6,194 each.'

'We haven't signed the agreement yet, but still you have the bill?'

'I can explain. See, well, it takes time to get them; they're custom-built in Toronto. I'd like to get a local preliminary test completed this year. Then we can spend the winter solving all the problems and planning our next excursion.'

'I thought you said the thing worked and there wouldn't be any problems.'

'Oh, yeah, that's right, but there are still calculations to solve. We've never actually done a real live test. I reckon Three units will be enough for a local assessment test and we should be able to get the software running.'

'So what's with the fencepost?'

Again he laughed; I think only to humour me. 'This is the gera.' He began unscrewing the 15-centimetre diameter tube to show me its intricate interior. The thing looked about a metre in length with a fancy plug arrangement at its top. Once the outer shielding had been removed he pointed to a complicated-looking device and said, 'This is the heart of it.'

'I'm non-technical. I can drive a car or fly an aeroplane, but I have no inkling as to how they work.'

'Ah, you see that's the pistol,' he said.

'Pistol? What is it? Some form of weapon.'

'No. I have three especially loaded 12 gauge cartridges. That's what makes the bang so we can record the echo.'

'Okay, but I don't see what that has to do with GPS.'

'The GPS is a very accurate time signal. That's how it navigates. I use the time signal to fire the cartridges in a rotation, one every 250 milliseconds.'

'Okay, I'll buy it. But don't plague me with technicalities. Remember, I'm totally green.'

'So I can go ahead and have two more built?'

'Sure. When's the test?'

Paul lit up like a kid with a new Christmas present. 'Great. I'll get them ordered and we'll have a test firing in less than a month.'

At dinner that night I asked Gran what she knew about this woman who was found just north of Arthur. She's a funny old girl – Gran that is. After I posed the question she carefully placed her knife and fork on the table and glared at me with deep furrows in her brow for a few moments.

'William,' she said in an admonishing voice. 'Why the sudden interest?'

'Why ... oh, that's easy. I thought it might make a nice distraction for Newf ... sorry, North.'

She smiled sweetly. 'Very well. At approximately 5.00 a.m. the post office intercity vehicle discovered a body on the Number 6 Highway about 5 kilometres north of Arthur. The woman turned out to be a young lady who had been missing for several years.'

'So what is so very different about this incident? It could be just a case of jealousy.'

'There are several peculiarities, William, dear. First, the lady was totally unknown in that area. Secondly, she was dressed only in a hospital nightgown. Thirdly, there had been no traffic on that part of the road all night.'

I shook my head in disgust. Gran of all people should understand the unlikelihood of such statements.

'Gran, there's no way they could know that no one used the road throughout the night.'

'Ah! but you see, the works department had a road traffic counter recorder running at Arthur and at the Damascus intersection. The instrument reported no vehicular traffic at all that very night.'

'Oh, well, I don't think being dressed in night gear at night is all that suspicious. Maybe she ran out of a house nearby.'

'It was a hospital gown, dear. No hospital has reported her missing and there is no house nearby.'

'Okay. So how do you know no one in that area knows the woman?'

'Simply because the police had difficulty identifying her. Strangely, the woman is originally from Dundas.'

I had to smile at that one, as I already knew it.

'So how d'you feel about a quickie up north, Newf?'

'Yeah, great. Me and you back on the trail ... great.'

'Have you ever heard of a place called Opinnagau, Gran?'

'No, dear, where is it?'

'That's what I need to know. How about the Cormorant Institute, have you heard of that?'

'No, dear, I have not heard of that, either.'

'Wow, that's unusual, Gran. I've caught you out twice in the same day.'

'Opinnagau sounds Indian,' Newf said. 'I reckon it must be a reserve or an Indian lake. I'll look it up on the Internet for yous. Why you interested in them two names?'

'I'll let you know when I have the answers, Newf.'

Sunday turned out to be a beautiful day, especially as I managed to deter both Deloris and Morag from accompanying us. This was to be a Newf and Bill affair, just as it used to be in the old days. Besides, I hate having to pull Morag off Newf's face every five minutes. I helped Newf into the passenger seat of the Rolls, folded his hand-operated wheelchair and put it in the trunk.

'It's great, ain't it, Bill. Just me and you togever again.'

'Yes. This one's just a quick look-see. There'll be no shooting or bashing involved, just a as you would put it, a quick butchers-hook.'

I drove directly to Greensville then to the 5 Highway, from which I went east to the 6 Highway. The 6 goes all the way to Tobermory for about 300 kilometres. Arthur sits just above Fergus about 50 kilometres from Dundas.

As I turned onto the 5, Newf said, 'I's found somefing out about the Cormorant place for yah.'

'Oh yes, what?'

'They's a medical research place. Guess where they is.'

'Are,' I corrected. 'Go on, then, where are they?'

'Them's at a place called Opinnagau. It's a lake T, H and G.'

'T, H and G?'

'Yeah, to hell and gorn.'

'Okay, like where exactly?'

'Hundreds of miles norf of Sault Ste Marie.'

'There isn't anything hundreds of miles north of the Soo. There aren't even any roads.'

'That's right, Bill, T, H and G. Remember Severn's Island?'

'Who could forget it?' It was in the middle of absolutely nowhere.

The local police detachment at Arthur turned out to be the next best thing to totally hopeless. Newf suggested we try a shop – like they'd know anything. Leaving Newf in the car, I walked into a local-variety corner store.

'Excuse me,' I started. 'I'm looking for information on the dead woman found –'

The shop lady, a young Asian girl, cut me short.

'Should speak to old Sam.'

'Sam? Where would I find old Sam?'

'Sits near the cemetery.'

'Great, thank you.'

Finding the cemetery was easy and correspondingly, finding Sam was also easy. An old fellow sat on the wall near the cemetery entrance. Fortunately for him, the weather was fine and quite warm.

'Sam,' I said, approaching the old man.

'Arrh. Like who's askin'?'

'I'm Bill Reyner.'

'Cop?'

'No, why, do I look like a cop?'

'Don't speak to no cops. I got nothin' to say to cops.'

I turned and there was Newf standing and leaning against the Rolls. Quickly, I paced out the couple of metres and grabbed his arm.

'I ain't no cripple, Bill. I can manage. Just keep your 'ands orf.'

'Yeah, you fall down and Morag will kill me. Hold me for support and shut up moaning.'

Old Sam laughed. 'Sittin' here, you gets to see it all eventually.'

'I'm told you're the expert on local affairs,' I said, addressing the old man. 'What can you tell me about that dead woman they found up the road a bit?'

'You a cop?'

'No; I told you that already.'

'Then what you want to know for?'

'I represent her father. I'm just doing him a favour as he's too upset to come himself.'

'It were the boaties.'

'Boaties? What exactly do you mean?'

'I tell yah, it were them boaties. Them's the only ones who don't register.'

'Have you any idea what he's talking about, Newf?'

'Yeah. Put me down, Bill. Let me sit on that wall by the old fellah.'

I eased him over and allowed him to settle beside old Sam.

'So, explain to me why a boatie doesn't register.'

'Them boaties bridge the counter. Don't want no cop knowing they's smuggling. It definitely were them; couldn't be no one else.'

'Oh, I get it,' I said as the light of dawn began to shine. 'You mean that Boaties is a family name and they somehow or other bridge the road counter.'

The old man turned to Newf. 'An' you let this twit drive you about. Is he safe?'

'Alright, enlighten me.'

Sam shook his head in disgust. 'I don't talk to no cops.'

'I'm not a cop, for crying out loud.'

'You're thick enough to be a cop.'

'I guarantee he's not a cop, Sam,' Newf assured him. 'He's my best friend and besides, cops don't drive Rolls-Royce cars.'

'Hmm, well, boaties be them that knocks off boats. O'Brien be the name.'

This time it was my turn to do the head-shaking. 'Knock-off as in a copy or imitation, or knock off as in steal?'

'I'd check his drivin' licence,' Sam said. 'What kind

o' bloody fool do you let drive you around, son?'

'Well it's 'is car, Sam, an' 'e is me friend. An' yes, sometimes 'e is a bit fick.'

'The O'Briens drive over to the lake and hauls boats out of the water. They takes them from tourists where they park. They takes them to their boat sales place. Ain't you ever heard of a chop shop?'

'Yeah, but not for boats.'

'They carries a bridge for crossing counters, false plates for cameras an' scanners to listen to the cops.'

'Okay,' I agreed. 'So you think they ran this woman down?'

'I don't think nothin'. I know they dun it.'

'So where would I find these O'Briens?'

'If yous got a death wish, you can find them at their sales place, on Fourth Concession.'

I took out my wallet, peeled off a fifty-dollar bill then handed it to Sam.

'Thanks, Sam. Buy yourself a few beers on me.'

He snatched the money.

'Thanks. I'll use it to buy a wreath for your funeral if yous visitin' the boaties.'

I helped Newf back into the Rolls then walked round and climbed in. Newf seemed a little nervous.

'You ain't gonna find these O'Briens, are yah?'

'Yeah, o' course I am.'

'But I can't give you any backup. If there's trouble, I can't 'elp.'

'I'm not going to start a war. I'll pretend to be interested in buying a boat; they are boaties, aren't they?'

'Just as long as yah don't start no fightin'.'

'Don't worry, Newf; we're customers, not competitors.'

'So 'ow's this gonna tell you what 'appened to that woman?'

'Who knows? We'll just nose around a bit and see if we spot anything suspicious.'

It turned out to be rather easy finding the Fourth Concession and even easier finding the boaties. A huge field absolutely filled with boats of just about every shape, size and description was easy to spot from a long way away. The main gate lay open and without hindrance, I drove up the boat-lined road to an aircraft hangar-sized building. On arrival two gentlemen met us, each with a shotgun under his arm.

'Hi,' I greeted, climbing from the car and putting the largest smile on that I could muster.

'What you want?' asked the taller and ugliest of the two.

'Hi. I'm looking for a boat.'

'So where'd you leave it?'

'No. I mean I'm looking for a new boat.'

'We don't sell new boats.'

'New to me, then.'

Ugly sighed. 'So who sent you?'

'Who? Oh no. I was just driving by, saw your sign and thought, well … I am looking for a new boat, why don't I just drop in and see what you have. Might even get myself a deal.'

'We don't have any boats in your price range.'

'Oh, I can afford it.'

Ugly came right up to me and placed the butt of his gun on his shoe and growled, 'Our boats are rebuilds. Ones that sank, burned or were grounded. They are all rebuilds; we don't have any new ones. You'll be looking fer brand names.'

'That's okay; I'm looking for something on the cheaper side. I didn't get rich by squandering, you know.'

'We only deal with dealers, not hobbyists. You'll have to check with a dealer, not us.'

I shook my head. 'Sorry, I just thought you might like to make a buck or two.'

'We do, we can and we will. But there ain't much profit selling *one*. If yous want three or four then we can maybe make a deal.'

'Oh.' I turned and looked at Newf. 'How'd you like a new boat, say one for you and your wife?'

Newf took up with the spirit of the game and grinning, he said, 'Me two sons might like one each if they's cheap enough.'

'Okay,' I said, turning to Ugly. 'I just might be in the market for three boats. Can you deliver?'

Ugly smiled, picked up his shotgun and tucking it under his arm, said, 'Then I'll show you around, mate.'

Chapter 4

Bang on Target

On our way home from the small town of Arthur, Newf seemed rather quiet.

'Are you in pain?' I asked.

'Nah.'

'So why the silent thoughtfulness?'

'I reckon old Sam knows what 'appened that night.'

'Why would you think that?'

'When you was off wiv that gun-totin' ugly fellah I saw somefing.'

'Go on then, don't keep me in suspense. What did you see?'

'One o' them geezers opened a door on that smaller shed. You know, the one opposite to the 'angar. When 'e slid the door open I saw a Land Rover.'

'Wow, that is suspicious. Perhaps I should have you investigated; after all, you have a Land Rover, too.'

'Just wait till I finish 'fore yah gets all snarky, Bill. Man, you do jump to conclusions fast.'

'Go on, then, and stop dragging it out.'

'Any'ow this geezer didn't see me sittin' in the Roller. 'e opens the shed … it's a garage where they do welding an' shit. Any'ow when the door opens wide I sees this Rover. The radiator had 'it somefing 'ard; it were all buggered up.'

'You mean, you think that was the vehicle that killed Jenny Stilton.'

'Wivout taking a close look I can't be sure. But it looks to me like old Sam is bang on target. See, 'e knows a load more than 'e says.'

'Okay, we'll pay these idiots a sneaky night visit.

Do you think you're up to opening a few locks for me?'

Newf chuckled and then said, 'I fort you'd never ask.'

At supper that night I thought I'd broach the subject of dead women lying about in unused streets.

'Heard any more on the Stilton case, Gran?'

'No, dear, but I know where you have been. I thought detective work was completely off your itinerary.'

'It was just a simple look-see. Newf and I think we've solved it already. As soon as we collect a little hard evidence, we'll tip the police off and that will be the end of it. No one'll get shot and the case will be solved.'

'Hard evidence, William? What exactly do you mean by hard evidence?'

'It was a couple of clowns called O'Brien who ran her down. For reasons of their own they steal boats, refurbish them and sell them on to legitimate dealers. One night whilst towing a stolen boat, they accidentally ran over Jenny Stilton.'

'Then why did their vehicle not trip the Ministry's vehicle counters?'

'Ah! you see, the counters only count the number of tyres that run over them. The O'Brien clowns used a cable bridge to cross without triggering the counter. They do that sort of thing so that the police won't be able to trace them or their movements.'

'What about Compass Cameras?'

'I don't think they have any on the 6 Highway in that area. The O'Briens would know that. These guys steal boats for a living; they're not amateurs.'

Gran smiled. 'Very good, dear. So what kind of evidence do you think you may be able to collect?'

'Newf ... I mean North and me are going to do a little snooping after dark. We'll be using our old black clothes trick.'

'No you're not!' Morag snapped. 'My North will be staying here where I can keep an eye on him. He's not going to put himself in any danger.'

I sighed to show my contempt. 'North is the only person who can open locked doors. He's coming and that's final.'

'Then I'm coming, too. Someone has to care for North.'

'I'll care for North,' I demanded.

Morag drew herself up to her full height and after hissing like a snake, she leaned across the table towards me and said, 'You ... you drive, I'll care for North.'

The drive up to Arthur only takes about an hour. We set out on the expedition at two in the morning and Morag insisted we all wear our Miguel Caballero vests, or perhaps I should say jackets. On this trip we mutually decided to use the SUV as it would be less conspicuous than a Rolls-Royce and there would be plenty of room for Newf's chair. I drove while Morag sat beside me dictating the rules of enemy engagement.

About half way to Arthur, she turned to Newf and said, 'You may as well carry this.' And then she handed him a parcel.

'So what's that for?' I growled.

'The doggies.'

'Dogs? What bloody dogs? We didn't come all this way to feed any dogs.'

'At the boatyard, d'yee ken?'

'No, I don't ken. There are no dogs at the boatyard. We were there earlier and there was no sign of any form of canine or even a warning sign.'

'Och!' she said in her sweet Scottish brogue, 'it's two poond of the best steak.'

'You mean a kilogramme,' I corrected.

'Noo. If I meant a kilogramme I would o' said soo.'

Of course we had to cross the Ministry of Transport's traffic counter. Just to give them something to think about, we drove back and forth over the detector several times.

Finding the boaties, or at least finding their storage yard, was simplicity itself. As expected, thieves never trust anybody; the place was lit up like the Second Coming.

'Now what are we going to do?' I hissed under my breath.

'Don't let it faze yah, Bill me old mucker. Thems is only lights. Drive up to the gate an' I'll open the lock for yah.'

'I'll old mucker you in a minute, Newf. If I stop at the gate anyone within 100 miles will see us.'

'I fink yous mean 160 kilometres, Bill.'

'Shut up while I think a moment.'

I concluded that it didn't matter either way. Waltzing up to the gate had to be the only way in. No one resided on the property, so there would probably be no one to see us trying to break in. As I stopped the SUV right at the entrance, two huge, tooth-bearing and vicious dogs rushed to meet us. Fortunately, there stood a very high and very strong steel wire mesh fence all the way round and the gate had no gaps, so the animals couldn't get to us.

'I don't see how we're going to get in there with those ugly dogs in the way.'

'Och! I'll show ye' a wee trick that any worthy Scotsman would ken.'

She opened her parcel of meat.

'But it's cooked,' I verbally noted.

'Aye, yah didna' expect them to eat it raw.'

Morag climbed out while I helped Newf over to the gate lock. In moments he had the simple padlock open and I helped him back into the SUV. Morag calmly showed the dogs the meat then placed the pieces on the ground about a metre apart in a line leading away from the main gatepost. She then walked over to the lock and removed it. For one horrible moment I thought she was going to open the gate. Throwing the lock into the bushes, she then wrapped the chain in such a way that it restrained the gate enough to fool the dogs.

Climbing back in the vehicle, Morag said, 'Now using a wee spot of brainpower, push the gate open with the motor.'

I inched the SUV forward until the gate opened. Immediately, the two dogs rushed out to inspect us, but were quickly distracted by the smell of freshly cooked beef.

'Now, get the motor inside quickly,' Morag snapped.

The moment I cleared the fence, she jumped out and closed the gate. Very clever! Now we were on the inside and the dogs were on the outside. She secured the chain to keep the animals from re-entering.

'Very clever,' I said as she climbed back into the vehicle. 'But now how are we going to get out of here?'

'Just drive through the gate. We willna' require to get oot and lock it.'

'It's not surprising you and Newf get on so well; you're both as mad as hatters. Newf, in which shed did you see that Rover?'

'It'll probably be locked; you'll 'ave to get me chair out.' He pointed to the appropriate building.

In moments, I parked right beside the huge door. In the middle of the large door was a human-sized one, and it had a simple padlock securing it. With a sigh of resignation, I extracted Newf's motor-powered chair from the back and helped him into it. It seemed very dangerous to me. What with all the lights on in the yard and on the buildings, you could sit anywhere and even read a book if you so desired. After only a few moments Newf tossed the padlock to the ground.

'You'll 'ave to lift me buggy over the gunwale, Bill.'

'The what?'

'The step. I can't motor over that; it ain't fer no disabled geezer.'

From the inside, I grabbed Newf's invalid carriage and hauled it over what he called the gunwale. It was as dark as the Black Hole of Calcutta inside the shed, not that I've ever been to Calcutta. Newf has a sixth sense when it comes to darkness.

'There'll probably be a light switch over there by the main door, Bill.'

He was right. Feeling all around the wall near the hinge of the door, I eventually found a utility box with a switch on it. Click! and the lights came on. There were four vehicles in the shed, one of which was the one we needed to look at. A Land Rover stood on chocks with two of its wheels missing. Someone had already started work on the front end, but traces of the dirty deed were still quite evident.

Newf examined the front damage while I opened the back hatch to see what I could find inside.

'Christ! If it isn't the cowboy and the cripple,' came a calm and almost quiet voice.

I turned and saw Mr Ugly leaning against the corner of a pickup truck and pointing a large shotgun at us.

'Your doorbell doesn't seem to work,' I said and smiled. 'And I'm not a cowboy.'

'An' I ain't no cripple,' Newf growled.

'Well, Doofus and Dingbat, just what exactly did you think you'd find?'

He was too far away for me take his gun away – somehow, I needed to creep closer.

'You shouldn't point guns at people,' I said and

took a step forward.

'I only point it at people I intend to blow away. One more step and you'll get the full meaning from both barrels.'

Suddenly, the flat of a shovel sprang from nowhere and clanged on his head like Big Ben striking one.

'I dinna like guns,' Morag said, stepping from behind the vehicle with a shovel in her hands.

Mr Ugly hit the floor with a thud and a rattle as his gun slithered under the pickup.

'Holy crap! I hope you haven't killed him; we don't want to get done for murder.'

She knelt down to examine the body.

'Noo. He'll probably live.'

Newf wheeled himself over to the prostrate gunman.

'Well 'e don't look too dangerous now. Chuck a bucket o' water over 'im an' we'll grill 'im.'

I retrieved the shotgun, unloaded it and put the cartridges in my pocket – the reasoning being that not too many people get killed by unloaded guns. With a piece of wire we found on the bench, I tied his hands behind his back and then rolled him over. At this juncture the man began regaining consciousness.

'So who are you?' I growled.

Ugly struggled to sit up but apparently he was too awkward to succeed.

'I'm the bleeding owner. Who the hell are you?'

'I'll ask the questions and if you have any ambitions left to fulfil, you'll answer them. Notice *we* have the gun now.'

'I ain't saying snot.'

'Maybe, but as I said, this here is your gun and I might just be of a mind to use it, if you're bright enough to follow my line of thought. Now, before I relieve you of a few litres of blood, who are you?'

'I ain't sayin' nothin' in this position.'

I handed the shotgun to Newf.

'Point this at that filth on the floor. If he does anything untoward, blow the sucker away and we'll get what we need to know out of the office.'

'Sure, great, boss, love to. I 'opes 'e tries somefin'; there ain't nofin' like the smell of fresh blood an' cordite.'

I walked over and hauled Ugly into the standing position then stepped clear.

'I don't want any of that buckshot spoiling my nice new jacket. Now who are you?'

'O'Brien. Who the bloody hell did you think I was? I'll have your hide for this. We don't keep any money on the premises, so you're out of luck.'

'I have enough money to buy this place and that's only this week's pocket change. What I want to know is what happened to that Land Rover.'

'Land Rover?'

'Yes, the one with the damage on the front end.'

'Bumped into something, didn't it.'

'I gathered that.' I turned to Newf. 'Seems to me this one's only going to drop us in it. He's not going to talk; we may as well kill him and go home. I'll count to four, Newf, and if he doesn't respond, pull the trigger and we'll leave. Someone will find the body eventually.'

'Love to, boss. Ready when you are. I don't like bein' called a cripple.'

'So, what happened to that Land Rover? One … two … three …'

'Alright, alright. So we hit something.'

'I know that. I want to know what you hit.'

'I told yah – a tree.'

'Okay, Newf, I'm tired of this shit. Blow this trash away.'

Newf lifted the gun to his shoulder.

'Alright, alright, wait a minute. I'll talk,' Mr O'Brien said excitedly.

'I'm waiting.'

'It was that broad, wasn't it.'

I walked in front of O'Brien. 'Good. I knew that; that's why we're here. Now, what I need to know is why.'

'Why?'

'Exactly, why?'

'There weren't no why.'

'So how come you managed to kill her and what was she doing in the middle of the road?'

'Ah, now you're asking real questions. I swear it was an accident. We didn't know she was there.'

'How do you mean you didn't know she was there? Didn't you have your lights on?'

'We drives over and grabs this boat. One of our lookouts reported an unattended boat up at Balmy Beach. We nipped up there and hoisted it. When we gets back we had to cross the Ministry counter in the road. I gets out and places the bridge. Roy drove the Rover and the boat trailer across. Anyhow, when I grabs the bridge, I goes to fling it in the boat ready for the next counter and whammo! This broad just about knocks me down and runs like shit into the darkness. Figuring she would blow the whistle, I jumps in and Roy guns it for a quick getaway. I guess we got up to about fifty and bang! This broad bounces off the front of the Rover. We didn't know she was there or where she come from.'

'Why, didn't you see her?'

'We was running without lights at this time. Didn't want any cops and snoopy bastards to spot us.'

'So what happened to the woman?'

O'Brien shrugged. 'How the hell would I know? We didn't stop. Weren't till we reads the newspaper we found she were dead. I swear it was an accident. We didn't know she was there. Nobody did it on purpose.'

I sighed very loudly. 'Then, Mr O'Brien, I reckon I can do you a favour.'

'Oh yeah, like what?'

'Me and my friends are going to drive out of here and leave you to consider your evil way of life.'

'What about the cops?'

'I would prefer to leave them out of this for the moment and I strongly suggest you find a different method of making a living.'

Without untying Ugly's hands, I placed the shotgun on the floor and walked over to the big door. Throwing the huge bolt, I allowed the larger door to swing open. Newf motored over to the SUV in his chair. In only moments we were on our way. The main gate offered no hindrance and with a slight nudge it burst open. The dogs were nowhere to be seen and moments later we were speeding northbound.

'What if that twit got our vehicle number?' Newf asked. ''e'll know where we live.'

'So what's he gonna do come after us?'

''e could come shootin'.'

'Unlikely. I would hazard a guess he'll pack up his bags and move off. Just now I figure we'll toddle off and take a look at this place Balmy Beach.'

'In the middle of the night?'

'It's coming up for five now. I figure by the time we get there it'll be around seven.'

'I'll die of starvation. I ain't ate nofin' fer weeks.'

'Shut up, Newf. We'll find a noshery on the way or when we get there.'

My ETA turned out to be only a little awry – we entered the near wilderness area on the Georgian Bay at seven fifteen.

'I wouldn't think anyone lives around here,' I

conjectured.

'Over there, Bill,' Newf said, pointing.

Sure enough, down the escarpment and on the edge of the lake we saw several boats lying at anchor. To put it mildly, it wouldn't be a likely spot for me to park any boat that I owned. A farm, or should I say a farmhouse with several wrecked boats, stood only a stone's throw from the water's edge. The road, which was nothing more than a gravel track, led almost directly to the house. I parked the car as near as I could to the front door.

'I'm still 'ungry, Bill.'

'Newf, just relax. As soon as I've made a couple of enquiries, we'll mosey back to Owen Sound and find a nice restaurant.'

Morag and I walked to the house leaving Newf in charge of the vehicle. I knocked several times with no response. Losing patience, Morag gave the door several hefty kicks, with some effect. A few seconds later we heard stirrings within. After what seemed an eternity, the door groaned on its ancient rusty hinges and an old geezer stood staring at us through thick bottle-glass spectacles.

'I told you lot afore,' he said angrily, 'no stuffing service till after nine.'

'Oh,' I said in surprise. 'We're not looking for a stuffing service. Just a couple of questions that I will be happy to pay someone to answer.'

'Pay?'

'Yes.'

'How much?'

'What's the going rate round here?'

'You bloody daft or something?' He moved to close the door.

Wedging my foot between the door and the frame, I said, 'How about twenty bucks an answer.'

The old guy smiled. 'You cops or something?'

'No, now do we look like cops?'

'So what you want to know?'

'I understand a boat went missing somewhere along this coast.'

'Yeah, so?'

'So you know about it?'

He eyed me up and down and then moved his attention to Morag. 'So who's she?' he asked.

'This is Morag, she is my … er, she's my secretary and helper.'

'The boat was here, but it weren't in the water. That'll be twenty dollars, please.'

'I'll pay when we've finished.'

He looked at me sort of sideways. 'No pay and we're finished.'

'Okay.' I peeled off a hundred-dollar bill and handed it over. 'Now you owe me four more answers.'

'Right, get on with it, then.'

'I see you have planes out there in the water, too.'

'Plane.'

'Alright, I see you have an aeroplane out there, too, Who's it belong to?'

'They comes and goes all the time. I looks after it when the driver ain't around.'

'Driver?'

'The guy who flies the bloody thing.'

'So whose is it?'

'Don't rightly know, but it's some kind of research institute.'

'Okay, now would you tell me who owned the boat that got stolen?'

'That's your hundred bucks spent, mister.'

'Sure, so what's the answer?'

'Bromley, Mr Bromley, 115 Acacia Avenue Toronto.'

'You know it by heart?'

'Sure. Answered enough cops asking damn silly questions; sure, I know it by heart. So why you asking all these questions if you ain't a cop? Like what's it to you?'

I peeled another note off the bundle, this time a fifty. 'One nice big question. Where were you when the boat was stolen?'

'I was in the hospital at Owen Sound. I fell and bruised my chest. They thought it might be heart troubles.'

'And that left no one to guard the boats and plane?'

'Right. Now I reckon you are spent out. Can I go back to bed now?'

'Sure, but here's a tip for you. I know who stole your boat and where it went.'

At last and without a single shot fired, we were getting to the truth of the matter. Mr Bromley would be the object of our next quest. Pity the old man didn't know the name of the organisation that owned the plane.

Chapter 5

Digging Deeper

After an all-night foray into the nether regions of Northern Ontario, we returned home for a well-deserved rest and of course something to eat. Newf seemed on top of the world. He appeared to have refuelled his ego with the excitement of the night – not that anything untoward happened. Unfortunately, I have to admit that the evening's happenings did rekindle my interests in the old gumshoe game. There's nothing like a little lawbreaking to juice up the adrenaline, particularly when no one is likely to report the incident. Top of my list and obviously the solution to this simple case is John Bromley of Toronto.

In fact, it turned out that John Bromley did not live in Toronto – he actually lived in a place called Mimico, which is a sort of suburb on the lakeshore. The house stood boldly in its own very green and manicured grounds looking like a small Victorian palace. Obviously, the man was not used to spending any time in employment exchanges – though I can proudly admit it was a shack compared to our house. A fairly modern BMW sat on the driveway and a Mercedes stood with its nose sticking out of the garage.

As I unloaded Newf and placed him on his manual wheelchair, a geezer who looked like the gardener came round the corner of the house. The man was wearing coveralls and heavy leather gloves.

'Can I help you?' he asked in what sounded like a South African accent.

'Sure, we're looking for Mr John Bromley.'

For a moment the man eyed me up and down and

then gave Newf the same treatment. After a very pregnant pause, he said, 'So if he's Ironside, who are you?'

'I'm Reyner, Bill Reyner, and this is my associate, Mr East.'

'I see. I am the said Bromley and it's Doctor Bromley.'

'Oh, right. We've come about your boat.'

He smiled and his eyes twinkled with what seemed to be delight. 'I don't have a boat.'

'Not now, no. I'm talking about the one you seem to have misplaced up in Georgian Bay.'

He grinned and shook his head. 'I never owned a boat; you must have me confused with someone else.'

'I fink this geezer's a bleedin' liar, Bill. Maybe we should duff 'im up a bit. You know, rearrange 'is memory a tad.'

'He's very brave for a cripple, isn't he. Or is it just Tourette's syndrome?'

'Mr Bromley, or should I say Doctor Bromley? We're here because of your boat. Now we can talk this out nice and easy, like, or I can go tell the Royal Canadian Mounted Police all that I have learned and let them continue this conversation with you.'

I could see I had hit the target in one salvo. The man visibly paled and he lost that twinkle in his eyes.

'Boat, oh yes, boat. You must mean the yacht. Yes, yes, I did have a yacht. Have you found it by any chance?'

'Not exactly. But I think I could put my hands on it.'

'Oh, very good. Would you like a snort?'

'Pardon?'

'A snort. You know; a snifter. Brandy, old man.'

'I'd rather have a beer.'

'Excellent, excellent. Let's enter from the

56

conservatory. We can get your friend in that way.'

He seemed jolly, but I saw an element of shock and surprise on his face. Considering we were total strangers, he was rather too friendly. I wheeled Newf in silence, following Bromley as we walked to the far side of the house. The conservatory turned out to be a king-sized greenhouse attached to the main building. The door seemed large enough for a small truck to enter and with no doorstep. Inside, we walked through an avenue of tropical-looking flowers.

'I collect and grow orchids,' he said, waving his hand at the strange blooms.

At the end of the avenue stood the house doorway and again no doorstep. A slight ramp led up into the next room, which looked like the scullery or servant's kitchen. We walked through and into a hallway then entered a large room with soft furnishings.

'No servants?' I queried.

'Not since the wife died,' he said. 'Please, make yourself comfortable. I don't actually have any ale, but I have ginger beer, if that's acceptable?'

I sighed. 'Whisky will do.'

'Rocks or soda?'

'Straight,' I said gruffly.

The room was obviously a lounge. It had a bar fully stocked with wines and spirits, and opposite hanging on the wall was the biggest flat-screen TV I've ever seen. I parked Newf and slumped down onto a divan-like seat. Bromley fiddled at the bar for a moment then brought the drinks over.

'I don't get very many visitors, you see.' After handing out the drinks he sat on an armchair opposite me.

I took a sip of my whisky and said, 'So what can you tell me about your boat?'

He looked puzzled for a moment then his brain

clicked in.

'Oh, the boat. I thought you said you had found it? Are you looking for a reward, perhaps?'

'No. Do you know what was found in your boat?'

He frowned and pretended to be totally ignorant of the facts. 'Nothing untoward, I trust? Surely not drugs?'

'So what you a doctor of?' Newf asked.

'Gynaecology.'

'So where d'you work?'

'Why all the questions? I thought this was about a boat, not my place of work.'

Somehow he looked worried. I reinforced Newf's query.

'So where do you work, then?'

'Not that it's any concern of yours, but it's a research institute way up north.'

'Cormorant?' I asked and watched him pale a little.

'As ... as ... well, yes, as it happens, I do.'

'So tell me about the woman in your boat.'

'Woman? What woman?'

I took a long, slow sip of the whisky and watched his worried expression for a moment.

'A couple of low-life boat thieves known as the boaties hauled your boat onto a trailer and drove it to their yard in Arthur. Just before arriving at their destination, they found a woman hiding in your boat. My question is, how did she get there in the first place?'

'Oh, oh! Really? Was she still there when they stole it?'

'Explain.'

'Goodness me,' he said, pretending to be shocked or surprised. 'Hmm, you see. How can I put it? I, er ... as a distraction – you know, a form of relaxation after a hard week's work – I often go to the bay and sail. Just for relaxation, you see.' He swallowed hard. 'I, er … I sailed most of the day and, well, suddenly there was this woman in the water. Heaven only knows what she was doing there.'

'So how come she was wearing a hospital gown?'

'Oh, yes, that,' he chuckled. 'Would you believe, she was totally naked! When I hauled her out of the bay, I gave her a gown to wear. Most embarrassing.'

'You just happened to have one handy?'

'Yes. I work at a hospital, you see. Just … just happened to have one handy, as you say.'

I scratched my ear for a moment. This story was so unlikely it could even be true. No one in their right mind would make up a dim story like this one.

'So how come she was still in the boat when it got hoisted?'

'I … that is, she was almost hysterical. Unfortunately, I had an imperative appointment to make. I gave her a sedative, put her to bed and told her I would return to help her. But … but, er … well, you see, I got delayed and when I eventually returned, the boat had disappeared.'

'Disappeared?'

'Yes. I thought she must have stolen it, as in sailed off into the sunset.'

'There was no report of a stolen boat.'

'Oh yes there was. I reported it the very next day. So do you have my boat or not?'

'No, the O'Brien brothers have it in Arthur.'

'Oh, may I retrieve it?'

'Probably not. I would recommend you call the cops and report them. The only thing that puzzles me is, if you left it in the water, how did the boaties get it out without being noticed? The night watchman said the boat was not in the water. I do believe it's a little difficult sailing off into the sunset still on land.'

'It most certainly was in the water when I left it. That's why I thought the woman had stolen it. I didn't want to get her into any trouble, poor creature. I thought, well, I thought someone would find it up the coast. She didn't look the type to go around stealing people's vessels, particularly being without clothing.'

'Didn't you think it a little suspicious, like, finding a naked woman in the lake?'

'No … actually, yes. She seemed very distressed. I thought she might be a little suicidal.'

'So you left her to it?'

'No, no not really. I talked to her and calmed her down. Then I gave her a sedative and put her to bed, thinking she'd be safe for several hours.'

'And then you left?'

'Well no, not immediately. I made sure everything was kosher then I drove to Owen Sound, where I had an urgent appointment. I wasn't gone more than six hours. I would have been back sooner, but as I said, I got delayed. Now, if you've finished, I have important work to do and perhaps a boat to reclaim.'

'Sure.'

Newf and I left him to it, but all seemed very suspicious. One doctor, a naked woman and boat thieves. Wow! talk about complicated lives.

'I fink I'll get a boat,' Newf said as we drove home.

'What for?'

'I reckon if yous can go around fishing naked women out o' the lake, seems to me to be a decent sort o' 'obby.'

'Morag would kill you if you started fishing for live bait.'

'I just fort of somefing, Bill.'

'Yeah, and?'

'The quack said 'e was only gone for six 'ours.'

'So?'

'Well, 'ow long do it take to drive from Arthur to Smelly Bay?'

'You mean, Balmy Beach?'

'Same fing. So 'ow long?'

'Maybe an hour, depending on the traffic. So what are you getting at?'

'Well if Mr Quack leaves 'is boat, surely somebody must o' known that 'e wouldn't be back for a long time. They then calls the boaties, so 'ow long is it before they can get the Rover ready? Then theys drive to Smelly Bay, hauls the boat out o' the water an' drives back to Arthur. So what you fink?'

'I think if you can pronounce "th" in Arthur, you should be able to pronounce it all the time.'

'Bill, you's beginning to get on my tit. Are you interested in solving this murder or are you just gonna pick me up on my words all the time?'

'I don't see what you're getting at.'

'Fink about it, Bill, six hours and they don't even pass on the road. See what I'm gettin' at?'

'No.'

'The old fart in the pyjamas, 'e weren't never in no 'ospital. There ain't no one else around. The old fart in Smelly Bay knows that the quack 'as gorn an' that 'e ain't gonna be back for a while. 'e calls the boaties and the boat gets lifted.'

Newf just doesn't get it. I don't think he'll ever make a decent detective. It's obvious even to an idiot; the boat keeper had to be in on it, but then what? I think the important thing is that the doctor is involved. Seems to me he knows a whole load more than he wants to let on. We actually never learned anything useful. It would have all remained that way but for a very peculiar set of coincidences. Newf was the first; he came into the drawing room where I just happened to be relaxing, speeding directly to me on his electrically motorised chair.

'Bill! Bill!'

'Yeah?'

'Crikey, Bill. I's bin on the Net.'

'I say! That *is* astounding. So what's so wonderful about the Internet?'

'Nofin'. But I found a news bulletin.'

I placed my drink down and prepared to be amazed. 'Go on, then, shock me.'

'Guess 'oo's dead.'

'King George.'

'No, the boaties.'

I sat up with ears pricked. 'The boaties?'

'Yeah. Some'ow the yard burned up in the middle of the night an' two dead fellers were found in the ashes.'

'I'd say that *is* suspicious, but I wouldn't have thought that Doctor John Bromley was the sort to go around burning down boatyards and killing thieves, would you?'

'Yeah, but 'e's got the money to pay a 'elper to do it for 'im.'

'A co-conspirator. That would mean he's not alone and has something else to hide. Why didn't he just go collect his stolen property? I bet that boat was evidence of something a load more sinister than a mere accidental abduction. He must have been lying about fishing for naked women.'

Gran walked into the room as I was speaking. For a moment she stood and listened and then said, 'Dear William, I fear you may have grasped the wrong end of the stick.'

'Meaning what exactly, Gran?'

She walked over to me and sat. 'I have discovered something that nullifies your theory in-totus.'

'In who?'

She smiled. 'In-totus, dear. Completely.'

'Oh yeah, like what, Gran? And I doubt you even know what my theory is.'

'Doctor John Bromley committed suicide. The man is quite dead and could not have started any fires anywhere.'

'And how do you know that?'

'I read the newspapers, dear. Doctor Bromley of the Cormorant Institute, a renowned and well-liked surgeon, was found dead in his house at Mimico and, my dear, that was before the fire. So it looks like someone else is cleaning up a mess that the good doctor may have created.'

My breath stopped for a moment. 'The Cormorant Institute. Man! that's the place Jenny Stilton was supposed to have escaped from. This is becoming a head-banging puzzle. I looked it up on the map and Lake Opinnagau is at least a couple of hundred miles from Balmy Beach. How did a scantily dressed woman fall in a lake hundreds of miles from where she supposedly escaped?'

'Kilometres, dear.'

'Whatever. Miles or kilometres, Gran, it just doesn't add up. She couldn't swim that far.'

'Be interestin' to know,' Newf said with a huge smile on his face, 'if that twit doctor could fly a plane.'

'What on earth has that got to do with anything, you twit?'

'Remember when we was in Stinky Bay and talked to that old geezer? There was a plane out in the water.'

'Okay,' I agreed. 'So she somehow smuggled herself aboard the plane, then he fishes her out of the water. That doesn't make any sense, either.'

'O' course. She tries to swim ashore. 'e spots 'er an' brings 'er back. 'e knows 'oo she is.'

'So how did she finish up at Arthur?'

63

'Cor blimey, Bill, use yours finker. The doc fishes 'er out o' the water, now 'e's gotta subdue 'er till 'e can get 'er back to the Institute. So 'e drugs 'er, plonks 'er in the boat, which ain't in the water, an' goes off to report 'is find to 'is boss. When 'e comes back, the bird an' the boat 'as flown.'

'Alright,' I agreed. 'So how come the doc is dead and the boatyard is just ashes?'

'I think,' Gran said authoritatively, 'we have all grasped the wrong end of the stick.'

'What do you mean by that, Gran?'

'Suppose the good doctor is … should we say, not completely in harmony with whatever happens at the Cormorant Institute and the girl had a little help escaping. Let me suggest that it is the Institute and not the doctor which has something to hide. It doesn't take a very large stretch of the imagination to think that a henchman could have tied up all the loose ends by eliminating the boat, the boaties and the doctor. Now there is no evidence anywhere of any crime that can be laid at the doorstep of the Institute.'

Trust Gran to turn a story upside down and inside out. A simple case of hit-and-run has become a major crime and a cover-up. But what are they covering up and why?

'Gran, at this point I think it's no longer of our concern. The only crime I know of is the one or ones committed by the O'Brien brothers. The boaties killed Jenny Stilton, they steal boats – there's nothing to incriminate the doctor except your guesswork.'

'What about the Cormorant Institute, dear? What part in this drama would you suggest they play?'

'Well, that might be worth a look. The Magnuscarter mob wants to do a field test next spring. I figure we'll do the test up at Lake Opinnagau and at that time I can give them the once-over.'

'How many people will die in the meantime, William?'

'Jenny died by accident. She possibly escaped and got herself run down by a bunch of criminals. It was a genuine accident. I don't think anyone else is in danger, Gran. I'm sure it can wait till next spring.'

And so be it. As far as I was concerned, solving the case would be postponed until we performed the Magnuscarter test. In the meantime I had a wedding, birthdays, and a birth to contend with. Oh yes! And a preliminary test of the geo-echo device. Life just seems to get more and more complicated. I tell you, the older you get, the less time there is. A very funny thing happened a few days later. Well … funny is hardly the term.

Gran came into the den where I was trying to understand the drawings of the Magnuscarter device. Suddenly I heard this noise. Looking up, I saw Gran was standing there watching me.

'So what's the prob, Gran?'

She walked over to me with a very stern look on her face. 'William, dear.'

'Yeah.' I stopped studying and slid the papers aside. As I sat to listen, Gran eased her weight by sitting on the edge of my desk.

'William, dear. You said this case could wait until spring as no one else was in any danger.'

I shrugged. Obviously, I'd put my foot in it again. 'Yes. What's happened now?'

'Do you remember Mr Stilton?'

'Sure. He was the one who started all this. His daughter was killed up at Arthur; the body on the road.'

'And did you not say there would be no deaths, no danger? In fact, you said that all would be calm until spring.'

'Yes, Gran. Please get to the point; the suspense is

killing me.'

'Apparently, Mr Stilton was found dead in his apartment in Dundas yesterday.'

'Oh! Murder?'

'According to the local newspaper, he committed suicide. Would you not think this is somewhat of a coincidence?'

'You're referring to Doctor Bromley?'

'Yes, William.'

Again, I shrugged. 'Gran, I can't prevent people from killing themselves if that's what's in their minds.'

'Do you not consider it a coincidence?'

'Sure. So it's a coincidence.'

'A very famous detective once said, "There are no coincidences in crime." It would seem we have two suicides, both closely associated with our prime suspect, both in connection to Jenny Stilton. And then there is the third coincidence of an accidental fire at the boatyard where two suspects just happened to die. William, I do believe you are totally blind, or is it that you do not want to see?'

'No, Gran, I can see what you're getting at, but what do you want me to do about it?'

'Solve this mystery before anyone else dies, William, that is what I want you to do.'

Chapter 6

Anomalies

Would you believe, my thirtieth birthday rolled around on 14 September – a miserable and rainy Monday. Already, I'm an old man. It seems like only yesterday that Mum and Dad died in that traffic accident, yet a lifetime has passed since then. I think Gran is beginning to show her age, poor old dear. She seems slower. Oh! not in her mind, but in her actions. The old girl's as sharp as a tack when it comes to puzzles. Newf, the old sod, is a little older than me and on my birthday as a present for me, he never once used his wheelchair.

What did I get for my birthday? From Gran, I got a new, very small and very complicated digital camera. She said it would be good for collecting evidence and that I should carry it at all times. Heaven knows why. I already had a phone that takes stills and movies and can send them over the air to almost any destination. But she means well. Of all things dangerous, Newf and Morag bought me a snowmobile. My dear wife handed me a card that said her present was on its way and that I should show some patience. What the hey! Who cares? I have her. I don't need anything else.

A few days after my birthday the three stooges turned up again: Or as I jokingly call them, Curly, Larry and Magnus. For eggheads they put on a real good comedy show. They arrived in an old, beat-up Ford towing an equally beat-up trailer. Unloading the trailer was a comedy act unto itself. Laurel and Hardy would have been proud of them. The greatest difficulty was the very tall drilling rig. Although the machine was self-propelled, none of them seemed to know how to drive it or, for that matter, how to start it. Eventually, they got it off the trailer and none managed to die or even sustain any permanent injury in the attempt.

'So what's all this junk?' I asked after a good laugh.

Magnus grinned. 'It's for the test.'

'Test? What test?'

'I've got three geras. I ... er, that is, we ... well, if you like, we can see what's under your house?'

'See what's under it? What on earth do you mean?'

'We'll do the test here.'

'I thought you said the echo thingies have to be a kilometre apart?'

'Oh no, they can be any distance. Don't you like the idea?'

I shrugged. 'Sure. You lot staying for supper.'

They all brightened up and nodded in the affirmative, looking like a load of school kids on a Sunday outing.

'Alright,' I said, raising my voice, 'I'll tell the servants to prepare three rooms. You guys may as well stay the night; unless you have other plans?'

You would have thought I'd offered them $100 an hour pay rise. The delight on their faces was worth the expense. I can only suppose that academics live a very frugal life or the thought of real food and a comfortable bed was new to them.

Magnus grinned like a Cheshire cat. 'Sir, oh, sir.'

'Don't call me sir. It's very ... well I don't like it. Call me Bill; everyone else does.'

'Yes, sir, Bill. Yeah, oh ... Bill, we need somewhere secure to put the geras; they are delicate and expensive. We also need somewhere secure to put the ammunition.'

'Ammunition? What ammunition?'

'The cartridges, which of course are explosives.

Don't want them falling into young hands.'

'Okay. We can use one of the garages round the back – they are lockable.'

As Raven House, that's my house, is larger than the hotel that I own there would be no problem putting up three guests. In fact, a dozen or so wouldn't make much difference. This evening we would use the grand dining room, much to Gran's delight. I think the old girl likes plenty of guests as it gives her an opportunity to show off her vast knowledge. The woman's like a walking encyclopaedia.

As usual Gran sat at the head of the huge 12-foot-long table. I do apologise – the huge, almost 4-metre-long table. I sat at the other end with Deloris on my left. Everyone else was scattered along both sides. After the food had been brought in Gran opened the conversation by posing a question.

'Which of you gentlemen actually invented this searching device?'

Paul Manningham, easily the oldest member of the group, timidly coughed and said, 'Well, madam. Actually, I did, but David was the one who put the finishing touches to it.'

'You're the engineer, Mr Manningham?'

'No, ma'am, just a geologist.'

'Oh, please call me Zelda; there is little call for formality in this house.'

'Yes, ma'am.'

'So, what makes your geophone so wonderful compared to those already in use by such as the oil companies?'

'Just two things, ma'am …'

'That's Zelda,' she interrupted.

'Yes, sorry. Well, two things. One, we use a device rather like a laser, but instead of light amplification it's sound amplification and phasing. The sound is directed into a vertical- or horizontal-phased wave. This gives us the Doppler effect we need. A computer actually measures all the waves and creates a three-dimensional representation of the world below.'

Gran's eyes lit up as if she understood what the geek was talking about. 'So you have virtually invented a radar that works like a bat's echolocation?'

'Even more so. The multiple phasing gives us a picture just like ultrasound, where you can see the baby right in the mother's womb. Well, our gera does the same thing to the soil or rock.'

'Fascinating. When will we see this marvellous device in operation?'

'First thing tomorrow we'll make the test and by afternoon we should have the pictures.'

I interrupted. 'For crying out loud, do we have to talk shop at supper? I'd rather eat. Anyhow, who cares how this gismo works as long as it does what it's supposed to do when it's supposed to do it!'

'William, dear, you are being very rude to our guests. I for one am interested in this device and how it works, as you should be.'

'Sure, Gran. But let's leave the details to the field of operation and concentrate on the consumption of this delightful meal.'

I don't think the three musketeers had ever had a proper meal before. Talk about getting stuffed. I would say that any one of them put away more food than the rest of my family put together.

The next morning turned out to be chilly and damp, but nonetheless the scientific trio were not only up before me, but they were also fed and working when I wandered down into the breakfast room.

'Good morning, dear,' Gran greeted cheerily.

'Hi, Gran. Where is everybody?'

'Deloris has gone to see her doctor –'

'She alright, is she?'

'Yes, dear, just routine. North and Morag are helping the Magnuscarter team to drill a few holes in your property.'

'Oh, what's for breakfast?'

'I can see, dear, that your enthusiasm is close to overwhelming. Is all the excitement too much for you?' she said sarcastically.

I had a good, hearty breakfast – one can't start the day on an empty stomach – then I donned my winter coat and walked out to see what the gang were up to. Newf and Morag were operating the little drilling rig out in the middle of our front lawn. Quickly, I walked over to them and shouted above the noise of the machine.

'What the bloody hell are you two doing to my lawn?'

Newf grinned. 'Would yah believe, drillin' a 'ole.'

'Exactly. Why are you drilling a hole in the middle of the lawn? Couldn't you find somewhere less conspicuous to do it?'

'They 'as to be a certain distance apart, so unless yous want a 'ole in the driveway, shut up and let us get on wiv it.'

'Where are the other idiots?'

'John, Dave and Paul are round the back loadin' the gera fings.'

Apparently, they had arranged the geras in a triangle of about 150 metres on each side with my house almost dead centre. One device had already been primed and stood guarded by a little red fence.

'I thought these things had to be about a kilometre apart?' I said, addressing Paul Manningham, the oldest of the bunch.

He shook his head. 'No, they can be any distance up to about a click and a half.'

'Okay, so when's the test gonna happen?'

'In about twenty minutes.'

'Okay, so I'll be in the swimming pool room; it's warmer in there. Call me before you do it. I'd like to see how things go.'

'Sure thing.'

Obviously, I was not needed. All these scientific brains worked well without my input and Newf seemed to be enjoying himself with the drilling rig. I like the swimming pool room – it's kind of soothing. Nice soft furniture and the gentle sound of rushing water, coupled with the humidity, makes for a pleasant and quiet atmosphere. I sat there reflecting on my life. Man! what a past. You would wonder what the future holds. Deloris is the best woman in the world but she didn't give me anything for my birthday. That kind of makes one wonder. Of course I know the reason – she's going to heap some outrageous surprise on me. Her excuse is the forthcoming birth.

'Wake up, Bill. We's gonna blow up yours garden.'

I jumped to my feet with the shock.

'I didn't hear you come in.'

'Nah, you wouldn't 'ear anyfing above all that snorin'.'

The team was assembled in the front yard on the lawn about 10 metres from the gera hole. Gran stood there with a grin as wide as the Niagara River.

'What's with the smile, Gran?' I asked, stepping onto the grass.

'Don't you think this is exciting, William? Our first test!'

'Our, what's with the "our"?'

'Oh! don't be so stuffy, William. It's our as in all of us. A test of the Magnuscarter.'

'Not really all that exciting; it's only a firing test.'

'You have no imagination, my boy. We are just

waiting for young William to arrive and then Mr Manningham will tell us what is to happen.'

I shook my head in disgust. What a load of crap. All this fuss for a few underground pops.

'Go on then, Paul. Get on with it before we all freeze to death out here.'

Miss Whine, William Tan's tutor and babysitter, came from the front door holding the boy's hand. Paul coughed and began his speech.

'Ladies and gentlemen, firstly I would like to say that we are all perfectly safe standing here. The explosive devices are only the equivalent of 12 gauge cartridges and will be fired at a depth of 3 metres. Mr Reyner, that is Bill, would you like to press the initiation button?'

I shrugged. 'Sure, I guess so.'

He handed me a little black box that had a small antenna and a large red button.

'Just press the button when you're ready, Bill.'

'Sure. Everyone ready? Okay, then. In ten, nine, eight, seven, six, five, four, three, two, one, zero!'

I pressed the button. Instantly, the hole nearest went bang like a small firework cracker and then with a sort of zip sound, the remaining eight cartridges fired at a rate of four per second. Then it was all over, like big deal.

'That's it?' I quizzed.

Paul seemed delighted and the other two clowns were ecstatic with joy. It sure doesn't take much to please some people. Paul came over and shook my hand.

'It's great, sir. I'll retrieve the memory sticks and Dave can start rendering immediately.'

'Rendering?'

'Yes, sir. The sticks have to be downloaded onto a computer and then the three-dimensional picture can be rendered. It should only take about three hours.'

'Your kidding. Three hours? Why so long? Can't you get a faster computer?'

'Our computer is not very fast and there are literally billions of vectors to calculate. Is it alright if we use your den for the rendering?'

'Sure. You got a computer with you?'

'Oh, yeah. I'll get right to it.'

I sighed and then said, 'You guys may as well stay for lunch. Morag, would you go inform Cook for me, please?'

After lunch we all retired to my den where the, quote, rendering, unquote, had been completed. You would think it was the launching of the *Queen Elizabeth III* or something. A great deal of fuss over a non-comprehensible load of coloured vomit on a computer monitor.

'That's it?' I snapped, observing the green-and-purple modern art.

David Carter, the computer-programming expert, excitedly began to explain what we were looking at.

'That's the three-dimensional view of the subsoil under and around your house.'

'So what's all those yellow balls?' I asked.

'Those are the result of glacial drift,' Paul answered.

'I hate to tell you lot, but there hasn't been any glaciers around these parts for about 10,000 years.'

Paul chuckled. 'No, that's what's left after they stopped. What you are looking at is a deposit of round stones pushed here from hundreds of kilometres away.'

'So what's all the grass doing up in the sky and, I may add, growing upside down?'

Again Paul answered. 'Those are the roots of trees. Dave, swing it round; let's see the house foundations.'

David Carter pressed a few keys and using the mouse moved, the scene to what looked like an upside-down building. I mean, you would expect to see a house at the bottom on the ground, not floating around in the clouds.

'Why is it floating in the air?' I asked.

Again Paul chuckled. 'You have to remember, Bill, you have a worm's-eye view. Look – that's the foundations. There's the swimming pool and that's the basement.'

'We don't have a basement.'

'I'm sorry but you most certainly do. Look, there it is. You can even see the stairs leading up.'

'I promise you; we don't have a basement,' I reaffirmed with emphasis. 'This is my house; I would know if there was a basement.'

Paul pointed to the screen. 'See there it is. The entrance is somewhere in the front foyer.'

'Do you know anything about a basement, Deloris?' I asked.

She shook her head and said, 'It should be easy to settle. Let's call Mr Post. He's the man who rebuilt this place – he would surely know.'

The gang was invited to stay for dinner again, which I prefer calling supper. Mr Post was out on a mission somewhere, but his secretary said she would give him a message. John Magnus –the leader of the three musketeers –never said very much, but he absorbed everything with keen interest. The funny thing was that just before supper he came to me and whispered in my ear.

'You've got a body.'

'Well of course I have; otherwise, my head would roll on the floor.'

'No, I mean you have a body in the grounds.'

I stared at him for a moment. 'Dead or alive?'

'Well, dead I would say. It's just a skeleton, really, but it's as clear as a pikestaff. You want to see it?'

I followed him back to my den. Newf and Morag were already there discussing the corpse. John pointed to the screen.

'Zoom into that bit, Dave.'

The picture rotated a little and then zoomed in on a skeleton. There, for all to see lay this dead geezer only 10 metres from my swimming pool – on the outside of the building.

'What's that misty orange square?' I asked, pointing.

'Looks like the coffin. Yeah, I would guess it's what's left of the coffin – most of it's probably rotted away. Must have been there quite a while.'

'Oh, so he's not a newcomer, then?'

Griffin came into the room. 'Excuse me, sir. Mr Post has arrived. Do you wish to see him in the drawing room?'

'Is he here or at the gate?'

'Here, sir.'

'Okay show him into this room. I'd like him to see what we've found.'

'Certainly, sir.'

A few moments later, Mr Post came into the room. His face immediately lit up with a huge grin and he slapped Paul Manningham on the back.

'I take it you two know each other, then?' I commented.

'Most certainly, Mr Reyner. I recommended Paul come see you about his geological work. Now, I gather you've found something of interest under the house.'

'Yeah,' I said drearily. 'Take a look at this and then explain it to me.'

He looked at the screen. 'I don't quite know what I'm looking at.'

'It's the underside of the house and there is a basement that Bill says does not exist,' Paul said,

76

indicating the shape with his finger.

'Ah, yes. Well, you see, the original house did in fact have a basement. They used it for a cold storage; ice, you see. The servants would gather blocks of ice and store them in the cold room so it would last them all summer.'

'So why don't I have a cold room?' I asked.

He grinned and said, 'Sir, you can afford a refrigerator. The cold room would only encourage vermin. I had it sealed off. But if you feel it necessary we could excavate it; the stairs are stone and still there.'

'No, don't bother. Now, would you like to explain the dead geezer in my backyard?'

'Oh dear, that is nasty. I do apologise for that, Mr Reyner. We had all the bodies removed. It would seem we must have missed one.'

'Missed one? What do you mean, missed one?'

'The original owners were Empire Loyalists and moved here in the late 1700s. They were trying to avoid the 1812 War, you know. In those days the rich always had their own cemeteries, usually on the property not too far from the house. There were eighteen graves and headstones, which I had removed to Woodlands Cemetery at Aldershot. This one must have been separate – probably the first, even before the house was built. I do apologise most profoundly.'

Mr Post seemed to have all the answers. At least this time it wasn't murder or stolen gold. Nonetheless, I really don't like dead bodies on my property.

'So, can we have this one moved and planted with the rest of his family?'

'Certainly. You do realise that it will be at your expense?'

'I don't care. I just want whoever it is off the property. How come there isn't a headstone for this one?'

Post smiled. 'I would suppose that the grave was marked by a wooden cross and merely got lost in time.'

The excitement seemed to be over for the time being and the three stooges took their equipment and toddled off home to plan the big test for the spring. Manningham wanted to do the test in February – his reasoning being that the lakes would be frozen and transport would be easy using snowmobiles or snowcats. Personally, I don't like the cold and up that far north we could easily see more than twenty degrees below zero.

Chapter 7

Taken by Surprise

Newf's birthday is on 17 January, which turned out to be a Sunday this year. I keep telling him only idiots are born in the month of January. Preparations for such a do that close to Christmas makes for some difficulty. This time the idea was to make it a surprise – like play it down and pretend nothing was going to happen. I decided that the celebration would be at the Canadian – my hotel up by the lake. This way I could make all the arrangements without a nosy birthday boy sticking his trunk in where it's not wanted. One problem – what do you buy an idiot for his birthday when he's already got everything?

Of late there seems to be an extraordinary amount of paperwork to complete. I get all the household accounts to clear, bills and receipts, then there's wages to organise and of course house maintenance, not to mention the Canadian. The den had become my office and all the paperwork somehow arrives on my desk. Oh, there's no problem – it's merely a load of work. I had just signed the last cheque when Gran walked in.

'Hi, Gran, what's up?'

'William, dear,' she said and eased herself into a chair opposite. 'I have been cogitating.'

Now to me cogitating had to be something to do with being a codger. I didn't answer but instead stared at her with a quizzical expression.

'You look stunned, dear. Even at my age it is possible to have thoughts.'

'Thoughts, Gran? What's that got to do with being a codger?'

'A codger, dear? Oh dear, you are such a simpleton. I thought you had been educated. Did all those years at McMaster's University do nothing for your intellect?'

'You said –'

'I know what I said, dear. Cogitation is thought, pondering. Probably something you should consider before opening your mouth, dear.'

'Doesn't seem to have softened your tongue, Gran.'

She sighed very loudly and deliberately. 'William, are you interested in what I have to say or not?'

'I don't know, what have you been thinking, Gran?'

'Oh, hapless William. I have been thinking about your case.'

'Case, what case?'

Again she sighed audibly. 'William, if you are not interested, then mayhap I should go talk to someone who is interested.'

'No, no, Gran. You just confuse me, that's all. So what is it you've been thinking about?'

'You do remember that a young lady has been murdered?'

'Murdered, no. Who was that?'

'Jenny Stilton, for heaven's sake. North of Arthur.'

'Oh! that. Sure, I know what you're talking about. So what's new?'

'Nothing is new, dear. I have been giving the puzzle a lot of thought.'

'Cogitation?'

'Exactly, dear. We have three versions of the story: one from the boat minder at Balmy Beach, one from Mr Stilton and one from Doctor John Bromley.'

'Four, then.'

'What do you mean four, William?'

'There was the tale from the boaties.'

'Yes, of course. Nonetheless, the stories do not tally. Neither do they add up to anything near to the truth.'

'Oh yeah? Go on, then, Gran, explain it to me.'

'Whether or not by accident, the boaties managed to kill Miss Stilton – this is a certified fact. The poor girl was ill clad, the doctor's excuse being that she had been fished out of the water.'

'Yeah, so?'

'The good doctor said his boat was in the water, yet the boaties say the vessel was high and dry.'

'So far, Gran, you've come up with nothing astounding. We know all this.'

'Indeed, William, dear. Have you ever extracted a boat from the water?'

'You know I have, dozens of times.'

'How long would it take an expert to pull a boat onto a trailer?'

I thought about it for a moment. 'Well if everything is prepared, including backing the dolly into the water, I don't know – say, maybe half an hour tops.'

'Where was the boat when you started, William.'

'Huh? Like what do you mean?'

'For a thirty-minute extraction, the boat must have already been at the ramp.'

'Oh, I see. Right, Gran. It could take a lot longer; especially if it's moored out in the lake.'

'Exactly, William. The boaties must have been informed. At least an hour's drive, an hour extracting the vessel and an hour home. Yet no one saw a thing. I suspect the boat was not in the water at all, then it would only take is coupling up the trailer and off you go. The doctor most likely is a liar. Next, peculiarity. Do you not think it is rather a stretch of the imagination for a doctor of the Cormorant Institute to find a patient of that same Institute by accident, just swimming around naked and hundreds of kilometres from the place she supposedly escaped from?'

'Sure, yeah. I suppose that is a bit on the fishy side.'

'Fishy, indeed, William.'

'But, Gran, what possible other explanation could there be?'

She smiled. 'I hoped you would ask. Consider this as a more feasible scenario. You saw an aeroplane in the water, did you not?'

'Yeah, so?'

'Does the good doctor have a pilot's licence?'

'You mean he was helping her escape, when the plan went pear-shaped?'

'No, William. Tell me, is there a public phone at Balmy Beach?'

'No idea, Gran. Why?'

'Then surmise this. Miss Stilton could not phone her father from the Institute, as there would be no repeaters or cell towers that far north. I would surmise the Institute uses radio, akin to the ship-to-shore you had on Fiend's Rock. Therefore, I reason she must have phoned from Balmy Beach. Then she was captured by the doctor and rendered senseless. He must have left to make a report or complete whatever task he was there to finish. On returning, he found the boat stolen and along with it the very woman he was going to return to the Cormorant Institute.'

'So how did she get in the water?'

'William, dear, the woman was never *in* the water. She must have stowed away on the aeroplane and was captured after calling her father.'

'Should be easy to find out, Gran. I'll have a search made for a pilot's licence in the doctor's name.'

'Good. Now, about young North's wedding.'

'I'll organise everything, don't you worry yourself.'

'No, you will not, my dear,' she said emphatically. 'I have arranged for a wedding planner to handle the entire thing. All you have to do is make sure North doesn't do anything stupid in the meantime. I want him healthy, sober and vertical on his wedding day. Can I trust you with this simple task?'

'Sure, Gran.'

The trouble with Gran is that she thinks I'm an idiot and incapable of carrying out simple tasks without her direction. 'Think outside the box, William,' she's always saying. Think outside the box, my foot. Who was it who solved the mystery of the *Serena,* a submarine lost for sixty years and the mystery of Fiend's gold? Me, of course. Like, I mean, it's obvious even to Newf that the good doctor is, or was a bad dude. The Cormorant Institute has something to hide and that quack was up to his educated neck in it. Why does Gran *think* I want the geological test done up at that particular lake? Now I'm so stupid I can't even organise a simple wedding. Wedding planner, my left foot.

One or other of the three stooges would pop in from time to time. Whichever one it was, they would always pretend to be overenthusiastic, tell me all the latest news and then present me with a bill. Would you believe, they rented an old store on King Street in Hamilton and purchased a computer I'd never heard of?

'We really do need it, sir,' David H. Carter said with as much bubbly energy as he could muster.

'What's wrong with a regular PC?'

'Oh, nothing. Except it would take a Pentium multiputer about a week to do all the calculations.' He grinned as if he'd cracked a subtle joke.

'And how long would it take this new thing?'

He smiled as though he was winning the argument. 'About fifteen minutes. And it can handle much better graphics. You'll love it. The Cray CX1 is the bee's knees. You'll absolutely love it.'

'At that price, I'll have to love it. What's it come with – a Rolls-Royce instead of a mouse?'

He forced a laugh at my puny joke. 'No, sir, but it will play games.'

'Great.' I snatched the detailed invoice from his hot little hands and wrote him a collective cheque for $10,000. 'If this Magnuscarter of yours turns out to be a damp squid, you guys will either have to live in Argentina or work the rest of your life for me as slaves.'

I mean like ten grand, Jesus! And that's only the down payment. I figured I'd pop in this cosy nest on King Street as a surprise. See just what my money was being spent on. I'm sure I could get a better return from the stock market.

As luck would have it on Monday, 11 January, Deloris decided she could no longer fit into her dress and needed something more befitting a pregnant lady of means.

'What's wrong with the other fifty or so you've got stuffed away in your closet?'

'Billy, dear. There are only five, not fifty. Look at me.' She cupped her bulging stomach with both hands. 'I need something more comfortable. Please come with me. I don't want the chauffeur and you can help me choose. I trust your advice.'

Like as if I had a choice. At least I would be able to drop in on the three stooges to see for myself what they were up to at the premises that I was paying for. The weather was cold but clear and the streets were well sanded. Driving in poor conditions with a very pregnant wife was not the pastime I really wanted. What if something were to happen? There were loads of stupid drivers out there. Within ten minutes we were on our way in the Rolls to wherever.

As we descended the mountain into Dundas, I said, 'I want to drop in on the Bobbsey triplets, in King Street. Where do you want to go?'

'There's a very nice shop for expectant mothers on Concession up Hamilton Mountain.'

'Okay, we'll pop in on the three stooges just before going up there. Is that alright?'

'Certainly, Billy, dear.'

The trouble with King Street is that the traffic flow is in the wrong direction. I turned onto Queen and headed back toward Dundas. Finding the place was easy and parking was round the back. Obviously one of the stooges spotted or heard the car, for as soon as I stopped, the shop back door opened and Magnus stood there waving and grinning like a schoolboy. I helped Deloris out of the car and we entered the techno-world of the earth-burrowing electronic rabbits. The place was filled with junk: old computers, discarded monitors, a three-legged table and three sleeping bags.

'You idiots sleep here?' I enquired.

Paul Manningham was the first to speak up.

'Oh, those. Well no, not really. If we work late … well … there you have it – you know, somewhere to crash.'

'When will you be ready for the big test up north?'

His face lit up like a navigation beacon. 'Oh, we're pressing ahead. Only waiting for the last few geras to be completed and tested now. Should I organise the expedition or would you like to do it yourself?'

'I suppose you seem quite capable; just give me a few days' warning.'

'Oh, sure, Mr Reyner.'

'So where's this super computer I've forked out a fortune for?'

Paul conducted us into another room, which looked more like Nasa space centre. At least a dozen active monitors of various sizes cast the only light in the otherwise dark room. In the corner of the room stood this thing half the size of a regular refrigerator, with more wires leading heaven knows where than you'd find in a twentieth-century telephone exchange.

'That's it?' I asked.

'Sure, isn't it great. Look, look,' he said excitedly. 'Here on this monitor you can see your house in detail. We can't wait to get a real ninety firing.'

'A what?'

'All ninety geras at once. Gonna be spectacular.'

Typical of the nerd generation, the man spoke in techno-riddles. It was all very interesting, but it meant absolutely nothing to me; other than that they were all engrossed in it. Suddenly, I noticed Deloris. She looked to be in pain.

'What's wrong?'

'Oh, nothing, Billy, dear. Just a twinge, that's all.'

'A twinge of what?'

'Oh, don't be such a fusspot.'

'It's not the baby, is it? You're not going to explode here on the floor, are you?'

'I'm not going to explode anywhere. Now stop being an old nanny and let's get to my shopping.'

'Okay, if you're sure you're alright?'

'Of course I am. You do fuss so.'

I drove up the Jolly Cut to Concession. It's only a rise in altitude of some 100 metres or so, but my ears always pop. The shop sold wedding gowns and baby things, including buggies and strollers. We walked to the preg-o-wear department and a young slip of a thing got all excited about Deloris, or maybe the thought of my money. Again, Deloris stopped in her tracks with a pained expression on her face.

'You alright?' I asked, beginning to feel a little hot under the collar.

She sighed and forced a smile. 'Just a twinge dear.'

'Twinge! Twinge. Should I call a doctor?'

Deloris laughed and said, 'Don't be so silly, Billy,

dear. The baby's not due for a month – it's just twinges, that's all. Nothing to worry about.'

Twinges, my foot. I can smell danger from two counties away. My heart began to race and I could foresee all kinds of dangers and disasters just waiting to spring up and bite me. Nonetheless, the shopping continued while I sat and chewed my fingernails. I think it was around the fourth or fifth fitting when it happened. Deloris was in that little changing room, when suddenly excitement broke out and people started rushing about. Like a sergeant major, the head shop assistant marched directly to me – back straight and head high.

'Mr Reyner.'

'Yeah?' I stood up, knowing there just had to be a disaster.

'We need to get your wife to the hospital promptly.'

'Why?'

'Her waters have broken.'

My knees buckled and if it hadn't been for her, I would have fallen to the floor. She eased me into a seat. Panic leapt up and surrounded me. My heart accelerated to a good 200 beats per minute.

'I'll get the car,' I said excitedly.

'Not to worry, Mr Reyner, the ambulance is on its way.'

'Ambulance, ambulance? She needs an ambulance?'

The world felt as though it had begun to spin faster and my thoughts fled from my head like sand from a broken egg timer. I couldn't stand up as my knees had turned to jelly.

Somehow or other, both Deloris and myself were bungled into an ambulance and whisked off to McMaster's Hospital. I really have little or no recollection of the proceedings. Deloris seemed to be in pain and my head had become filled with living-daylight nightmares.

At the hospital Lori was whisked away while a nurse tried to calm me down. Again, I have little recollection except somehow I arrived in a waiting room and only a few seconds later Newf hobbled in under his own steam with a crutch under each arm.

'Well look at you. So where did yous get shot?'

'I didn't – it's Lori.'

Newf laughed and came to sit with me. 'Don't worry, Bill. She's only gonna pop a sprog. Mrs H is here – nothing can go wrong. Loads of broads do it all the time.'

'Pop a sprog, you idiot? The baby's not due for a month. Something terrible's gone wrong.'

'Bill, relax afore yous blow a gasket or two. Deloris is in the right place – theses geezers are experts. You know, once, when I was little, a cat 'ad kittens on my bed. I wakes up an' 'ears all this racket, so I 'elps 'er. Twern't nofin' to it. Piece of cake.'

'Deloris isn't a cat. And I don't want any cake.'

'Same fing. All mammals is the same.'

'Well thank you, Doctor Spock.'

'Come on, me ol' mate. Buck up an' look on the bright side. Yous is gonna be a dad, ain't yah.'

'I'm already a dad.'

'Ah, but yous is gonna be a double dad.'

At that moment a nurse came into the waiting area. She walked directly to me with an ear-to-ear grin.

'Mr Reyner?'

'Yeah.' I stood up and began to feel a little wobbly again.

'There's nothing to worry about. Mrs Reyner is in the first stages. Doctor Reynolds thinks the baby has decided it has been hiding from us long enough.'

'Oh, God! You mean she's going to … going to … oh, God!'

'Relax, Mr Reyner. There is absolutely nothing to worry about; everything is progressing normally.'

'But she's a month early.'

'Come along, Mr Reyner, I'll take you to see your wife.'

I knew I should have gone up north. Oh heck! I'd rather be staring down a gun barrel than being led to this torture chamber. Talk about medieval, man! The torture instruments were all set up on a table in the room and three green-coated dungeon masters standing by. Mr heart leapt into my mouth as I saw Deloris lying on a bed. She didn't seem concerned. The guide led me to a chair beside Deloris. Thank goodness! Another few steps and I would have fallen over.

I didn't understand the proceedings but no one seemed very concerned. After a few minutes all the experts left the room and I was alone with Deloris.

'Where's everybody gone?' I gasped. 'Is it safe leaving you all alone like this?'

'*You're* here, dear.'

'But aren't you supposed to start screaming or something? I mean, what are we waiting for?'

She chuckled then winced. Instantly, I began to perspire. What if she had it now? I couldn't do anything. To my great relief, one of the nurses came back into the room. About four agonising hours later, things really began to happen. I remember sitting there holding her hand, when she said, 'Now!' and began to scream. My blood froze in my veins and my hair stood on end. The room darkened and when I opened my eyes, Newf was sitting beside me.

'What's going on?' I managed to wheeze through my very sore throat.

'You chickened out, Bill. What a geezer.'

I sat up. 'Chickened out, what are you talking about?'

'First grunt and yous hit the floor, like a pancake that missed the frying pan.'

'Oh! Deloris.'

'Yeah right, oo else?'

'Has she given birth yet?'

'No, just relax. I reckon they ain't gonna let you in there no more; yous is too much trouble.'

'It's not my fault. I was taken by surprise.'

Newf laughed. 'Don't worry, Bill. It'll all be over in awhile.'

I slumped back onto the bed. 'Thank God. If I'd have known it was this easy I'd have fainted at the dress shop.'

Chapter 8

Nuptials

Somehow it tickled Newf. The thought of me fainting fired up his imagination. He stood there glaring at me. It took a moment or two to recollect what had happened, plus the fact that Newf loved to rub it in. A young and pretty nurse walked into the room with a smile as large as sunlight.

'Mr Reyner, sir. How are we feeling?'

'Oh, hi. I, er … I guess I'm okay.'

'Excellent. Doctor Reynolds gave you a sedative.'

'Sedative?'

'While you were out – nothing to worry about. It should slow your heart a little. If you feel faint, just take a deep breath. Now, are we ready to return?'

'Ready to return? You mean it's not all over yet?'

Her grin would melt a dairy full of butter.

'Come along, Mr Reyner. Your wife needs your support.'

'Go on, Bill. Chin-up; you've faced worse. Just fink, it ain't Wilson.'

'Yes, but I have a phobia. That's what it is – I have a phobia. I'm allergic to women giving birth.'

'The best way to 'andle a fear, Bill, is to face it. Grits yours teef and pretend you's 'avin' a grand ol' time. Pretend you's got a coat 'anger in yours gob.'

'I'll stick a coat hanger in your mouth in a minute, Newf. I can't go back in there, I just can't.'

The nurse took my hand and again lit up the room with her smile.

'Come along, Mr Reyner. There's absolutely nothing to fear.'

She was perfectly right – there was nothing to fear. Still trembling all the way down to my roots I allowed the nurse to lead me back into the torture chamber. Thank God! it was all over. Everyone stood around with beaming expressions and there laying on Lori's chest was this little bundle: a hairless and wrinkled little imp.

'It's a girl,' said the chief surgeon.

I think my heart stopped. There was a sudden rush of blood to my feet and I almost fell over again.

'A girl!'

They certainly don't keep people in hospital longer than necessary these days. Lori was given a clean bill of health and allowed to leave only two days later. Our newborn, however, was a little premature. Fully healthy but severely underweight. Apparently, they don't like to let children out until they match this scale of weight or size they have, which was why the two-day stay.

It still shocks me – older you get, the faster time seems to pass. Like in ten minutes I was married, had solved the mystery of a missing submarine and increased the family by one. Although I saw William Tan just after his birth, I didn't remember the smallness. Have you ever looked at a newborn and held their little hands? She had ten perfect miniature fingers with beautiful and perfect little fingernails. Lori wanted to call her Christi after her mother. I agreed as long as the little mite had two names. I wanted Zelda. I thought Christi Zelda Reyner sounded good. I know the modern thing is to give the poor kid a dumb fruit or place name like Apple or Paris, but I don't like that. Christi Zelda sounds fine.

The next and biggest problem I had to face was to get that twerp, Newf, legally hitched to his Scottish face-sucking attachment. Newf wanted to walk down the aisle unaided, but Gran and myself didn't want to wait forever – we decided to go ahead with the arrangements as soon as possible. Being only a registry office affair, if he couldn't walk all that way on his own, well I'd be there to hold him up or even carry him if I had to.

The Stilton case had to be put on the back-burner. After all, there were no real clues. I knew the Cormorant Institute seemed to be at the centre of it all, but of what? Jane Overland, oh, now she's Jane Asquith, she used to be my best source of information, but she'd married my partner in the helicopter company and moved to England. Maybe a phone call would arouse her interest. The problem with calling England is that noon here is five in the evening there. Nonetheless, I managed to get up early enough to phone at noon, English time.

'Hi, Jane. It's me, Bill.'

'You darling boy. How have you been?'

'Great. I need your help, Jane.'

'Oh! my goodness. This is new – you actually asking for my help. Is the world about to end?'

'No. What do you know about the Cormorant Institute?'

She chuckled for a second or two. 'Never heard of it, my love. What are you hot on the trail of?'

'Don't know. One dead female so far. I'm sure the Cormorant Institute is at the centre of things but, I don't have anything.'

'Well, darling, I'm at a bit of a disadvantage over here, but I'll call a few friends and see what I can dig up for you. Any clues as to what you're looking for?'

'No, not really, but I feel they are up to no good. The Cormorant Institute seems to overshadow some skulduggery,'

A couple of days later the leader of the three

musketeers turned up at Raven House. Paul Manningham never looked happy; he would make a perfect funeral parlour attendant. He walked into my study and appeared to have the weight of the world on his shoulders.

'You look worried,' I said. 'Take a seat. I suppose you bunch want more money, is that it?'

'No, Mr Reyner, Bill. There's been a break-in.'

'A break-in. What d'you mean?'

'Someone broke in the lab and … and …'

'Yes, spit it out.'

'You see, they stole a gera and smashed the main computer.'

'And you guys didn't notice?'

'Well of course we did.'

'I thought I said the place was never to be left unmanned.'

'You did and we didn't. David's in hospital with a fractured skull.'

David H. Carter was or is our computer expert – the typical geek with thick glasses and a smooth, hairless head.

'So when did all this happen?'

'Last night.'

'What about the cops, anybody told them yet?'

'They were told, but what can they do? I think it's industrial espionage. Someone's trying to steal our idea.'

'Espionage? You mean piracy. Okay, that settles it. I'll hire a security company. We'll have two guards on site at all times.'

'But they've already got the gera.'

I shook my head. 'So they have one. I'll fly you up to Owen Sound and we can get my lawyer on it. We'll have to get patents and copyrights immediately. It won't do thieves any good. Also I'll get Mr Spadafora

94

on the job, to see if anyone is trying to sell our device on the black market. If I catch them, it won't be just a fractured skull. Now, what can I do for Dave?'

He shrugged his shoulders. 'He's in hospital.'

'Alright. See to it he gets whatever he needs. Private ward, whatever. Send me the bill. So how come I was not told of this affair earlier?'

'You were. Well, you are. I thought it best to come over here as soon as possible. We thought a phone call would look cheap or petty.'

'If anything, you guys are not cheap; particularly with my money. Which hospital's he in?'

'General, on Victoria Street.'

I couldn't imagine why anyone would want to steal an earth X-ray device and wreck our computer. There must be more to it than that. I phoned Mr Post the moment Manningham left my house.

'Ah, Mr Post. I need you to visit me as soon as possible at the house.'

'Oh dear, more trouble?'

'Yes and no. I want you to convert one of my garages into a research lab for the three musketeers.'

'The three musketeers? Who are they, actors?'

'Oh! sorry. I mean Paul Manningham and company.'

I should have done that in the first place. If the boys were here within the house grounds the likelihood of a bandit or vandal showing up would be greatly reduced. Somehow, I seemed to be doing nothing but organising things since the new baby arrived. The world would have appeared to have stopped and only I had the power to push it on its way. Newf is a pain and an annoyance, now the musketeers were having troubles. I'd have to employ a business manager or someone with a very large whip.

Post is a good man and he quickly organised a

building company to set up one of the garages as a research centre for the gera project. I arranged for a security man to be on duty 24/7. The computer company agreed to replace or repair our old machine and all would be set up in the new lab: my garage. The trouble with all this is that the clock never stopped ticking – the year was growing older at an alarming rate. With a new baby in the house, Gran was kept occupied. I think she thought she was the nanny.

Though everything seemed to be in a muddle, in reality all was proceeding according to plan. The gera test would definitely have to be held in the spring and not the fall. Nobody in their right mind goes up north in the dead of winter. But there again, nobody said I was in my right mind. There was the small inconvenience of a break-in and the boys having to move up to my house, although this would not really do any harm to the project.

Oh dear, the wedding. I do so hate having to organise things like that. My wedding to Deloris was hard enough, but Newf was marrying a girl from Scotland. Suddenly and like a bolt from the blue, an idea struck me. Here in Canada, Newf only has a handful of friends, but in Scotland Morag has a family and friends. Not too much of a stretch of the old imagination, but Gran owns a castle there.

'Newf, you old sod,' I said when I eventually found him in the swimming pool room as usual sucking face with his Highland lass.

'Yes, Bill?'

'I had a thought. How would you like to get married at Cromlet?'

His eyes lit up like a shipping beacon. 'Like, be the guest of honour, you mean?'

'Whatever.'

'Yeah, when?'

I had to think about that for a moment.

'I'll talk to Gran and see what she thinks; it is *her* castle.'

'What abart the fingy test?'

'The three musketeers can wait. Besides, the test may be delayed owing to a small problem with vandals. We have to get you all legal and above board. You did get your divorce through, I take it?'

'Yeah, course I did.'

'Okay, I'll see if I can't oil a few wheels and get this party on the road.'

'I don't wanna get married on no road.'

'Shut up, Newf.'

I smiled at myself. I'm not just a pretty face; he can have the wedding and the honeymoon in the same place. What better venue than a beautiful old castle in Scotland? My partner in the helicopter business, Reggie Asquith, could supply all the transport.

Fortunately, Gran turned out to be most agreeable. In fact, she acted as if it was all her idea. Great, at least most of the responsibility for organisation was taken from me. Now I could concentrate on the important things in life, such as the three musketeers and their project.

One of the garages was a double and plenty large enough to be converted into a research centre. Unfortunately they are not heated, but Mr Post soon found a reasonable temporary answer. While the three musketeers stayed in Canada and improved their invention in my garage, I was off to Scotland. I booked a first-class flight for my darling little Christi – my new daughter – and Deloris had found a nurse-cum-babysitter to go with us. So that meant we had William Tan and his minder, Mrs Whine, as well as the new lady, Mrs Evelyn Parker.

I should have chartered a plane, as all together there

were nine of us, including the baby. Getting through customs and immigration was awkward, what with all the newfangled rules. But eventually we made it aboard. The big problem would be the other end. Reggie might have to make two trips to get us all safely to Cromlet.

To say the crossing was without incident would be a falsehood. Newf, the prat, left his folding chair in the departure lounge. He managed to remember somewhere mid Atlantic, then he lost his walking stick on the plane.

'How the crap could you lose a stick on a plane?' I bellowed.

'Must o' left it somewhere.'

'Please, William, modify your language.'

'Sorry, Gran.'

Eventually, a steward found Newf's stick; he'd left it in one of the toilets. The trip was bumpy and when we descended over Scotland we came down through cumulonimbus cloud, which was almost like a roller-coaster ride. Needless to say, it was pouring with rain when we landed at Prestwick.

Both Reggie and Jane were waiting for us in arrivals. Man, it was good to see both of them.

'We're rather a large party,' were my opening words.

'Happy to see you, too,' Jane said and then gave me an enormous hug and a slobbery kiss. God, I wish she wouldn't do that.

'Not to worry, old bean,' Reggie said.

He looked great, standing there like the very pillar of society – dead straight back, smart uniform and a moustache that could sweep both sides of the room in one pass.

'But there's nine of us,' I complained.

'Not to worry, old bean.' He grabbed the trolley

with all our luggage on it and began leading us away from the crowds.

It felt a bit reminiscent of the time I first met Reggie at Bristol Airport. He led us out of arrivals and onto a concrete pan or dispersal area, and there stood one of the largest helicopters I have ever seen. He had arranged a portable tent-like apparatus on wheels close to the helicopter's entrance to keep us dry.

'So what do you think of our new baby?' he said, waving his hands at the monster machine.

'Holy cr … Good heavens.'

'Janey darling got us a new contract with National North Sea Oil. We service four rigs and have two new elephants like this one.'

'Wow!' was all I could say.

'She's a Eurocopter AS332. Carries up to twenty people and their luggage. This one's set up for passengers. Has a 540-mile range and a hefty top speed of 166 miles an hour, old bean.'

To say I was impressed would have been an understatement. The machine was beautiful – if only I could fly one! Man, it would be so much better than a floatplane.

'You can be my co-pilot, old bean. Just be polite to Sikorsky.'

Sikorsky is a huge, flat-faced smoky Persian cat with vicious claws and temperament to match. Reggie uses the cat as a sort of watchdog. Amazingly the cat remembered me and unlike the first time we met, he purred and brushed up against me in a friendly way. I climbed onto the flight deck and fussed the fur ball while our captain arranged the passengers and luggage.

'The old bugger remembers everything,' Reggie said as he climbed aboard. 'Your suit will get all hairy if you're not careful.'

'So how many of these machines have we got?'

'This one and two other windmills of the same ilk. We only own this one; the other two are on a sort of rent-to-own basis.'

I'd never seen Cromlet in the winter before. As we approached from the air the world looked frozen – a wonderland of snow. The entire scene looked like something from a Disney fairy tale. Cromlet looked beautiful and totally unreal as it nestled in a field of white with its many roofs covered in the same sparkling whiteness. The vision below told me that this was going to be a wedding to remember. The noise of the machine woke people up on the ground, for as we descended onto the snow-covered front lawn, people began coming out of the castle to meet us.

We blew up a minor snow squall as we settled down, then the blades were feathered and the engine shut down. Peace and quiet reigned. Sikorsky was the first out; I think he remembered Cromlet, for he surely knew where the kitchen was situated. Quickly, we all poured into the warm castle. At least all but Reggie, who took off again to deliver the helicopter to another pilot so it could be flown out to one of the oil rigs. Surprisingly, Sikorsky stayed with Jane and the rest of us.

Gran's a real whizz when it comes to accurate organisation. The wedding had been arranged for 20 December – only five days before Christmas. While Newf and Morag were on honeymoon, we would all spend the holidays at the castle; at least, that was the plan.

As they say, it never rains but it pours. Like Cromlet Castle is not good enough for a honeymoon, the twits – now married – wished to go on a holiday in the Shetlands. I have to get me a new aeroplane. Fortunately for everyone, Reggie came to the wedding in one of our smaller helicopters and could ferry the newlyweds to some place on the Shetland Islands.

Gran's a clever old girl. When Newf demanded to go to the Shetlands, she smiled and said, 'Certainly, my boy. I think it would be a grand idea for you and your bride, but do you think you are up to it? Can you walk or would you need the chair?'

'Oh, I can walk okay, Mrs H.'

'Good, then I'll book you on the ferry from Aberdeen; you'll love the sea voyage.'

I think the older you get the more hectic life becomes. Everything seems to happen at once. Newf goes on his honeymoon in the beautiful Shetland Islands then only two days after Christmas I'm on my way back to Hamilton; that's Hamilton in Canada. The brainy trio were apparently having trouble that needed my expertise.

The chauffeur picked me up at Pearson Airport and drove me back to Raven House. The weather for Canada was amazing – probably the first January I could remember with no snow on the ground. Although the house looked welcoming and warm, I felt that it was empty – no Deloris, no Gran and no Newf. The brain brigade was waiting by the front door as we pulled into the yard.

Paul Manningham rushed to the car and opened the door for me. 'Oh, Bill, are we ever glad to see you!' He looked like the rag doll that the dog brought home. His clothes were wrinkled and somewhat dirty.

'Can I at least go into the house?'

'Sure. We've run into a problem.'

'Please, allow me to unwind. I'd like a little rest then I'll sort your problems out. Okay?'

Like a scolded puppy, he slunk off with his tail between his legs. Griffin was, as ever, the perfect, stoic fortress of pure gentlemanliness.

'Would sir like a nice hot bath before supper?'

'Yeah, that sounds good.'

'Come this way, sir. We'll handle your luggage. I'll see to it that there is hot cocoa and a whisky awaiting you in the den, sir, after your refreshing bath.'

It's nice to be pampered, but it's no substitute for family. Dressed in my best silk robe, I wandered into the den after my bath. Just what I needed – the Brains Trust was waiting for me.

'Okay,' I grouched as I entered. 'So what's all this distress?'

Manningham decided to be the spokesman.

'Well, sir, I mean Bill, sir. Space Tech will not give us the GPSs we ordered. We can't do anything without them.'

'You had me travel 7,000 kilometres just to tell me that?'

'Actually, no, not just that. The police caught the person who stole our gera.'

I sighed deeply and looked at my watch. 'Well, I would imagine that the staff at Space Tech are off until after the New Year. Don't worry; everything will be alright. I'll see to everything myself. We can't do the test until later in the year, anyway.'

'Oh, no! I've arranged it for Groundhog Day.'

'Groundhog Day, February second. There'll be 1,000 foot of snow up there.'

'It's alright. A bit cold, but snowmobiles and planes with skis will work. That's another thing. Could you talk to Grundy and Brown Air for us? I can't seem to explain what we need.'

'So what *do* you need?'

'I've rented two caterpillar boring machines; they'll be here in a week or so. We need to carry them to Lake Muswabik.'

'Ah, yes,' I said. 'We'll be doing the test at Lake Opinnagau. That's where I want the test.'

Manningham shrugged. 'Okay, you're the boss. Either way, we'll need a way to get the stuff there. Would you talk to Mr Grundy?'

'Sure; leave it all to me.' At least I would have something to do until the others returned. 'So, where are you guys living these days?'

'Ah, well, your butler said it would be alright if we … well, if we sort of live in the garage. He said we can use the bathroom in the swimming pool area. That's okay, isn't it?'

I shook my head in disgust. 'I suppose so, but I would like to see you guys dressed more like scientists than hobos.'

'Oh, yeah, sure, sorry.'

Chapter 9

Lake Opinnagau

New Year's Day was a miserable affair with no family. I should have stayed in Scotland with them. There is absolutely nothing I can do on the gera project until everyone returns to work after the holidays. They do say that new year in Scotland is something else! Oh well, such is life.

I wandered into the garage where the Brains Trust operated. All three were huddled around a new-looking box of tricks.

'So, what yah got?' I asked.

Like a schoolboy caught peeping in a porno magazine, they scattered and pretended to be doing something else. David Carter almost dropped his glasses.

'I, er … er, that is ... we …'

'Never mind the excuses, what's happening? Why the red faces?'

'It's just a bit of fun.'

'Then cough up, what's happening?'

Carter cleared his throat then coughed a couple of times. 'Go on then, take a look for yourself.'

I walked over and he pressed a few keys on his keyboard. I looked at the screen and saw a cloudy, indistinct mosaic of brilliant colours.

'So?'

The other two crowded round and Dave tickled his keyboard. The cloudy image cleared a little and looked like a woman standing in an orange fog.

'So?'

'Wait a minute.'

He continued to manipulate the keys and shades of colour ran through, rendering the picture. After several changes, a picture of a naked woman appeared in a light green fog. Nothing clear but the picture was fairly obvious as to what it was supposed to be.

'Okay, so you've produced a Picasso version of some nondescript woman walking in a pea soup mist. What's so clever in that?'

'Well … er … well …' Dave stuttered and scratched his head.

'For crying out loud, man. Spit it out, will you?'

'Er, yes, while you were in Scotland we needed to test the timing and distance accuracy of the geras.'

'And?'

'Well, we fired three in the air to, well, to … as I said, to test the timing and distance measurements.'

'Yeah, so?'

'And, your maid was crossing the green on her way to work when we fired it. That's her on the screen.'

I craned a little closed and examined the display. So it looked like a naked woman, but you couldn't be sure.

'So it's rubbish.'

'Well, apart from being an exciting picture, it tells us that it can be used to find living tissue in the air.'

'Meaning what, exactly?'

'It means that a series of geras could be fired in the air to find lost people.'

I shook my head. God, save me from engineers.

'At multi thousands of dollars and weeks to set up, it has less use than a rusty police whistle in a desert.'

'The sound waves travel slower in the air, but they'll carry several kilometres. The transducer is fast enough and sensitive enough to do the job.'

'Yes, but looking for lost people is out of the question. It takes you hours to get a rendered picture. Just use your brain, man.'

'Ah! but in the air we can use a QR.'

'What's a QR?'

'Quick rendering. Like the first one I showed you on my laptop. I still have that program and it only takes a few minutes to detail something as simple as an air shot. You see, we wouldn't be looking for complex structures and densities; we'd only be looking for flesh, a silhouette.'

'Whatever. I've got an interview with a rep for Grundy and Brown Air Service. The meeting's at Monroe Airport, tomorrow at noon. The man is just passing through. So why did you pick such an unknown company?'

'They're not unknown for the haulage of gear up on the permafrost.'

Knob-twiddlers and gadget-fixers should leave planning to the experts. Carter was right in only one respect: yes, Grundy and Brown did run an air company that specialised in the great white and frozen north. But Robin Grundy turned out to be a woman, not a man. She certainly knew her flying machines and the North and had an air of power and an unpleasantly overbearing presence about her.

'I'm just passing through,' she snapped as though I were something that was only causing her a bother.

'I would like to rent a plane,' I protested.

'We don't rent planes, only services.'

'You only fix them?'

She looked at me as if I had passed wind or something equally unacceptable.

'Fix them? God! of course we fix them. We rent a service, pilots and machines. Planes for hire, not for rent.'

'Oh! I need a plane to carry drilling equipment up north; must be able to land on ice.'

She shook her head in disgust. 'Weight?'

'Weight? Like what?'

'What weight is the drilling rig?'

'Oh, there's two at 8,000 pounds each.'

'Hmm. The only ship we have to carry that would be the old Packet; needs a runway. What have you got in the way of runways?'

'You see, the other end is a lake – frozen, of course – and, well … this end would be Monroe Airport, here in Hamilton.'

'Hmm. Not interested. We don't do bush flying or barn storming – what you need is a helicopter.'

'They couldn't carry the load.'

'Hmm … I'd, call this number it I were you and tell Johnny I recommended you.' She handed me a small business card.

You could say I went home with my tail between my legs. That woman could eat a dragon *and* use the tail to pick her teeth. Not wanting to let the boys think I had failed to get us a plane, I went directly to my den and called the long-distance number on the card she gave me.

'Hi,' came a sleepy male voice.

'Oh, hello. This William Reyner. I'm looking to hire a helicopter for a prospecting expedition up into Northern Ontario in the winter.'

He suddenly seemed awake. 'Expedition? Ah! Great! When, where, how long and what'll we be carrying?'

'I thought you might like to know where we'd be landing?'

'Land anywhere. Water, ice, desert, you name it.'

'Okay. I need to carry 8,000 pounds – that's about 3,700 kilogrammes – to an icy destination, plus passengers, food, camping gear and so on.'

'No sweat. How far?'

'Just over 1,600 kilometres.'

107

'Hmm ... can't make it in one hop. Is there somewhere to refuel en route?'

'Sure, Sault Ste Marie, about halfway there.'

'Great. What's your local?'

'Well, I'll tell you what. I'll get one of my subordinates to call you and between you, you can make all the arrangements. Money's no object. I'll foot the bill. My man will pay half upfront if that's satisfactory?'

'Great; I see we'll get along admirably well.'

He certainly seemed a very nice gentleman. I gave all the details to Paul Manningham and told him to complete the deal on my behalf. It looked like everything was set to start on Groundhog Day.

I hate being alone. Well, the house is full of servants, but without Gran or my wife, it just isn't home, it's only somewhere to sleep. The phone rang and Griffin quickly found me and handed me the wireless.

'Hello, Reyner.'

'I bloody knows who yous is, Bill. Yous don't 'ave to shout.'

'Newf, you old sod. Where are you?'

'Shetland Islands. Neat place, Bill; you should come for a visit.'

'Never mind that, when are you coming home?'

'Miss me, does yah?'

'I'll miss you in a minute! Now, when are you going to stop farting about and get your hide back over here?'

'That's why I phones yah, Bill. Reggie's gonna take us straight to Prestwick. We's comin' 'ome tomorrah.'

'What about Gran and Deloris?'

'Them's already on their way. Just fort I should warn yah.'

'How's the walking going?'

'Dunno, Bill. This is a 'oneymoon, not a walkin'

108

'oliday.'

Newf is an idiot, but just talking to him brightened my whole day. I was rather surprised that neither Deloris nor Gran had phoned to say they were on their way. Still, good news is good news, no matter how one learns of it. Now I could apply my full attention to the three musketeers and their project. It's real nice not being a detective – simple and quiet treasure hunting is far more relaxing.

Late that same afternoon, Gran and the whole family arrived by private taxi. My heart leapt with joy when I saw them all. William Tan seemed the perfect little gentleman, dressed in a smart pale blue suit and baby Christi looked a picture of health, with rosy cheeks and a beautiful smile.

'Oh, don't fuss, William,' Gran said as I tried to usher them into the house and out of the cold.

I kissed each and every one in turn; not the servants, though. Although Deloris rescued me from a dangerous situation in the past and I know she can take care of herself, I still worry when she's out of my sight. Mostly, I can't get her out of my thoughts. That goes for Gran, too. As soon as Newf gets home the family will be complete – maybe now he's married he won't have Morag stuck to his lips all day like an oversexed limpet.

It's surprising how boring life is when there's not a good mystery to solve. The scientific bunch in the garage are hard to talk to – they have their heads stuck firmly up there somewhere in the clouds.

First of February and the weather seemed quite favourable. This was a record year with very little snow and quite warm weather for Canada. Around nine I yawned and staggered out of bed. I like a nice long, hot shower before breakfast; it sort of wakes me up. As usual, I was the last to arrive in the breakfast room –

everyone had eaten except Newf. He doesn't take any longer than anyone else to eat; he just eats three times as much.

'Mornin', Bill. Yous managed to fall art o' bed, then?'

'Shut up, Newf. Where's your Highland face attachment?'

'Me what?'

'Morag. Where's Morag, your wife?'

'Oh, yeah. You seen what's out on the front lawn?'

'Snow, maybe.'

'Bloody big snow; you should take a butcher's.'

The man's an idiot. I wandered over to the window and pushing the curtain aside, I peered out. Holy mackerel! The biggest helicopter I have ever seen was parked there right in the middle of my front lawn.

'How the hell did that get there?' I demanded.

'Language, dear,' Gran said as she entered the room.

'Sorry, Gran. But it's not every day you see a sight like that. Where did it come from?' I returned to my seat as the maid came in with my breakfast.

Gran smiled. 'The Magnuscarter boys ordered it, dear, on your behalf.'

'What they do, carry it in? I didn't hear it arrive.'

'You must be the only one in the entire house who did not hear it, dear. The thing fair shook the building with its thundering roar as it settled down on the lawn, blowing the snow everywhere. I thought we were having an earthquake.'

'When, Gran?'

'At five o'clock this morning.'

I looked at my watch. 'It's not the second of February, what's going on?'

'You should talk to your boys, William. The pilot has had his breakfast and is now with your lads in the garage.'

'The cheek of it. I'll have my breakfast first. Can't start a day on an empty stomach. Where's Deloris and the kids?'

Gran smiled that "I know everything" smile of hers. 'William, dear, what day is it?'

'First of February.'

'Yes, dear, but what day is it?'

I shrugged and consulted my watch again. 'Oh, crap, it's Wednesday. Oh boy, now I'm in for it.'

She smiled. 'Fortunately for you, William, I told your wife you needed the sleep. The chauffeur has taken her and your young daughter on their regular Wednesday medical appointment.'

'Thanks, Gran. What with this big test coming up tomorrow I clean forgot. There's been so much to do and there just doesn't seem to be the time these days.'

After finishing my breakfast I proceeded to investigate the helicopter. As I had been told the pilot was in the garage that was our heading. Newf, using his walking sticks, one in each hand, hobbled along with me. Paul Manningham met me at the door.

'Oh, great. I was just coming to get you.'

'Why, what's happened now?'

'Johnny needs clearance for a fuel deal.'

'Clearance? Fuel deal? What on earth are you talking about?'

'Up at the airport, they want your clearance to set up for refuelling that helicopter.'

I shook my head in disgust. 'Doesn't he have the ability to buy his own?'

This tall, good-looking fellow came out to meet us. He looked barely out of high school.

'Hi, I'm Johnny. That's my machine in your front yard. So you're the boss, eh? Pleased to meet you, sir.' He stuck out his hand.

I shook it. 'Yeah, so what's this I hear about fuel?'

'I need your say-so. I don't have an account in this province.'

It was all very simple – they know me up at C. Monroe in Mount Hope. I gave them all the particulars over the phone and everything seemed kosher. They even arranged for refuelling at Sault Ste Marie. Even before I turned my back I heard the scream of the turbines – the helicopter was already leaving.

'So where the hell's he going?'

Manningham grinned. 'He's going to fuel-up. We're taking the first load in the morning – tents and stuff – to set up base camp. You wanna come on the first run?'

'Well of course.'

Johnny whatever-his-name certainly knew how to handle his 234 Boeing Chinook helicopter. For all its size, he could throw it around like any of the smaller machines.

When I woke up on Groundhog Day, most of the work had already been completed. The Chinook was loaded with a large amount of freight. I was at breakfast when the boys marched into the breakfast room.

'We're ready for the first trip, Mr Reyner,' Manningham said shyly.

'You don't have to be so formal, Paul. Where's Mr East?'

'He's already aboard and raring to go.'

'Damn,' I said in anger. 'I told him he wasn't coming – what about Mrs East?'

'She's there, too. We're ready for take-off. Do you want to come on the first trip?'

'Sure, what about food and drink?'

'All taken care of, sir. Shall I tell Johnny to wind her up?'

'Sure. I'll get my coat and be with you in a few minutes.'

Although I have headed into the unknown many

times, this trip seemed different. I felt somewhat apprehensive. Johnny was standing at my front door and the huge, twin-rotor helicopter was quietly whistling away with stationary rotors.

'You sit up front with me, Mr Reyner.'

'Sure.' I climbed in and Johnny ran round and climbed in the other side, just like a good chauffeur.

'Slip the latch,' he said. 'Don't want anyone falling out. The weather report's good, plain sailing.'

'You do know where we're going, then?'

'All programmed. Would you like to put the headset on? I'll start winding her up.'

I put the headset on – something I'd done many times before. Johnny fiddled with a few switches then eased the throttle forward. The rotors began to thrash the air and in seconds we were rising like an express elevator over my house. The feeling of doom seemed to grow stronger.

'You wanna take the cyc?' came Johnny's voice over the headphone.

'What, me?'

'You're a pilot.'

'Planes, not helicopters.'

'Easy – any kid can do it. Just hold the cyc nice and steady; the old whirly knows what she's doing.'

With a deep exhalation, I took the epicyclical-control and thus became the pilot. I had flown before – Reggie let me do it several times back in England.

I would never have agreed to this insanity if I'd known just what was going to happen. After a brief stop in Sault Ste Marie, we headed out for Lake Opinnagau. It was a lot farther than I had thought. You look at a map and don't really get any idea of distances. We seemed to fly forever over nothing but whiteness. White stretched from horizon to horizon, with very little to distinguish the route. Rivers, lakes and mountains or hills covered in featureless snow.

Johnny seemed happy. He sort of reminded me of Newf in the old days. Suddenly, I noticed we had stopped in mid-air.

'What, need to change a wheel or something?'

Johnny pointed to the ground. 'This here is the place. Looks like someone got here before us.'

At first I couldn't see what he meant – then I saw it: oil drums and with no snow on them. Johnny gently settled us down on the flat, frozen surface of the lake. My God! what a wilderness we had landed in. The lake spread out before us like a smooth plateau and the surrounding countryside, though hilly, looked barren – just whiteness everywhere. A well-used road, though white, was quite plain to see once you got out of the helicopter.

Manningham came running round the machine and smiling through his fur parker, said, 'Man, you sure know how to pick 'em.'

'Sure,' I said, shading my eyes and scanning the horizon. 'The Cormorant Institute is supposed to be here somewhere. I don't see it.'

'Yeah,' he said and pointed east. 'I saw some buildings over in that direction several kilometres over that rise.'

The more I learned about this experiment, the less I liked it. I thought I'd take a trip to the Institute and introduce myself, but it was unnecessary. The helicopter had gone to collect more equipment and the drilling derricks. We were left to set up camp. Manningham and company were so excited they were behaving like little children on a Sunday outing. Mostly, I stood around freezing. The temperature was -15 Celsius.

Suddenly, I heard this noise like a farm tractor running at high speed. Looking up, I saw this snowcat bearing down on us like one of Rommel's panzers. The machine was making good speed along the mystery road, with snow flying off its tracks and a haze of disturbed snow in its wake.

As the machine stopped with a squeal of brakes only a couple of metres from me, two fur-coated individuals leapt out. They didn't look too pleased or even very friendly. I walked over to meet them.

'Hi,' I greeted.

'What the hell are you doing here?' the tallest and grumpiest man demanded.

'Freezing my ass off,' I said. 'Why? Does it bother you?'

'This is private property.'

'No it isn't. It's government land and I have a permit to prospect here.'

'Prospect for what?' Grumpy asked.

'Anything we can find.'

'This lake and this road are for the exclusive use of the Cormorant Institute; you have no right setting up camp here,' Grumpy snapped. 'I want you out of here immediately.'

'Tough,' I said. 'We're here to do a job and we'll go when it's finished. So shove that up your exhaust pipe and melt snow.'

Without another word, they jumped into their snowcat, swung around and sped off in an easterly direction.

When Johnny returned we already had the tents up. Man, you should try living in a tent when the temperature has already fallen out of the bottom of the thermometer. Unloading the rigs was not easy. The helicopter could lower its back door like a ramp and all we had to do was drive out. Simple, you would think. First, we couldn't get the diesel engines to start. Eventually, we got the rigs out and work began immediately.

'What about some sleep?' I yelled at Manningham as he joyously began driving one rig up the road.

He shouted over the diesel engine, 'Now we've got going, we may as well complete the work.'

'It'll be dark soon.'

He grinned. 'Doesn't get really dark; just dims a bit.'

The first caterpillar-tracked rig took off in one direction and the second in the opposite. They intended to sink a hole every kilometre, in a circle some 10,000 metres in diameter. There were thirty holes and thirty geras in a massive circle. Looking at the map and an aerial photo Carter took, I could see that they would include the Institute on the eastern edge of the ring of holes. My main interest was precisely this – I would like to drop in unexpectedly and give them a shock. I smiled as I considered my plan.

A couple of days later we were frigidly ready for the first full test of the geras. Carter took charge, like some over-fussy nanny. Eventually, we all assembled in the control tent and Carter did the Huston countdown. 'Fire.'

Most disappointing – it sounded rather like a cheap two-stroke engine failing to start and it was all over. Johnny and I walked to the helicopter; it would be much faster to reload if he delivered us to the sites. We had just reached the machine, when Carter came running like a dog expecting a bone.

'So what's the hurry?' I asked.

'One gera didn't fire.'

'How d'you know that?'

'The fire sequence is timed by the GPS and it reports to the main computer – one didn't fire.'

'Oh boy! Do you happen to know which one didn't fire?'

'Sure.'

'Will it ruin the test?'

'Well, we can still get results but, well ... not a complete picture. It's not a really good test.'

'So can we do it again?'

Carter scratched his head. 'Well, we only brought 180 rounds of ammunition. It takes 90 for one shot.'

'Really? I thought there were only thirty geras out there.'

'Yes, but the firing goes round three times.'

'So if you've got the ammo for another shot, what's the problem?'

'I wanted to do an air run as well.'

'So send Johnny for some more ammo,' I said, finding this conversation boring.

'Can't do that. The ammo is especially made – takes a couple of weeks.'

'Okay, then you can strike that. I'm not staying here any longer than we have to; it's bloody cold. Make up your mind if we do it again or go for the airburst.'

Chapter 10

Fatal Airburst

The cold was slowly but surely getting to me. I like to sleep-in, but not when you have to snap the icicles off your face first. The weather took a nosedive and bottomed out at around -22 Celsius. Nothing in its right mind can exist in those temperatures.

'I think we'll do the airburst,' Carter said. 'It would be quicker and easier.'

I sat in my tent shivering with a bottle of whisky in one hand and the other holding my fur collar around my face.

'Whatever! Just hurry up and let's get the hell out here before we get frozen to death. How's that helicopter holding up in this weather?'

'Johnny likes to keep moving. He's ferrying the heavy equipment back to Hamilton. We don't need to drill any more holes, so he's taking one of the rigs back.'

'Are we ready for an air shot, then?'

'Paul and John Magnus have gone out to reload. We should be ready for the shot in about four hours or so.'

As he said that I heard the helicopter making a landing not far away on the lake. At least inside the helicopter was warm. Newf and Morag managed to stay hot, snuggled up in a single fur blanket with an aluminium liner. I walked out to meet Johnny as there was nothing else to do.

'That's about it,' I said, meeting him halfway to the machine. 'Can we sit in the helicopter for a moment? the weather's getting to me.'

'You're paying the bills, Bill. Huh! I cracked a

funny.'

'Tomorrow we'll be leaving. I'd like to go on the first trip and leave these eggheads to clean up the site. They really don't need me, anyway.'

'Whatever you say; you're the boss.'

I sat in the machine for awhile just thawing out my bones and gazing at the featureless vista before me. Johnny sat in the seat opposite me.

'Why do I get myself into these situations?' I said, thinking out loud. 'I think I'd rather be out there chasing the bad guys; it's safer and a whole lot warmer. If the helicopter crashes in this wilderness, they'd never find us in a month of Sundays.'

Johnny grinned from ear to ear. 'I went down once; it took three days for them to find us. It's no big deal as long as you tell everyone where you're going and which route you're taking. Sooner or later they'll miss you and come looking.'

'That's easy for you to say. So what *is* your real name?' If it wasn't for the accent he could double for Newf. He even had some of the same mannerisms.

'Me real name is Cedric Corner,' he said and brushed his hair with both hands as if sprucing up to use his proper name.

'Corner, like as in round the corner or the corner shop?'

'Yeah, exactly.'

'So where does Johnny come into it?'

'Johnny Horner.'

Not only does he act like Newf, but he's also obviously just as daft – Johnny Horner, indeed. I should have thought they'd call him CC, after all his real name is Cedric Corner

'Come on,' I said eventually. 'Let's go eat some frozen groceries, Johnny Horner.'

The following day which, incidentally, I had hoped

119

would be our last in that frigid wasteland, I sat in my tent shivering and cursing the great frozen north – that's the area not the person. I wanted to get into the Institute just to see what they did there, but as yet there hadn't been an opportunity. The whole idea of coming here was to get a look at that place. We'd driven past it a couple of times and flown over it once, but not actually entered the grounds, if that's what you'd call it up here. I made up my mind that I'd go and knock on their door just after the upcoming gera test. Next time we come, we'll either bring an Inuit to build us an igloo or we'll bring a fully lined shed to live in. Tents don't have any insulation whatsoever.

At that point in time Newf came wandering into my tent looking like the dog that just lost the rabbit.

'Bill.'

'What?'

'I fink Morag wants to go 'ome.'

'You think so, do you? Well that'll be a first if you actually *think*.'

'I don't like this project, Bill. There ain't no excitement an' it's bleedin' cold.'

'So, I could always go berserk and shoot a couple of those insane boffins, if that would give you a little excitement?'

'Nah. When we going 'ome, Bill?'

'Johnny's about to take the last of the heavy stuff to Hamilton. By the time he gets back, we'll be ready to leave. You can go with him now, if you want.'

'Oh, no. If yous stay, I stay.'

Manningham walked into the tent.

'Johnny's left and we're ready for the airburst. You wanna come over to the control tent and watch the action?'

I nodded in agreement and we all walked over to the control tent. Morag, Magnus and Carter were already there.

'It's a wonder that stuff works in this cold,' I commented.

John Magnus was really the boss of the little fraternity, but he never did more than politely ask. David Carter was the real egghead – he lived and breathed computers. This time he sat pensively looking at his laptop, which was on a temporary table.

'So let's get this show on the road,' I encouraged. 'Then we can burn something to get warmed up.'

'Okay,' Carter said. 'We're ready. I was just checking the GPS. No anomalies noted. In five, four, three, two, one, fire.' He pressed the button.

Man! talk about make you jump. An in-ground firing sounds like a distant Honda motorcycle having trouble with a hill, but an airburst! Wow! With a very peculiar, almost machine-gun sound, the noise zipped up and around like a swarm of very angry and giant bees. It was all over quicker than you can say "balderdash".

'That's it?' I asked.

Carter looked like the monkey who had just found a 3-foot banana. 'Great, lovely. Now we must collect the chips and I can begin rendering.'

'Okay. For something to do, I'll take one of the snowmobiles and collect half.'

'I'll come wiv yah, Bill.'

'You're crippled; you stay here.'

'I ain't no cripple an' I ain't stayin' 'ere.'

'I'm sorry; the cold's getting to my brain. We'll take one snowmobile and Carter can take the other.'

I climbed into my winterised travel suit then helped Newf into his. It was cold enough just being there, but whizzing around on a snowmobile was even colder. The thing handles rather like a motorcycle, something I'm not familiar with. The boys had made a trail around the circle of geras. All we had to do was drive to each of the devices and collect the computer chip from each one. At least we would be going home soon. Johnny would collect the geras with his helicopter and we'd be off. As far as I was concerned, the tents could stay – the polar bears could use them.

The first gera was easy. Carter had arranged the thing to be upside down, so the sound tube was in the air instead of at the bottom of a hole. I took the chip and drove off into the wild white yonder. Newf seemed happy enough just hanging on. At about the eleventh one on our route, which happened to be the closest to the Cormorant Institute, things started to go pear-shaped.

I stopped, just to get a look at this mysterious Institute. Why would anyone build a thing like that here in the middle nowhere? The place looked rather like some medieval fortress with a high stonewall all the way round. I wonder where they got the stone. The main building looked like an extension of the keep and believe it or not, there was a small tower at each corner of the outer wall. The entrance from where we stood seemed to be directly into the main building, with a door large enough to take a fair-sized truck. What looked as if it might be a road came from the building and divided into two roads: one east and one west.

'So what we stopped for, Bill?'

'Just a look-see.'

'We goin' in?'

'Not this time.'

I throttled up and headed for the red flag that marked the gera's position. It was at this point the bottom dropped out of the expedition.

'What's that?' I said, slowing down and indicating with one hand.

'Looks like some old rags,' Newf said.

I changed direction and headed for the bundle. When we arrived, I jumped off the machine and knelt down to examine the body. A woman, scantily dressed in only a light blue hospital gown, lay face down in the snow with a gera pole lying beside her. When I rolled her over there was no mistake that she was dead. Her face had been virtually blown off by the gera firing.

'Oh crap!' Newf exclaimed, climbing off the snowmobile. 'I fort you said there wouldn't be no dead 'uns.'

Of course at that moment my world fell apart. However, it did have one bright side: it gave me an excuse to visit the Institute. I looked over at the castle-like structure. Owing to the walls there were no lights visible or even any signs of life, just a dirty great grey dollop in the middle of a white desert.

'We'll have to report this to the RCMP,' I said softly.

'Yah want me to stand guard while you buggers orf an' reports it?'

'No.' I took out my radio and called home base. Morag answered. 'Hi, Morag. We've unfortunately found a dead body. Can you call Johnny and tell him to report it to the RCMP?'

She didn't answer.

'Morag, are you still there?'

'Yes.'

'Well get to it. We've got a corpse on our hands.'

'You're nay joking, then?'

'No. Now call Johnny asap; I don't want to stand here all day.' I handed Newf the radio. 'I'm going over to the Institute; maybe they have a landline or something.'

'So you wants me to stand guard?'

'I don't think she's going anywhere, do you?'

'No, but if yous call the fuzz an' a ruddy great bear

123

finks she's a packed lunch, you're goin' to look really dim when the cops ask what you've did wiv the corpse.'

'Oh, that's okay. I just don't want to have to tell Morag that the very same bear thought you were a snack.'

'Oh, well maybe I should be yours backup.'

We both mounted the snowmobile and sped over to the main entrance. The place could easily have been Fort Knox, as there was no method of entry that I could find. The main gate was large enough to admit a sixteen-wheeler, but it was firmly closed with no obvious way of opening it. Another thing that was conspicuously absent was any form of doorbell or buzzer.

'So har we gonna get in?'

'Bang on the bloody door until someone opens it, I suppose.'

I commenced kicking the great door. It had little effect, it being so heavy that my kicks only resulted in soft, dull thuds. Suddenly, a woman's voice barked from nowhere.

'What is it you are looking for?'

'Have you lost something?' I answered.

There was silence for a moment.

'What do you want?'

'To use your telephone.'

With a click and rumble, the great door slowly began rising and as soon as it was high enough, I drove the snowmobile through and into a large forecourt. A massive building stood only 3 or 4 metres away. At least it looked more like what you'd expect a hospital to look like. A woman emerged from a central door wearing a heavy parka and walked towards us.

'You're the intruders from up on the lake,' she grouched.

'Yeah. Anyway, we need your phone.'

'Why?'

'We've found a dead woman out there in the snow. Looks like she came from here.'

She glared at me as if I were some filth that had as yet not been collected up.

'Go away; we don't want your nonsense here.'

'I have to call the Royal Mounted.'

'So where is this woman from?'

'From? From? How the hell do I know? She's out there and frozen stiff. Maybe you think we should just go home and forget all about it.'

'This is a secret establishment,' she said in a haughty tone of voice. 'We neither want nor accept strangers. You may have noticed the locked entrance.'

'Can I use your phone or not?'

She glared at me as if thinking or maybe planning a way to get rid of us. Eventually she spoke, preceded by a deep sigh.

'Very well. We have satellite communication with our head office in Toronto. Follow me and I'll put you through.'

She marched back to the building. Newf had difficulty getting off the snowmobile. I helped him and we followed the woman. She led us into a small room off the main corridor. It looked like a small office but one wall had commercial equipment racks, rather like a telephone exchange from the old days. A desk supported several microphones and two telephones. She picked up one phone, flicked a few switches on a little panel then handed it to me.

'Which service do you require?' said the phone operator.

'Service? Oh, well, we've found a body.'

'Ambulance?' she suggested.

'No, I don't think that'll do any good. I really need

to talk to the RCMP.'

'RCMP, sir? I'm afraid that's not possible. I can put you through to Toronto Constabulary.'

'Nah, it's okay, thanks.' I placed the receiver down and looked at the woman who had led us into the room. 'So, who do you call out here?'

'I think it's about time you left, Mr Reyner.'

'What?'

'Let's stop playing these silly games. Please leave these premises or I'll have to call security.'

It was worse than a nightmare. The local inhabitants were unfriendly and unhelpful – we had a very dead woman on our hands and no one was interested. Newf and I motored back to the body and stopped.

'Maybe we should take her with us,' I suggested.

'I ain't sittin' wiv no corpse.'

'So what do you suggest?'

'Call Johnny an' get 'er art o' 'ere wiv the 'elicopter.'

'Okay.' It was then that a thought struck me. 'She called me Mr Reyner.'

'So that's yah name, ain't it?'

'It is, but how did she know that?'

'A good guess?'

'Idiot.'

Using the radio again I called Morag.

'Morag, where's Johnny?'

'Auch,' she said. 'He's on his way to the Soo, but the police are on their way here. You are to leave the body where you found it and get back here soonest.'

I have no idea where they came from of how they got there so fast, but less than an hour after we arrived back at home camp, a military helicopter landed. A very officious Mountie in a fur parka and leather boots ordered us to be taken to a place called Moose Factory – an outpost some 400 kilometres away; about two hours flying time.

As we sat in the helicopter the thoughts struck me: how did they get there so fast? And how did they know exactly where to go?

On landing, I was led to this oversized room in an otherwise innocuous building that could have been any office block. Then into a room that looked only a little less barren than the Sahara Desert. It was a damn great expanse with one little table in the centre of the floor and four chairs.

'Sit,' said the Mountie.

'Where?'

'On the floor, if you like. Take your choice.'

I wandered over to the table and eased myself down onto one of the chairs. Man! the times I'd been through this routine. Eventually, this wizened little bespectacled fellow in a wrinkled suit crept in with a very tall young woman. All were dressed in civilian clothing.

'I thought all you lot all wore red?' I said and smiled.

'No,' he snapped. 'We see it, we don't wear it.' He plopped down in a chair on the other side of the table. The good-looking woman sat beside him. 'So why did you do it?' he said and looked rather like an unhappy bloodhound. He had this faint hint of a French accent.

'Do what?'

He pushed his nose up with the flat of his hand and snorted. 'A frozen land, not a bloody soul for kilometres around, and you manage to murder some woman in broad daylight. And you say, "do what?" Are you a madman, Mr Reyner?'

'If you mean angry, yes. I always thought the Royal Mounted were intelligent and always got their man. Obviously, it's just propaganda. Do you have any idea who I am?'

He scratched his forehead as if trying to encourage a

thought.

'Mr Reyner, let's stop sparing and trying to be clever. You found a corpse, you say. Convince me.'

I sighed as I could see this was going to take a long time.

'Johnny took off for the Soo and that left six of us in that frozen wasteland, sitting on the edge of a frozen lake.'

'Johnny?'

'Our helicopter pilot.'

'Go on.'

'We did a firing, then Newf, that is Mr East, and I went out to collect the chips.'

'Chips?'

'The computer chips in the geras.'

'Geras?'

I looked at him and strained hard to prevent myself from bashing his little brain out.

'Do I have to explain every word?'

'When you talk twaddle, yes.'

'Maybe I can explain it to her – she looks a load more intelligent – then she can explain it to you.'

'Continue, Mr Reyner.'

'So as I said, Newf – er … North, that's Mr East, and I drove off into the tundra on a snowmobile and collected the chips from the geras. Somewhere around the tenth or twelfth, we found this bundle of rags. I walked over and it turned out to be a dead woman.'

'Killed by one of your cartridge devices.'

'So you say; though I can't see how you could know that – you don't get rifle marks on a shotgun blast.'

'Then what?'

'I called the fuzz. Your boys arrived a little later in a helicopter and I get arrested.'

'You've not been arrested; you are here merely to assist in our enquiries.'

'Did you question anyone at the Institute?'

'Institute?'

'Tell me, have you actually been to the crime scene and looked around?'

'I ask the questions, you answer. That's the way it works around here.'

'Okay, let me place a few easy-to-read cards on the table. In the first place, there were only seven of us up there. One left in the helicopter, which leaves six. Newf … er North and I find a dead woman. Now that makes seven. How do you *think* she got there? Maybe we took her along, just in case we needed to murder someone. Don't you think it's a little suspicious that there are two dead girls associated with that place?'

'Two?'

'Oh, heavens. You cops just don't talk to each other. Jenny Stilton – she was found just about naked, very dead and also from the Institute.'

'Institute?'

'You mean you haven't heard of the Cormorant Institute? So how you gonna solve this case when you simply and actually don't have a clue?'

'Tell me about this Institute.'

I sighed. 'Well, right opposite where Newf and I … I mean North and I found this dead broad, there's this humping great castle-like place with hundreds of suspects crawling all over it.'

'Up North?'

I shook my head. 'Can I go now? I have a plane to buy and a life to live.'

The man was less of a detective than Mickey Mouse. As I was about to expound my contempt for his methods, a thought flashed through my mind. All this time I probably had the answer and was too angry to realise it.

'May I speak freely?' I asked.

He looked at me almost sideways. 'Good grief, haven't you been?'

'No, what I mean is, may I give you a little … well, not exactly advice, but instead a good lead?'

'I'm all ears.'

'Yeah, well … we were up there on legitimate business. Our object was to test a new invention; it's called a gera. I'll not bother to explain what or how it works, but just to say that it can create a picture of the rocks and stuff under the ground. Well, to cut to the chase, we did an airburst. And before you ask, it's the same as a subterranean burst except it's in the air. That's how that woman was killed by it.'

'Did it rape her, too?'

'What? Oh, never mind. Anyhow, we did an airburst which kind of takes an X-ray picture of the entire area. Do you get it?'

'No.'

'The picture would have been taken the moment she was killed, if she *was* killed by the gera – see what I mean?'

He looked puzzled. 'A picture?'

'Yes. If you let my boys render the burst, they probably have a picture of the murderer, just as it happened.'

Chapter 11

The Great Wash

After a large amount of hassle and statement-signing, we were all released and Johnny flew us home to Raven House. He landed right in our front yard – fortunately, we have no neighbours. Exhausted, cold and thoroughly annoyed, I entered the house. Deloris stood in the front hall with Christi in her arms.

'Look, Daddy's upset.'

'I'm not upset,' I grouched.

She smiled sweetly. 'You look it. I heard that you all got arrested and thrown in jail.'

'Yeah. I'm going to my room. When's supper?'

'Usual time, Billy, dear.'

The following day I had hardly climbed from my bed, when Griffin knocked on my door.

'Come in.'

'Excuse me, sir, but there is a gentleman who wishes to see you. It all seems rather urgent.'

'When?'

'Right now, sir.'

'Oh, crap. Where is he?'

'In the den, sir.'

I exhaled in disgust – there doesn't seem any time to do anything these days.

'Alright, tell him to wait; I'll be there directly.'

'Very good, sir.'

I had a quick shower, dressed casually then walked to the study – my private study, I might add. Who should I see when I opened the door? It was that wizened little RCMP twit from Moose Factory.

'Christ! How did you get here and at this time of

day?'

He had been sitting at my desk. Slowly, he stood up and contorted his face, which I suspect might have been an attempt to smile.

'We have a crime to solve.'

'Oh yeah, and the Mounties always get their man; least, that's what I'm told.'

'Or woman,' he added dryly.

I walked to my side of the desk and signalled for him to sit somewhere else.

'So, what do you want this time?'

He quietly and slowly eased himself into a chair.

'Mr Reyner, the only reason I let you and your people go is that it would create too much paperwork for me should I charge you with something.'

'So you are still convinced I dragged some poor female into a frozen wilderness and killed her on the doorstep of the Cormorant Institute as … well, maybe a sort of joke or something?'

'No. Let us be serious. We have a mega-conundrum. I know you and your reputation. A man of your means and certainly a man of your intellect would not, could not and did not commit a stupid and obvious crime like this one, unless you deliberately intended to create a puzzle for me?'

'So why are you here?'

'It's a sort of … you know, you could say a political problem.'

'Political? How?'

'The Institute you refer to is not only a legitimate private company, but they are also strongly affiliated with the powers that be.' He sighed. 'Furthermore, they have an inscrutable security system that records everyone's movements and time stamps it. The woman in question at this moment has no identity and has never been in the Institute; at least not that we can prove. Magically, she turns up dead – killed by one of your mining devices and coincidentally just outside the Institute.'

I could see the general gist of this conversation and I didn't like the way it was moving.

'Well I can't time stamp my movements or the movements of my crew, but I know for sure both Mr East and I are the innocent victims of some outlandish plot.'

'You mentioned that you took pictures at the time. That's why I'm here. I'd like to see these pictures.'

'Oh! I see. Ah, they aren't actually pictures like, well, like what you'd take on holiday. They are more like X-ray images. I'll take you to meet the gang. Have you had breakfast?'

'No, I came here directly from the airport.'

'Okay, it's your choice. Breakfast then the pictures or pictures then breakfast?'

For the first time he actually moved his face in a recognisable smile. 'Very well. Breakfast first.'

I picked up the phone and dialled the garage. Manningham answered.

'Hi.'

'Paul, have you rendered the airburst, yet?'

'No, Mr Reyner. We were working on the subterranean burst and it's beginning to look very interesting.'

'Okay. I have an RCMP detective here who's interested in the airburst, can we render that?'

'Sure, I'll get to it, but it'll take a couple of hours; there are thirty chips and ninety shots.'

'Okay.' I put the phone down. 'Right, they'll get to it. We have time to take a leisurely breakfast.'

'By the way,' he said. 'I'm Commander Pierre LePort.'

'Figures. So what's your theory of what happened

up north?' I started leading him to the breakfast room.

'I have no theory. What's yours?'

'Hmm … firstly, I guess breakfast. I can't think on an empty stomach.'

As usual everyone had finished breakfast by the time I got there, with the exception of Newf. I led LePort in and indicated for him to sit.

'Hmm, now I see how the other half lives,' he said, trying to force a smile.

'I fort you Frogs always dropped your aitches,' Newf said and grinned as if he'd cracked the gag of the century.

LePort sat almost directly opposite Newf. 'It's breeding, you see.'

'So where's your portable face attachment?' I asked.

'What?'

'Morag.'

'You should learn English, Bill. An' it ain't nice to be rude.'

'Yeah, so what's your theory as to what happened to that dead girl we found?'

Newf put his piece of toast down and glared at LePort.

'You fuzz should arrest one of them buggers at that Institute. Thems 'as to be to blame. I reckon it were them that buggered up our first shot.'

The maid came in and handed both myself and the Mountie a small card menu.

'Goodness me,' said LePort. 'My wife would die if she saw this. Thank you. I'll have the English, please.'

'Me, too. Double the sausages.'

'Yes, sirs.' She curtsied and left.

'Come on, LePort, you must have a theory?'

He brushed his eyebrows with both hands and his eyes closed as he encouraged a thought out into the open.

'Yes,' he said eventually. 'You see, I have a dilemma. One group of suspects wouldn't be so stupid as to take a girl up there for the sole purpose of murder, and the other group of suspects couldn't have done it.'

'So?'

'So, my dear Mr Reyner, knowing that the impossible is just that, I have to group you all under the heading "possible". I do not believe in miracles or magic. I'm fairly certain we can rule out the Abominable Snowman.'

Breakfast arrived and our maid carefully served.

'So, you're telling me you have an open mind?'

He nodded and smiled at his plate. 'This I shall consider as a bribe. You see, Mr Reyner, there are some powerful political people associated with the Institute and even some very high foreign dignitaries.'

'So what do they do there that's so secret?'

'Medical research. Apparently, that is why they are so far up north. The idea, I am told, is so that they have less contamination and no public interference. That is why I thought it strange you received permission to do mining in that area. That would be the last thing they wanted.'

'We weren't mining, just prospecting.'

After breakfast we all retired to the garage, where the eggheads were playing with their computers.

LePort was suitably impressed by the science fiction-like atmosphere of my garage. The boys had all this computer stuff with many screens. Man! I could see where my money was going. David Carter was our computer expert but not a very good talker. Paul Manningham, the geologist of the team, was eager to explain.

'This is the subterranean shot,' he explained, pointing to a very large, flat-screen LCD monitor. What you're looking at is the rendered subsoil. Just as if you could X-ray the planet, that's what you see here. That clump there is igneous quartz; an enormous field of it. There, that's the Institute. The rendering isn't all that good because one gera failed, so the result is slightly distorted in that area.'

LePort leaned in close to scrutinise the images.

'I can only see strange streaks of colour. Where was the dead girl found?'

'Oh!' Manningham said, 'this is the underground rendering; we're still working on the airburst.'

The Mountie shrugged. 'I'm afraid it's all a little over my head, but while we are waiting for your pictures to develop, explain this to me,' he said, indicating a point on the screen.

David Carter eased himself onto the seat in front of the screen.

'Well … I, er, well, you see, this is only a test. But if you look closely, you can see stratification – blue-and-green stripes in the rendering. That's the quartz bed over there. I'll magnify the Institute for you; it is rather interesting. There, now you can see the foundation of the huge wall and that appears to be a cemetery.'

'So what's that?' I asked, pointing to misty-looking blobs directly beneath the main building.

'Don't know. Could be basements or cellars. Would have had a clearer image if the one gera hadn't failed. Oh, and by the way, I found out why it failed.'

'Yeah, why?'

'The microchip had been eased out of its socket. It recorded nothing at all.'

'How could that be?' I asked.

'Don't know. Couldn't happen by accident. Someone must have done it on purpose.'

'You wanna see what we got?' called John Magnus.

We all walked over to another huge display screen.

'What have we got?' I asked.

John said, 'Let Dave squeeze in; he knows this software better than I do.'

Dave quickly took control of yet another expensive computer and began manipulating the mess on the screen.

'Bloody marvellous,' he said excitedly. 'Amazing! Look, there's the Institute as clear as a bell.'

The picture was quite a surprise to all of us. Even with one gera out of position and supposedly killing a woman at the time it fired, the picture looked like a poor-quality, overexposed shot of three men, one large snowcat and a female. The woman looked to be supported by two of the men.

Manningham said in a low tone, 'I think you'll find there must have been more than one corpse out there.'

'Why?' I asked.

'The way they are holding the gera, it must have blasted at least two people, three cartridges and in quick succession. Maybe it was an accident – they were just looking at the device when I fired it and killed the woman.'

'This is most interesting,' LePort said with his face almost glued to the screen. 'Is it possible that I may have a digital copy of this picture to take with me?'

John smiled and said, 'I'll run one off for you.'

The strange little Mountie detective left us with a promise to solve this baffling case. At least he didn't arrest any of us. Now I had an aeroplane to buy and a trip to England to prepare. This summer we intended to find King John's lost treasure once and for all. Dead women in the snow or even lying in the street were not my problem. The three musketeers were excited by the results we had achieved and felt confident that if anyone could find this royal treasure, we certainly could.

A couple of days later my heart leaped into my

throat as Newf and I arrived at Monroe Airport, Hamilton, for there standing on the tarmac was a beautiful white and red dream. The Learjet-70 looked like it wanted me to own it.

'Christ!' Newf exclaimed. 'You ain't gonna buy that fing?'

'Yes, I am.'

'If yous crash that one, there'll only be a 'ole left, it goes that fast.'

'I can cross the Atlantic. Just think of the advantages.'

'But it's a jet.'

'So?'

The sales rep greeted me like royalty and led both Newf and myself on a tour of the plane. He let me sit at the controls. Man! the beauty, the splendour, the smell of newness – my heart thrashed in my chest like a wild animal trying to escape. The instrument panel looked like something from outer space, all colour LCD complete with colour maps and talking GPS. The pilot's seat was luxurious enough to have in the living room.

'I wouldn't flog it to 'im,' Newf said. ''e'll only prang it.'

The sales rep-cum-pilot spoke with a really thick Quebecois accent. 'I will tak' you on a short trip, no?'

'Sure.'

'You sit in dee co-position, yes?'

'Sure.'

He explained his movements. Man! the engines started like a Rolls-Royce car, quiet and easy. When she rolled it felt like an upholstered dream. He talked to the control tower and after a short delay taxied to the north-eastern end of the runway. The take-off was supreme, quiet and powerful. Once airborne, he let me take the yolk. *Cloudier* was a beautiful plane, but this

... well, she defies description – it was love at first sight.

The test flight was enough to take the nastiness of the last few days away. All the way home in the car I dreamed of that beautiful aeroplane. Gran was against it; she said it's nothing more than a rich boy's indulgence. Who cares? I can afford it. I wanted to fly everyone to England in it for the upcoming gera test in the Wash area, but unfortunately the one I flew was just a demo model. My aeroplane would be delivered later in the year and I had to take a one-month course on jet flying.

Gran seemed to have lost all interest in both the gera tests and the mystery of the dead girls. Intrigued by the mysterious Cormorant Institute, I phoned Jane.

'Well hello, William, dear,' she said, putting on that silly, sexy voice of hers.

'Hi, Jane. We're all coming to England to test out the new invention for finding treasure.'

'Invention, no less,' she said mockingly. 'I thought the great Reyner did it all by himself.'

'Never mind that, Jane. When we were up north testing the device, we found a dead woman or girl. It was up by a place called the Cormorant Institute, only a stone's throw from Lake Opinnagau.'

'You do rather have a habit of finding dead people, William. How long had she been dead?'

'Just a few minutes. Anyway, that's not the point. I would like you do a little nosing for me – you have all the right contacts.'

'Oh dear, this does sound serious. I thought you had given up being a detective.'

'Jane, are you going to help or not?'

'Certainly I'll help, dear boy. What exactly do you need to know?'

'You see it's like this. There was only me and my

crew up there. No one else for 1,000 miles, except the Cormorant Institute. Suddenly, this mysterious woman or girl gets killed, right on our patch. No one around, but it was right outside the Institute. I know I didn't kill her and I know none of my crew did, either. We were all together in the control tent when it happened.'

'And so you deduced that it had to be someone from the Institute?'

'Obviously.'

'So, dear boy, what do you want me to do about it?'

'Find out what that place does, why it is in the middle of nowhere and who works there.'

'Hmm, a bit of a tall order, but I'll do my best. You know, I have already made some enquiries, but nothing useful so far.'

It was late August when we finally landed in the British Isles. This time we arrived in Manchester. Still, it made little difference as Reggie met us with one of his larger machines – or should I say, in one of *our* larger machines? We managed to put up the crew in the tiny and picturesque town of Sutton Bridge. Newf, Morag and I stayed in one of the more upmarket hotels in King's Lynn on the other side of the Great Ouse, while Reggie flew Gran, Delores and the children up north to Cromlet.

At least on this quest there were no mad gunmen or motorcycle gangs after us. Hopefully, the only problems would be political and mostly they could be solved with a little money placed in the right palms. Although it was peak holiday season, we more or less commanded the hotel. I used the main lounge as a strategy office and headquarters for our project.

England is a small place on the map, but in reality when you're actually there it seems to stretch forever. We had a very large table on which we spread the large scale, 5 millimetres to the kilometre map.

'So where are we going to plant the geras?' I asked.

John Magnus was our history expert. He scratched his chin thoughtfully and eyed the map.

'We know that King John's entourage was heading to Sutton Bridge,' he said, drawing out the words. 'What we don't know is where Sutton Bridge was in those days. My best guess was that the town was probably coastal at that time. Again, we're not sure of the exact position of the River Ouse as it was then.'

'So?' I encouraged.

'I would hazard that the commander was not an idiot and would have started his journey when the tide was at its lowest, giving him the best chance of crossing.'

'Yeah, so?'

He leaned over the map and traced the probable route with his finger.

'Assuming a walking speed of maybe only about a kilometre and a half per hour, they would probably have reached ... oh, say 9 kilometres before the swamp opened up. That would mean they would have been within about a kilometre and a half of Sutton Bridge. I think we should make Sutton Bridge the centre of our circle of geras.'

The other two eggheads seemed delighted at the decision. Personally, I think only a kilometre and a half per hour rather slow.

'Okay,' I said, raising my voice over the excitement. 'Draw the circle on the map, and let's get out there and rent the ground for this experiment.'

'Don't yah fink this is kinda borin'?' Newf said, eyeing the map suspiciously.

'So, it was your idea in the first place.'

'Yeah, but there ain't no excitement in a miserable firework display that's underground, nah is there?'

It always helps to be in the know. Carter got a local college interested and we soon had a whole crowd of willing young helpers. Then the newspapers got hold of the story and we were inundated with reporters eager for a scoop. But, like me, they couldn't see how it was going to work.

Our 10-kilometre diameter circle of geras looked really small and ineffective on the huge map. In my mind, we would probably have to do a firing in ten different locations if we were going to cover all possibilities, but Carter seemed sure we could hit the target in one shot.

Man, the gera firing was a real pain in the butt. The British authorities made us use a locked security fence around each and every gera, with a warning "danger" sign. Needless to say, this added greatly to the expense and a delay in the actual firing. Another costly item was the rent of the firing zones – apparently, English farmers have this thing about their land. You wanna use it, then you have to pay for it. Each gera site – and there were thirty of them – had to be rented. You'd think they would have been eager to find King John's treasure – like it is British heritage.

It was the first week in September before we were fully licensed, rented, governmentally cleared and ready for the firing. Man! this is going to be a damp squid if anything goes wrong. The mayor of Kings Lynn was invited to be the man to press the button – a clever piece of politics on Carter's part. The BBC turned up in force and at least a dozen newspaper reporters.

To put it mildly, I was not impressed. I wanted to go home and learn to fly my new aeroplane. On the evening before the stupendous gera test, none other than Reggie Asquith came to see me. He found me with a good English pint in my hands sitting in the bar area.

'Ah, just the man I was looking for, old bean,' he said and slid into the seat opposite. 'Where's your partner in crime?'

'Newf's at a place called Tydd Gote checking the last of the geras for the morning's test.'

He stroked his huge moustache and his eyes twinkled with delight or intrigue.

'North tells me you're buying a new aeroplane.'

'Yeah. You wanna a beer?'

'No, I'm flying to home base in a short while. What I wanted to ask you was …' He paused for a moment, trying to think how to broach the question. 'Well let me put it this way. Janie, dearest, came up with a scheme – through necessity, mind you – and well, it's a scheme that alone I can't afford.'

'Why don't you get to the point, Reggie?'

'Well, old bean, my heliport has enough land to pop in a 700 metre runway – it used to be an aerodrome during the war, you know.'

'So?'

'Yes, well, Janie, dear, gets loads of requests for executive flights to Milan, Paris, Rome and tons of other places. You see, a helicopter is too slow and sometimes lacks the range.'

'Go on.'

'Yes, well, if you're buying a Learjet, you won't be using it all the time. We could use it for commercial executive flights.'

I had to smile – he looked so guilty. 'How would it get here?'

'Ah, we'd have to have a pilot. They could pick it up when you're not using it and we can make a packet out of it. Help you with the payments, no less.'

I laughed. 'Reggie, me old sport, what would be your contribution?'

'The runway, old bean – 700 metres of runway

would probably be as expensive as the plane itself.'

'Let me think about it.'

Think about it was all I intended to do. *Cloudier III* would be my toy, not a commercial venture. But I had ninety small explosions to worry about. And a king's treasure to find.

Chapter 12

Intruder

England's a great place and I love it, especially Norfolk, but with three eggheads hanging around your heels it becomes more of a drag. The firing went well, with all ninety rounds going off in the correct order and on time. Reggie and Paul collected all the chips using the helicopter. The big problem being that the team could only do a rough rendering using small computers. For the final look, we had to take the chips back to Canada and have them assembled on the monster in the garage. It was time for me to pack up my toys and head back to Canada. I phoned Cromlet.

'Hi, Gran. Everything alright up there?'

'Yes, dear. Young William is having the time of his life. The gillie is teaching him how to play the bagpipes on a goose.'

Now that brought a strange vision to mind. Why would anyone sit on a goose and play the pipes? And what the hell's a gillie?

'That makes very little sense, Gran.'

'Oh dear, William. A goose is a special set of pipes for training a player. Young William Tan is a natural. You should hear him play.'

'So where's Deloris?'

'She has taken Christi for a leisurely boat ride on the loch.'

'So what's a gillie?'

'It's a lord's right-hand man. I think it also refers to a general handyman and gamekeeper. You should know things like that, William; you are supposed to be a man of substance.'

'Yeah, right, Gran.'

'Are you coming up here to Scotland, dear?'

'Oh, Gran, I just called to say I'm heading back to Canada. What about you?'

'I'm a little under the weather, William. I think I'll stay a week or two – the air up here is much better for my health.'

'Okay. Give everyone my love. I'll call when I get home.'

Although I didn't want to hang around with those eggheads, I didn't want to go home alone, either. Travelling by one's self is a miserable pain in the butt. I thought Newf would come with me, but he decided to see the project out to the end.

'But they can't read the results without that monster in the garage,' I argued.

'I know, Bill, but Morag is going to see her muver an' well, I wanted to spend a day or two afore she goes.'

'Oh! for crying out loud.'

And so it was that the lord-of-all-he-surveys had to fly back to Canada all alone. This high-tech treasure hunting isn't all it's cracked up to be. It's boring – no pun intended – and there's no excitement. Oh, Paul and the others act like kids on Christmas morning every time they see some blotchy image on a computer screen, but I can't get excited over a splodge of useless electronic colours. I need action, real action. I began to think that I should drop this King John crap and go and find out what happened to Jenny Stilton or, for that matter, the boaties. Someone wiped them off the map for an unknown and probably foul reason.

The plane ride over the Atlantic was calm, boring and definitely lacking in any form of excitement. I sat dreaming about my new plane and slowly, my thoughts drifted to Jenny Stilton. The boaties killed her by accident, but what was she doing on the good doctor's boat in the first place? If she was from the Institute, then how did she get in the Georgian Bay? Obviously, she must have travelled with the doctor, but how and why? He was knocked off, too; maybe it was some form of love triangle or he was going to spill the beans. One thing is for sure, you can't ask a dead man any questions.

At long and boring last, we landed at Pearson Airport in Toronto. Like a regular jerk, I had forgotten to call the house and ask the chauffeur to collect me. Having already landed, it would be quicker to take a taxi and just arrive unannounced.

I'd barely got in the door, when Griffin came toddling up.

'Sir,' he gasped rather breathlessly. 'Oh, sir, Madam Jane called; says it is most urgent. And Mrs McPherson called saying it is most urgent. And now we have that RCMP gentleman waiting for you in the study.'

'Oh, crap! What's he want?'

'Wouldn't say, sir. I don't really like him, sir. He seems to think he owns the house – or at least acts in that manner.'

'So who's Mrs McPherson?'

'Mrs McPherson is your lady manager of Pitcalver Castle, sir.'

'Oh, yeah, that McPherson, right. I suppose I'll see to that twit from the Mounties first. The man's a menace.'

'Very good, sir. Would sir like a wash and brush-up before the meeting?'

I sighed loudly. 'Nah, I may as well get him off my back first.'

Talk about make yourself comfortable. When I walked into my den – that's *my* den – this RCMP with the ugly face and squinty eyes was sat in *my* seat with

147

his feet up on *my* desk.

'So what do you want *now*?' I growled in an unfriendly voice. 'And that's *my* desk you've got your filthy feet on.'

'Ah!' he said, slowly removing his feet. 'The elusive yet ubiquitous Mr Reyner.'

'So what do you want?' I walked round the desk with the intension of crowding him out, in the hope he would take the hint and accept another chair. Mounties don't take hints. 'Would you please remove your ass and allow me to sit in my own chair at my own desk and would you believe, in my own house?'

With a face like a lemon after it had been squeezed, he slowly eased himself off my chair and meandered to the other side of the desk. I sat and glared at him. But as far as intimidation goes, it was totally hopeless. Mounties don't get intimidated.

'Have you come to arrest me?'

'No.'

'So what do you want? I'm a busy man and haven't the time to play silly games with a bunch of redcoats.'

He carefully wiped his teeth with his tongue and glared at me as though he could see right through me. Eventually, he spoke.

'I'm only one redcoat. Anyhow, that picture you gave me ...'

'Yeah?'

'Can you enhance it?'

I shook my head. 'I haven't the faintest idea – my crew is still in England looking for King John's treasure. I guess I could ask them when they return.'

'When will that be?'

'Soon; they need to use the big computer in my garage.'

'You have to see it from my point of view.'

'Which is?'

'I have a boss to please and a puzzle to solve. So far, the Institute have better evidence than you. They can prove to my satisfaction that no one from the building was outside when this ... this ... let's say "lady", died.'

'First, we didn't have a snowcat, they do. All we had was a helicopter and snowmobiles.'

'A ghostly image with a doubtful time code supported by uncorroborated witnesses tends to look a little bad for you and your men.'

'You're calling me a liar?'

'No, I'm asking for ... for more evidence.'

Again I sighed deliberately loud. 'You know as well as I do that none of my people were near that place when she died.'

'It was your device and remotely activated.'

'Okay, okay, so what would you have me do?'

'What about the device you say someone tampered with. Could I have it for fingerprint analysis?'

'Gord! as my friend Newf would say. Have you any idea what you're talking about? The temperature up there is around twenty below – nobody in their right mind is going to walk around without gloves, especially if they intend touching metal.'

'Well I'm sorry, Mr Reyner, but my boss wants action. I have to arrest someone.'

'Why me?'

'I'll give you a couple of days then – well ... I'll have to start putting the law to work.'

'Is that a threat?'

'Please, Mr Reyner, you're a smart man. Come up with something I can use – at least something to delay the inevitable.'

As soon as he'd gone I phoned Mrs McPherson at Cromlet Castle. She answered the phone in person.

'Oh, hi, this is Mr Reyner. You asked me to call.'

'Oh, yes, sir. I'm very sorry that I had to have you

call. It's your grandmother, sir.'

'Gran, what's up with Gran?'

'She seems fine now, sir, but we had to call the doctor.'

'Why, what happened?'

'Please, not to worry, sir. The doctor said she'll be fine in a few days, but they have taken her to the infirmary for observation, sir.'

'Observation, what observation? What's wrong?'

'Nothing serious, sir. It's just that I thought you should know.'

'I'll fly to Scotland first thing in the morning.'

'Don't worry yourself, sir. I'll let you know everything as soon as I hear anything.'

'What about Mrs Reyner?'

'Nothing to worry about there, sir. Your good lady will probably call you when she gets back from Edinburgh.'

'Edinburgh? What the hell's she doing in Edinburgh?'

'That's where your grandmother is, sir.'

As if I hadn't enough to worry about with Gran, Jane didn't answer her phone. Now, LePort had left me with another headache. It was obvious that someone of power was giving the orders behind the scenes. I'm sure that somehow the Institute faked the time code on their security cameras, or no one actually looked at them. How could I prove they were lying? Firstly I needed to know what they were up to. Why were they hidden away in the frozen north? The place was like a fortress up there – even an army couldn't break in.

However, things heated up a couple of days later, just before the gang was about to return to Canada. I'd been to downtown Hamilton to see my bank manager to free up some more money for the eggheads and to make sure Gran was well cared for. On returning home,

I walked to my room with the intention of changing for supper. Just after I closed the door, a voice said, 'Don't panic and no one will get hurt.'

Turning round, I saw this young lad pointing an old-fashioned revolver at me. He was tall and gangly and only looked about seventeen or so.

'So what do you want, boy?' I growled in an annoyed tone of voice.

'Don't boy me. You're sticking your nose in where it's not wanted. It has to stop or else.'

'Or else what? Do you really know how to use that pea shooter?'

He waved the pistol nervously. 'You have to stay away from up north or your family might come to some harm.'

Now threatening me makes me annoyed, but threatening my family … well, in Newf's words, it really pisses me off. I noticed that the twit's pistol was not cocked – he was a rank amateur. I calculated that if I could get within a metre and half of him, I could take the gun away before he could fire it. Gently, I eased my way toward the lad – I needed this one alive.

'Don't try to be clever or I'll shoot,' he growled and backed up a little.

I looked over to the bathroom and said, 'Oh, hi, Newf.' The idiot gunman turned and in that instant I leapt at him, grabbing his pistol arm with my right hand and adjusting his jaw with my left fist. Amazingly, the tough little fellow didn't go down and neither did he release the pistol. I must be losing my touch. In one quick move, he somehow or other twisted me round and threw me to the floor. I found myself lying on my back with a cocked pistol stuck up my nose.

'Now, Mr Hotshot,' he said in an angry tone. 'You're nothing but trouble. For the safety sake of my sister, stay away from the Cormorant, or next time I'll pull the trigger. Do I get my point across?'

'Most eloquently,' I said, hoping not to hear a very loud bang.

He suddenly snatched the gun away from my face and before I could collar him, he'd opened my door and fled into the depths of the house, never to be seen again. Feeling rather like the dinner that the dog wouldn't eat, I sat on the floor a moment pondering the circumstance. How did that little shit get into my house? Who the hell's his sister? And why pick on me?

LePort had left me his card just for such an occasion. Of course, the little twit was not in his office, if he actually had one. I told the man who answered the phone who I was and what had happened. He said he'd report the incident – great! fat lot of help they turned out to be.

Loneliness is the shits, especially when you have a house full of servants – they are just not the kind of people you want to confide in. Maybe I should call Spadafora and see if he'd like to pay me a visit or even help with this case.

Whilst I was sitting at supper, Griffin came to the table with the portable phone in his hand.

'I'm sorry, sir, but you have a most urgent call from a lady.' He handed me the phone.

'Hi, this is Reyner.'

'Reyner, indeed,' said Jane. 'Silly boy, this is Janey.'

'Oh! hi, Jane. I tried to call you but you were out. What can I do for you?'

'Don't ask such questions, darling boy, you're a married man and I'm a married woman.'

'I mean … well – well, you know what I mean.'

'I have some interesting information for you, darling boy.'

'Okay, so what time is it there?'

'Time for you to listen.'

'Okay, so what've you got?'

'It's a little past one in the morning – now be quiet and listen. You asked me to ask around about the Cormorant Institute.'

'Yeah, right.'

'It's a very hush-hush place, but one contact of mine has it on good authority that it's a baby factory.'

'You what? Like they're into cloning?'

'No, silly boy. They engineer pregnancies. You name it and they'll make it happen.'

'I don't understand, Jane.'

She sighed. 'The place is so secret, even the people who go there don't know what they do. The very rich that need heirs, or just want to get pregnant, you see the Cormorant is the place that can make it happen for anyone who can afford it.'

'Is it legal?'

'As far as I know, there's nothing on the books to say pregnancy is against the law. But in some countries engineering the sex of a foetus is illegal.'

'Hmm … then why have they sent someone to threaten me and why all the secrecy?'

'Threatening behaviour, I know nothing about that, darling boy, but secrecy – well, you can imagine that if Princess So-and-so isn't up to the job, they don't want the public to know all about it. Or the sheik of somewhere isn't up to the job … secrecy is utmost.'

'Oh, right. I get your drift. But they seem so … well, so uptight, so secretive and, I have to say, somewhat threatening. I still think there's something sinister going on up there. Oh yeah, and how do you explain two dead women?'

'You're the detective, sweetie, you figure it out. Now I'll keep trying, but it doesn't look like there's much chance of me getting any closer to the truth.'

My eyes almost fell out of my head with surprise. As I was talking with Jane, Newf wandered into the dining room. As quickly as possible, I closed the phone down and leapt to my feet.

'You old bugger,' I yelled. 'What the hell are you doing here?'

'Well if that's yah attitude, I'll go back, then.'

I grabbed him and gave him a bear hug. 'Man, am I ever glad to see you. Where's your Highland face attachment?'

Newf wriggled free and eased his weight onto a dining chair. 'I don't like the way you talk about Morag.'

'I'm sorry.' I plopped down beside him as the maid came in.

'Would sir like supper?' she asked politely.

Newf smiled and nodded. 'Anyfing yous got going.' As the maid left he said, 'Wouldn't mind 'er fer supper.'

'You're married; surely Morag's enough for you?'

'Yeah, but I mean, just look at ... oh, 'ere she is.'

The maid placed the plates of food on the table and curtsied. 'There is more, sirs; I'll bring it through.'

'I'm glad you're home, Newf. So what happened to Morag?'

'She's gorn to 'er muver's, ain't she, so I says I better give Bill some support. Them brainiacs of yourn gets on yah tit after a while. Anyway, I fort me an' you, yah know, ... why not crank up the 'eat on them buggers up norf.'

'Great, I've done a load of thinking on that subject. Oh! by the way, did you hear about Gran?'

'Mrs H – wha's a matter wiv 'er?'

'You haven't heard, then?'

'No, what?'

'Apparently, she's in Edinburgh Hospital.'

A look of shock snapped onto his face. 'She's o'right, ain't she?'

'Mrs McPherson says she's alright, just a rest and routine checks.'

He relaxed. 'I wouldn't like anyfing to 'appen to Mrs H. Maybe we should go to Scotland.'

'No, I don't think so. Deloris would have phoned if it was serious.'

'Okay, so what'll we get up to?'

'Right, Newf, I've made a decision.'

'Wow, Bill, I fort you'd never come to a decision. So what is it?'

'We're going to set up a permanent camp up at Lake Opinnagau,'

'What for?'

'Firstly to keep warm. This time, I want a wooden and insulated building to sling my hammock in.'

'Yeah? Then what?'

'We'll dig out those Cormorant vermin and expose them to the fresh air. This time, we'll crack that fortress and find out once and for all what's going on up there.'

'Well you'll eiver need dynamite, a big bulldozer or maybe a parachute. There ain't no way I can open them big doors.'

'How about a ladder?'

Newf looked at me and slowly, a sly smile slipped across his face. 'Like assailing a castle in medieval times? You's gonna 'ump over the wall wiv a ladder?'

'Sure, why not?'

'Morag'll never let me go.'

'She won't know.'

'So 'ow 'm I gonna git up a ladder wiv my gammy legs?'

'I'll throw you over my shoulder like a sack of spuds and – as you would say – hump you over.'

'Well you know me, Bill. I'm wiv yah all the way.'

155

'I'll call CC.'

''oo's CC?'

'CC – you know, Cedric Corner; the helicopter lad.'

'Oh, you means Johnny.'

'Yeah. Why the hell they call him Johnny beats me. I always think of him as CC.'

'Ain't you ever 'eard of Little Johnny 'orner?'

'If you mean the nursery rhyme, yes, of course. But what the hell does that have to do with anything?'

'Cor, Bill, talk abart fick. Cockney.'

'Cockney? Cockney what?'

'Cockney rhymin' slang. Johnny 'orner – corner. You, know like apples and pears – stairs.'

'Christ, listen to the kettle calling the pot black. You're as daft as he is, but he can fly a helicopter.'

'So what's the plan, an' why?'

'I thought we'd get him – Johnny – to carry up a shed, an insulated shed, so we can at least have a little comfort.'

'A shed?'

'Yeah.'

'Wiv your money, yous should fink big. Har abart a trailer?'

'A trailer, what do you mean?'

'Like the movie stars, a trailer wiv proper beds an' cooking an' a toilet an' stuff.'

'Alright, I'll call Johnny and ask what he can do for us. This is going to be fun. Between us, we'll show these Cormorant Institute dickheads how a real detective team operates. I know they're up to something and we're going to find out what. Did I tell you, a twit broke in here and threatened me with a gun?'

'Nah. What yah do, fix 'is wagon?'

'No, he got away.'

'You's slipping, Bill. Fancy lettin' 'im get away. So

when's this expedition to the great white norf?'

'I've got to check on Gran and talk to Johnny, but ... well ... I figure we should get up there asap, if not sooner – preferably before the three musketeers get back. We have an excuse.'

'Oh aye, like what?'

'Crikey, they cocked up the test last time so we need to repeat it. I'll make like the road manager and plan ahead. As soon as they get ready, we'll do another firing.'

'What abart King John?'

'He's dead.'

'Bill, I know that. What abart the gera firin'?'

'Well as soon as they've rendered it, we'll fire again up north. Meantime, you and me'll do some snooping.'

Chapter 13

Another One Bites the Dust

First thing I phoned around for a mobile hut. I discovered that a company right on my doorstep specialised in huts for drilling companies. Apparently, the buildings come ready assembled with chemical toilet and lifting rings. All you need is a helicopter and you're away. Johnny was eager to help and said he would be free in a couple of days. In the meantime, I planned the campaign – the three musketeers could play with their explosive toys while the real men solved a crime.

Whilst deep in thought, Griffin walked into the den with the mobile phone.

'A call for you, sir, from England.'

'Oh, right, thanks, Griffin.' I took the instrument. 'Yeah, this is Reyner.'

'Oh, Mr Reyner, sir,' came the voice of Paul Manningham. 'I thought we should report before we packed our bags.'

'Yeah, and?'

'I'm sorry to report, sir, well … but … well …'

'For crying out loud, get on with it – and drop the "sir" bit.'

'Yes, sir. I mean Bill, sir. Well, there's a problem with the gera system.'

'What do you mean, there is a problem with the gera system? For crying out loud, elucidate, man.'

'Yes, sir … er, Bill. Well, you see, the math is wrong. We have to be deeper, I think, and closer, maybe.'

'What do you mean?'

'Well, the results are not very useful. The shot up north failed. Not because someone interfered with it, but because the math was wrong or maybe the spacing.'

'So, correct it.'

'Yes, sir, Bill, sir. It's going to cost money and, well … well, you see, we'll have to start again. It won't be so expensive this time as we've already got the holes. Just need to be a little deeper, I think.'

I sighed to show my boredom with the conversation. 'Listen, you guys are the geniuses, get geniusing and make this thing work before I go broke. You've already cost me just over a million dollars. Now if the thing doesn't work, it's money down the drain. We can't sell an idea that is only an idea. How much is it going to cost to make it work and when can we have good results?'

'We'll be returning in the next few days, sir. We need to consult our big computer to make the calculations, but I know it will work; it's just a matter of tinkering with the math. It only needs a little adjusting.'

'Okay, thanks for calling. I'm going up north to the Lake Opinnagau site. I have a little business up there that needs attending to.'

'Yes, sir.'

I put the phone down and went in search of North. I found him in the swimming pool relaxing in the water.

'Hi, Newf. When Johnny gets here, I want to go up north and set up a more permanent camp for us.'

'So at least it ain't frozen up there at this time o' year. What abart that dead broad?'

'What about her?'

'Well, ain't yah gonna do somefin'? You knows as well as I does who's guilty. I fink we should go smash a few 'eads in.'

'Yeah, see, I'm working on that angle. The gera

159

thingy failed in England. I figure we'll have to do the whole thing all over again, both up north and in England, but this time I'd like to have my own plane, a new and shiny *Cloudier III*.'

'I fink Reggie's got the best idea. You should give 'im the plane an' make a profit wiv it.'

'Yes, well, thanks for your advice, but I'll spend my money how I think best.'

Somehow I couldn't come up with a decent plan of action. The gera experiment seemed to worry me – it was always at the back of my mind. Oh, the money angle was nothing, but those overgrown schoolboys running around spending money and exploding things that were beyond my understanding felt upsetting, somehow. I really needed a long talk with Gran about this Institute business and the RCMP who seemed to be taking an unnatural interest in my affairs.

The days seemed long without Deloris and the kids, so I decided to go to bed early and try not to worry about anything.

At breakfast I was surprised to find Newf finished.

'You must have been up early,' I said, taking my seat opposite him.

'Yeah. Mrs H is art o' 'ospital.'

'Oh, good. I'll call her after breakfast.'

'That ain't all.'

'What d'you mean?'

Newf chewed his bottom lip for a moment. 'Well, there's uver news.'

'For crying out loud, stop being so melodramatic – spit it out, will you?'

'You's got a visitor.'

'Oh, crap. Not another beggar looking for a handout, is it?'

'Nah, it ain't.'

'So?'

'It's that ugly little RCMP wallah.'

'Oh, crikey. So when is he coming?'

''e's bin an' gone an' come.'

'Would you translate that into English?'

''e's 'ere. In yours den.'

'Oh, crap! Postpone breakfast; I'll sort him out first.'

If there is anything I hate it's uninvited cops, especially the RCMP. When I arrived at the den, LePort was making himself perfectly comfortable with a bottle of whisky – my whisky – and sitting in my seat.

'So are you enjoying yourself?' I said, trying to sound forceful.

He cracked a grimace and poured another glass for himself.

'Perfectly,' he said. 'Cheers.' He raised the glass and then took a sip. 'You know,' he said, squinting at me as though the light was too bright, 'you are nothing but trouble for me.'

'Are you pissed?'

'I have arrested the young thug who assaulted you in this house.'

'Well I have to admit, *that* was fast. How come?' I sat down on the edge of the desk and stared hard at this little twit.

'Simple deduction. A patrolman noticed the possibly abandoned car up on the Highway 8, not far from your driveway entrance. He made a note of it and the time. Simple, cooperation.'

'In that case, what do you want with me?'

'The lad said you assaulted him.'

'Oh, right! Of course I did. I invited him here, handed him a revolver then took it out of his hands and sent him home. What do you eat for breakfast, sour pills and hot vitriol?'

'Only occasionally and usually when I'm feeling a

little down.'

'So what do you want with me this time?'

'I have been given strict instructions to warn you off. You are not to contact the Cormorant Institute at any time, for any reason. In fact, your licence to prospect in that vicinity has been revoked. Stay away. Now, having done my duty, how can I help you?'

'What?'

'When someone behind the scenes starts to pull my strings, I get the distinct feeling the puppeteer has dirt on his or her hands. Why do you think you should stay away from that place, Mr Reyner?'

I had to think about that for a moment. This little policeman was not as thick as he pretends to be.

'Well,' I said, slowly getting into gear. 'The first thing I ever heard about that place was Jenny Stilton. She was killed by some boat thieves, 1,000 kilometres from the Institute and wearing one of their hospital gowns. Strangely, the doctor who claimed to have pulled her out of the Georgian Bay died shortly thereafter, and he was from the Institute, too.'

LePort scratched his nose with the glass and eyed me suspiciously. 'You tell a fine tale, Mr Reyner. So what are your thoughts on the body you found in the snow?'

'I haven't a clue – no name, no reason. It has to be the Institute; there was no one else there. Have you questioned them?'

He sighed deeply and stared into his glass, slowly rotating it between his fingers.

'You know,' he said, still gazing at the whisky, 'there are things in heaven and on earth that mortal men should avoid.'

'Meaning what, exactly?'

He stared me straight in the face. 'Who do you think could have the power to take me off this case?'

'Your boss.'

He smiled. 'And who do think could give him such orders?'

'What are you getting at?'

LePort downed the whisky in one gulp. 'You, Mr Reyner, have stuck your stick into a hornet's nest, now you have to extract it without getting stung to death.'

'You talk in riddles,' I complained.

He put the glass down and looked at me with a very serious expression on his face.

'I don't like any malefactor to get the better of me, no matter how powerful, rich or clever he – or she – may be. The Cormorant Institute carries a big stick, a long stick and a swift one. I've let the lad go who broke in here. He's nothing, but letting him go looks good. I know your world record, Mr Reyner. Remember, I have officially forbidden you to continue your work up north, but I can't police the whole country by myself.'

'Are you saying that I should ignore your warnings?'

'Mr Reyner,' he said, standing up, 'I have officially warned you, just remember that. I have been given strict instructions and instructions that I cannot ignore.'

I nodded in agreement. This little policeman was telling me not to take any notice of him. Even without Gran, I realised the instructions were coming from the top, maybe the prime minister himself.

'This isn't Russia,' I said. 'The people run this country, it's a democracy.'

LePort grinned. 'Exactly.' He handed me a card. 'Call me if you get arrested, which you probably will. *Ravi d'avior fait votre connaissance.*'

Everything started happening at once: the eggheads arrived and only five minutes later, Johnny landed his helicopter on the front lawn. He seemed to have more in common with the Bobbsey triplets than me – he shut

163

his machine down and went straight to the garage lab. When I wandered in, everyone was relaxing still dressed in their wrinkled travel suits.

'So what am I – chopped liver?' I demanded in a gruff voice.

Paul stood up. 'Oh, sorry, sir, Mr Reyner, sir. Well … we, that is I, thought you'd be resting.'

'Resting, resting? I don't draw a pension yet. So what happened in England?' I walked over and sat on a chair next to one of the computer displays.

Paul grimaced and looked rather forlornly at David Carter. Dave meandered over to me and, placing his hands behind his back, chewed his bottom lip for a few moments.

'Well,' he began slowly. 'The math is all wrong.'

'The math is all wrong?' I echoed as a question.

'Yeah. I think I've figured it all out, but I have to run it past the big boy.'

'Big boy?'

'Oh, the Cray – it can do the calculations for me.'

'Okay, so why all the sad faces?'

'The gera has to be redesigned and the timing is all wrong. We need to fire a shot every four seconds or so. It's too fast, you see. Too many unidentified echoes.'

I sighed. 'No, I don't see. So what's the problem?'

'Money.'

'Money?'

'Yes, sir. Every gera has to be rebuilt.'

I brushed my hair back with one hand. 'Okay, stop the farting about and get to the point.'

'We'll redesign and have thirty new ones built at something like $36,000 per instrument.' He hurriedly added, 'But then we'll be able to find *anything* underground.'

'Okay,' I said without blinking. 'So what's the bottom line? How much and when?'

He coughed. 'Well, a little over a million dollars and about September or November.'

Before I lost my temper and hit someone I left the room. I needed space to think about it. These guys were rapidly becoming a money pit. Newf met me at the house door grinning all over his face.

'So what's tickling you?' I barked.

'They're coming home.'

'Who is?'

'Everyone. Yours Deloris just phoned. Mrs H an' all. They'll be 'ere tomorrah.'

To put it mildly that changed my mood. The thought of putting my arms around Deloris again and being able to kiss my children is a big morale builder and to cap it off, Gran's coming home, too. If anyone can make a sensible decision I know Gran certainly can.

Deloris was as good as Gran at organising things. The entire entourage arrived at Pearson Airport in Toronto and a minibus awaited them, all arranged by my dear wife. No one bothered to tell me when this momentous event was to take place. My first inkling was when the bus arrived at our front door.

Delores looked wonderful, but Gran was definitely showing her age. I needed to talk to her about the case I was working on but, well, I just didn't want to worry her. I figured it could wait until after Newf and I had done a little scouting up north, we wouldn't be up there very long. Unfortunately I had arranged the trip for the very next day. We decided to go ahead with the plan. Morag had come home with everyone else, but I put my foot down and refused to take her on this trip.

When we finally arrived up north the tundra looked so different without all the snow. Apart from the mosquitoes, the place seemed quite pleasant. Johnny had placed the hut on a small promontory some 50 metres from the edge of the lake. The road to the

Institute made an excellent landing area for the helicopter.

'I never noticed that before,' I said to Newf, pointing to a small wooden jetty running out 20 metres or so into the lake.

'Nah, it would o' bin buried in the snow. Do you fink that's where the planes tie up?'

'Planes? What planes?'

'The doctor geezer and the dead broad.'

'Ah, you mean Dr John Bromley, deceased.'

'Yeah, that's the geezer.'

I nodded in agreement. 'Yeah, could be and somehow she was either put aboard the plane or she stowed away on it – poor kid. I wonder what she was running from.'

'Same as the uver one.'

'The other one?'

'Yeah, the one who was blown away by Paul's toy up by the Institute.'

'Oh, that one. You reckon she was running away, too?'

'O' course she were. We should break in an' bust a few 'eads. Get the troof art o' 'em.'

We climbed out of the helicopter and proceeded to the cabin. Now this is what I call camping. You can stick your canvas tents where the sun don't shine. We had a nice little stove – propane operated – a chemical toilet, proper seats and four single beds.

'I'll put the kettle on,' Newf said and dashed to the little sink.

'We got water?'

'Course we 'as.'

I looked at Johnny. 'You know those eggheads will have to do another firing here?'

'Sure, why not?'

'Yeah, well, I guess as long as you get paid, what

166

the hey? You know it's going to be in the winter again. Several reasons. One – they think transport is easier in the snow and two – they like the frozen ground. Is that okay by you?'

'Sure, you pay, I'll fly – no sweat.'

Newf came and sat down again. 'This is great, ain't it, Bill?'

'Sure.' I looked a Johnny again. 'You know, there's something fishy about that Institute up the road.'

'If you say so.'

'Yeah, I'd like it if you sort of pop off and go do some shopping or something while Newf and I do a little fishing.'

'Fishing?'

'Yeah.'

'Like you want me out of here?'

'Yeah.'

Johnny shrugged. 'You're the boss. So when should I be back?'

'Say tomorrow morning. That'll give Newf and me almost a day to … to … well, to fish.'

'Sure. Okay.'

'Have your tea first.'

Although we had brought two ATVs, I figured it would be best if Newf rode with me as pillion passenger. After the roar of Johnny's helicopter and as the thrashing of the blades faded into the distance, I felt strange. The silence was deafening, with only Newf and I standing on the edge of a brilliant blue lake of crystal water.

'You know,' I said slowly, 'it's as if we're the only people in the world.'

'Yeah, great, ain't it. So when we gonna break a few 'eads?'

I looked at my watch. 'Don't know, what d'you think? Should we go at suppertime when they're all

167

busy or maybe after dark when they're all asleep?'

'We'll 'ave to leave the bike some distance from the Institute.'

'Why?'

'Cuz they'll 'ear us comin'.'

'Nah! That place has walls at least a metre thick. The ambient noise in the building will hide the sound of the helicopter, never mind an ATV.'

'Then, do it matter what time we go?'

'You're right. There's no time like the present. How you feeling?'

'Feelin'? What yah mean?'

'Are you up to it? If you like, I'll go on my own and you can stay and look after home base.'

Newf looked at me with thunder in his eyes. 'I ain't come all this way to sit an' fart around in no 'ut. If yous is goin', so 'm I. An' remember, we didn't bring no bulletproof vests, so don't ask anyone to shoot yous.'

We hopped onto the ATV and I started the engine. In moments we were sailing merrily down the road someone cut through the scrub. Although the road was not metalled, it was very smooth and well worn. Shortly the Institute appeared as we reached the top of a rise. It looked a lot closer without all that snow, but it still looked just as ugly and sinister. Not freezing to death or having any geras to look for, I could give the building my full optical attention. The massive four walls completely surrounded the main structure, which poked up above the wall rather like a medieval castle. There were two turrets or towers on the wall and a square block with a dome on the main building.

The tundra scrub grew all around the base of the wall, making close inspection on a vehicle impossible. We would either have to wait for the snow or walk all the way round. I decided the frontal attack was the best policy and drove directly to the front door.

'Now what?' Newf asked as I parked the vehicle by the door.

'Knock.'

'I fort you was gonna break in?'

'How do you suppose I might do that? If you hadn't noticed, the place is impregnable.'

Newf sighed loudly. 'Go on, then, knock like a pansy.'

I gave the huge door a few hefty kicks but, as last time, with little or no effect. After a short time the voice barked out at me again.

'What do you want this time?'

'Can I come in and talk?'

Click and huge door released its lock and slowly began to rise.

I jumped on the ATV and motored into the indoor courtyard. The yard had a glass roof on it to keep the snow out in the wintertime. A regular door opened in the far wall and a woman emerged. Newf and I walked over to her. She glared at us with eyes like deadly lasers.

'Who have you killed this time?' she snapped in a very angry tone of voice.

Somehow, she looked stern and matronly, with a floor-length skirt and all black garments exposing only her face and hands. Her hair was pulled tightly together at the back like a black hot cross bun and she had three pens in a breast pocket.

'Truce,' I said.

Her eyes flashed like a laser about to deliver the fatal blast of light.

'What do you mean, truce?'

'We come bearing the olive branch; after all, we're your only neighbours.'

Suddenly, her attitude changed. I wouldn't say she thawed, but the outer icing did melt a little. She smiled.

'Please, come into the office.'

Wow! what a shocker. We both followed. Again we went to that room with the electronic stuff in it. I guess she didn't want to give us a guided tour. She picked up a phone and mumbled into it for a few moments. Although I heard some of what she said, it made no sense; it was either code or a foreign language, or maybe a bit of both.

'I am Dian Morningblood,' she said, putting the phone down and staring directly at me.

'Hi, I'm Reyner, Bill Reyner, and this is my associate, Mr East.'

'Please, follow me, gentlemen.' She led us back to the courtyard and then through another door, which opened into a long corridor. About the third door down, we entered an office of considerable luxury. She closed the door behind us, smiled and said, 'Please, take a seat.'

For the next half-hour she lectured us on the sterility of a humanless area, which she called her own domain. We apparently were unwanted intruders who would ultimately contaminate the surrounds and ruin the puerile work being performed at the Cormorant Institute. Newf and I were not allowed a word; she would cut us off and continued the lecture. At great length, the woman stopped gabbing.

'I appreciate your work,' I lied. 'We won't interfere in any way. Our tests are merely geological. We are not prospecting, only testing a secret device.'

I seemed to have hit the right note. She smiled and said, 'Let me give you a short tour.'

Wow! Eagerly, we followed and were led to a hospital-like area that had ten wards, five on each side. Each ward had only two women, all of whom were either pregnant or had a baby with them. Everyone seemed happy, well fed and cared for. Some of the women joked and giggled at us. Apparently, males were few and far between.

At long and puzzling last, Ms Morningblood led us back to the ATV.

'Now, gentlemen,' she said. 'You have seen all. Please leave the area and do not return.'

I drove us back to base camp in silence. I think both of us were confused by our tour of the mystery palace in the great, uninhabited north.

I parked the ATV and Newf walked over to the hut to make a welcome cup of tea. In moments, he hobbled back and glared at me in silence.

'So what's wrong now?' I demanded.

''ow many of us come?' he said.

'What do you mean?'

''ow many of us is there?'

'You gormless twit. You and me, that's two.'

'Oh, well, 'oo's the dead geezer in the 'ut?'

Chapter 14

Cloudier III

To say the least, finding a dead man in our cabin was the very last thing I had expected. Newf led the way and opened the door. Sure enough, sitting in my chair by the table sat, or slumped, this well-dressed fellow with a large hole in his head and a very ugly pistol lying on the floor.

'This is insanity,' I said. 'Someone's trying to frame us for this person's death.'

'Yeah, I know. You couldn't 'ave done it, cuz yous was wiv me. And I couldn't 'ave done it, cuz I was wiv yous.'

'Newf, your logic is impeccable. Notice how wet he is.'

'Wet?' Newf walked over and felt the body. 'Not only wet, Bill, but 'e's also bloody cold.'

My mind began to race – obviously, this was another set-up. The Institute was using us to get rid of their old corpses.

'See if he's got a wallet, Newf.'

Carefully, Newf frisked the dead man and eventually extracted a wallet.

'There's bleedin' ice in the wallet, Bill, an' a driver's licence. Holy crap! Says 'ere 'e's a bleedin' doctor. Oh, an' no prize for guessin' where 'e works.'

I tried to remain as calm as possible and to think logically.

'I figure we got three choices, Newf. We can bury the body and pretend we've never seen him, or we can take him back to the Institute and hand him back.'

'That's only two.'

'Sure. Or, we can take him home with us.'

Newf tossed the wallet onto the table and glared at me. 'What we want to take 'im 'ome wiv us for?'

'So the Institute loses control of the situation.'

'So, like. I ain't flyin' 'ome wiv no dead feller. I votes we take 'im out into the lake an' dumps 'im wiv a loada rocks in 'is pockets, then denies any knowledge of the geezer.'

'Yeah,' I said slowly and trying to think of something sensible at the same time. 'He's obviously from the Institute, but why? Maybe we should take him there and dump him on their doorstep, sort of payback.'

'Now you's finkin', Bill.'

'Okay, grab his head and I'll take the feet.'

Newf stood and glared at me. 'I ain't touchin' no 'ead. 'e's all slippery an' 'orrible. You take the 'ead an' I'll take the feet.'

Reluctantly, I walked to the head of the corpse and grabbed it under the arms.

'Well come on, then,' I demanded as Newf just stood there.

'Listen,' he said and strained to hear something.

I listened and sure enough, the welcome sound of helicopter blades thrashing the still air grew louder and louder.

'Wow!' I said, dropping the body. 'It's Johnny; he's back early. Now we can call the RCMP.'

'Or just drop this geezer in the lake an' go 'ome.'

Walking outside, our hearts sank in unified despair, for there, rushing in at low level, were two helicopters and neither were Johnny's. One sported the word "police" on its side.

'Oh, crap!' I groaned. 'The bloody Institute got their vote in first.'

The two machines landed fairly close together on the hard roadway. As the rotors began losing speed,

173

several people climbed from the first one and made their way over towards us. A very large, burly and smartly dressed RCMP officer grinned at me and beckoned his fellow from the second machine.

'Reyner,' he barked like some wild sergeant major from the war of 1812.

'Yeah, we got a b –'

He cut me off mid sentence. 'You seem to make a habit of creating havoc,' he growled in a none-too-friendly tone.

'You're under arrest for the murder of Doctor Henry Drummond.'

'What?'

'Anything you say may be taken down and used in evidence …'

'Oh! quit the crap. Who the bloody hell's Henry Drummond? And how did you get here so fast?'

He ignored me and repeated the charge. Another cop grabbed me and slapped handcuffs on my wrists.

'Like I'm going to make a run for it in the middle of the bush.'

Without answering, I was hustled into the nearest helicopter. Moments later, Newf arrived in a similar condition. We sat in silence awaiting some form of explanation, but none was forthcoming.

'I reckon we's in the shit this time, Bill,' Newf finally said.

'For what? There's something fishy going on here.'

'Quiet, you two,' yelled one of the cops.

The engine revved up and the rotors thrashed the air. Now, the noise was so intense that talking became next to useless. Even in the warm weather the view was almost as boring as in winter – thousands of kilometres of nothing with the occasional lake or river. Hills that all look the same.

After a while I could see the ocean. It looked like

they were taking us to Moose Factory again. Suddenly, we changed course and a short time later landed at a lonely outpost, literally in the centre of No-where-ville.

We were hustled off the helicopter and into a large shed. Big Brute ordered everyone about and then said to me, 'You'll be taken by plane to Ottawa.'

'Ottawa? What for?'

'Sentencing, I shouldn't wonder. We take a distinct dislike to murderers.'

'Then you should go back there and catch a few.'

'I don't like that geezer,' Newf said. 'Ain't yah gonna call yours lawyer?'

'This is crap – they can't pin that murder on us, if it *was* murder. Doctor Whatever-his-name-is had been dead long before we even arrived on the scene. As soon as the coroner gets to work, they'll let us go.'

'I 'ope you're right, Bill. I don't fancy spending the rest of me natural in a cage.'

A small jet, something like the one I intended to buy, ferried us to Ottawa and there we were met by the Black Maria and hustled off to police headquarters. Almost without seeing daylight, we were hustled into some dark corridor then separated. I was led into a standard interview room, with video recorder, the works. The cop pushed me down into a seat then left, but the door was guarded by an equally tough-looking ruffian in uniform.

The procedure was always the same, the whole world over. I was left to sweat awhile, though I had nothing to sweat about. Eventually, a burly, plainclothes cop and his very attractive blond assistant walked into the room. They marched to the opposite side of the table and sat.

'Now, Mr Reyner,' said the big guy. 'I need an explanation from you.'

'Really?' I scoffed and raising my hands, said, 'My

mouth doesn't work worth a shit when my hands are tied.'

He looked at me as if I had just accused him of passing wind. After a good stare, he nodded at the guard, who came over and produced a key to release my hands.

'Thanks,' I said and smiled as nonchalantly as I could muster. 'Now, what can I help you with?'

'I know all about you, Mr Reyner, with your very rich and cocky ways. Here, you're nobody and your money means nothing.'

'Okay, if you say so. So what's your problem?'

'What were you doing up north? You know very well it's a restricted zone.'

'Restricted zone?' I said, slowly trying to think of a good and funny answer. 'I ... well, you see ... Who said it's a restricted zone?'

'You have been warned before.'

'Hmm, well, it's Crown land, I know that, but you aren't the Crown. As far as is known, anybody can do as they like.'

'Not mining,' he growled.

'I wasn't mining. We were testing a device that would be dangerous in town, that's all.'

'And the dead man – was he helping you?'

'Helping? I've never seen the geezer before. Why don't you go ask them at the Institute?'

'Institute?'

'Oh, God, not another one. It's that bloody great building just over the hill from where you arrested me. Go ask them.'

'The Minister of Northern Affairs has issued this order restricting you from entering that area. Are you telling me you didn't know?'

'Yes.'

He pushed the written order in front of me and then

with his beautiful assistant, left me to read it. It had been signed by a Mr François Quiberon, or should I say Monsieur?

Eventually, the big guy returned. He just leaned in the door and said, 'Formally charge him and throw him in the slammer.'

'What!' I yelled, jumping to my feet.

The guard quickly apprehended me and formally charged me with murder.

'You're all nuts,' I complained. 'This is total madness.'

'I'm sorry, sir,' said the guard. 'You can argue your case before the magistrate in the morning.'

After a very rough night in primitive and appalling conditions, I was finally led to the small courtroom.

'I want my lawyer,' I moaned at the guard.

'Don't worry, sir. Just relax and don't cause us any trouble.'

In the courtroom were a couple of officials, a court recorder, the magistrate and couple of cops.

'Ah,' said the magistrate as I entered. 'The accused.'

The whole affair seemed rather primitive and not really like any normal court.

'So what's it all about?' I demanded.

'Silence,' shouted the bailiff. 'You are charged that on the said occasion, you did wilfully kill Doctor Henry Drummond. How do you plead?'

'It's a load of crap. What is this – a kangaroo court?'

'Please control both your emotions and your language,' said the magistrate, grinning, 'and we can get this over without too much fuss.'

'Too much fuss?'

The magistrate glared at me. 'Mr Reyner, please – how do you plead?'

'Not guilty, it's a set-up.'

'Excellent,' he said and read a few more of the papers in front of him. 'It seems to me that what you say is true. There is no evidence whatsoever to support a charge of any more than trespass.'

'Trespass?' I bellowed in anger.

'Silence,' yelled the bailiff.

The magistrate continued. 'Doctor Henry Drummond would appear to have met his demise some time ago. This puts you and your companion completely out of the frame. As for the charge of trespass, fine $500.' He slammed his gavel down, making me jump.

I figured $500 was nothing to worry about and no amount of arguing would get me out of this nuthouse any faster. At the front desk they gave me all my stuff back and as I was about to leave, Newf wandered in.

'Mornin', Bill.'

'So what they charge you with?' I demanded angrily.

'Nofin'.'

'Nothing, so where the hell have you been all night?'

'Let's go, Bill, an' I'll explain on the way.'

Together, we walked out of the building.

'Well?' I demanded.

'Yes, fanks, Bill.'

'Idiot, I'm not enquiring of your health. Where were you last night?'

'I stayed in a 'otel an' guess 'oo I met?'

'I don't give a shit.'

'You will as soon as yous calm down.'

'I am calm. So who did you meet?'

''e's in that car over there.'

Inspector LePort climbed from the car and opened the rear door for us.

'Good morning, gentlemen. The RCMP is at your

service.'

'I knew you'd have something to do with all this,' I said as I flung myself into the vehicle.

'I'll take you to breakfast,' he said dolefully. 'We're a bit too late for a flight to Hamilton; the next plane's at eight o'clock in the morning.'

'You mean I'm stuck here for another stinking day?' I moaned.

LePort took us to a hotel, where we all ordered a late breakfast; though, it was more of a brunch, I would say. The clock was creeping up towards eleven.

'You know I've been suspended,' LePort said as he eyed the menu.

'Suspended? For what?'

'It's all to do with you and your interference. My boss has a boss and pressure is descending from a great altitude.'

The waiter arrived and we all ordered.

LePort continued. 'Normally, I wouldn't dirty my hands with a case like this one, but I know your reputation. You have put more people behind bars than any five active policemen all together.'

'I'll take that as a compliment.'

'Good. I can't help you but, well, I can at least guide you.'

'Guide me? What do you mean?'

'I have information that may be useful to you. If you get into trouble, like yesterday, I still have friends who can help. For instance, Doctor Henry Drummond – the actual autopsy report was hijacked and a friend of mine managed to swap the envelopes. That's the reason you got off this morning.'

'Oh! For that I thank you.'

'Doctor Henry Drummond had been frozen, stored – God knows why. You popped up and they delivered him into your hands. You were supposed to go down for his death.'

I shook my head. 'Why, who have I upset and how?'

LePort tried to smile – obviously something he never usually does. 'Well, François Quiberon, Minister for Northern Affairs, seems to crop up in the oddest of places. I checked him out and he has no criminal affiliations.'

The waitress arrived with our breakfast and we all got stuck into a well-deserved meal. I felt as though I hadn't eaten for weeks.

The following day, bright an early, Newf and I set out for Hamilton by air. I simply hate it when we get a case that makes no sense. I strongly needed to talk with Gran. If anyone in the world could make sense of this ridiculous affair, she certainly would.

The quickest way from Monroe Airport was by taxi. Newf remained quiet and thoughtful – I also had a lot on my mind, like what happened to Johnny, for instance? That question quickly answered itself, as when we drove up the driveway there on the front lawn stood his helicopter.

'Oh, great,' Newf said. 'I reckon 'e'll be wiv the brains. See you in the 'ouse, Bill.'

Deloris met me at the front door. 'Oh, William,' she said as if she hadn't seen me for months. 'I thought we'd lost you. I was going to get Daddy's lawyer to come over.' She flung her arms around me and we hugged for a moment.

'Where's Gran?'

'Oh, yes, you'd better let her know you're alright. She's in the lounge. I have to see to the servants. I'll meet you in the lounge in few moments.'

Gran was, as stated, resting in the lounge. Well not exactly resting, she was knitting.

'Hi, Gran,' I said softly as I walked into the room.

'Oh, William, dear, where's North?'

'He's gone to see the three stooges.'

'The three stooges, dear?'

'Oh, sorry. I mean the boffins in the garage.'

She smiled sweetly. 'Oh, sorry, William, dear, but they have gone to England.'

'What?' I said, raising my voice in shock and surprise. 'What do you mean, they've gone to England?'

'Oh dear! You said they were to have a free hand and they had found a company that would make those things for them on the spot. The company is in Ipswich and so your boys took the next flight out there.'

'But they didn't ask me.'

'Of course not, dear; you were in jail.'

'So who's paying for this trip – the one that I didn't approve?'

'You are, dear. Or at least I understand you will get the bill.'

I was about to explode in a cascade of angry flames, when Newf stormed into the room.

'Them buggers is gone,' he said. 'Oh, sorry, Mrs H.'

'I should think so, North. There are children in the house, you know.'

I shrugged in despair. 'I know; they've gone to Ipswich.'

'Where's 'at?'

'Somewhere in England.'

'So is we gonna go after 'em?'

I shook my head. 'Nah, I've got to go to Quebec for flying lessons. Did you find Johnny?'

Newf shook his head in disgust. 'Nah, and you ain't really gonna buy that plane?'

'Yes, all arrangements are made. All I have to do is get my jet licence. Do you know where the helicopter pilot is, Gran?'

'Yes, dear. He's gone into town to buy something. He's staying in the garage until you return, William, dear.'

I sat down. 'Gran, I need your help on this Jenny Stilton case.'

She carefully stabbed the ball of wool with the needles then sitting upright, she glared at me.

'I thought you didn't do that kind of thing any more, dear?'

'Yeah, so, it sort of forced itself on me.'

'Then what's your problem, dear?'

'There's something fishy about the Cormorant Institute. Not just the fact that it is in the middle of nowhere, but because the entire staff and inmates are either mad or too crafty for me to comprehend.'

'Yes, William. I heard about your newest dead man. I spoke to Jane and that cheeky RCMP gentleman. I think what you have stumbled into is a government secret establishment for some form of medical research.'

'Really, so why don't they just say so?'

'I would suspect the place is more than likely quarantined and that is why there is such secrecy.'

'So what about Jenny and the other woman who died when the gera fired? Oh, yes, and what about that doctor who turned up dead in my hut?'

Gran stroked her chin thoughtfully as she mulled over my questions. Eventually, she said, 'William, dear, one terrible problem with remote government agencies is the possibility of corruption. I think you have stepped on someone's toes who is deeply involved with some skulduggery at this Institute. Perhaps it was the beginning of this conspiracy unravelling when John Bromley died or was perhaps murdered. He was, after all, responsible for Jenny Stilton being in the wrong place at the wrong time.'

Gran's a clever old duck. In just a few seconds I'm sure she had put me on the right road. It slowly began to make sense – François Quiberon, Minister for Northern Affairs, of course he was somehow tied up in this mess. I smiled to myself as I realised what I should do, but first I needed to learn how to fly a jet aeroplane.

In a way I was looking forward to the idea of becoming a jet pilot, yet at the same time I felt nervous at the prospect. A jet liner, even a small one, was a huge responsibility compared to my earlier flying. I had expected the training to take place in Quebec, but the arrangements were for Ottawa, at a private airfield some 12 kilometres out of town. What a coincidence, the Houses of Parliament are in Ottawa and that's where François Quiberon would probably be hanging out. With a little luck, I may be able to kill two birds with one stone.

My course turned out to be entirely different than I had expected. I had to go to school every day, brush up on my navigation, and learn all about air lanes and airport procedures. It was just like being back at McMaster's again. Eventually, I did get to see my new baby and I spent almost thirty hours flying it. At long and tedious last, I received my ticket to fly. Of course that just added to my problems, as now I needed a ground crew and somewhere to keep her.

I don't think I have ever been so excited in my life as when we went to the hanger to actually fire up my new *Cloudier*. My heart thumped out a rhythm that would put jungle drums to shame. The Bombardier people said they would make arrangements for my plane to berth at Hamilton until I could make my own arrangements.

I registered my flight plan and shook hands with my teachers. Then I boarded my plane for a solo flight to Hamilton. I felt excited and yet afraid. It was almost embarrassing as I taxied my beautiful girl to the take-off point. My transponder was Reyner-1. I trembled as I awaited the go.

'Reyner-1, you are clear for take-off.'

'Roger that, Tower.'

It was almost like making love for the very first time – the thunder of those engines and the feel as she began to grip the air. To be honest, I was so excited I very nearly threw up as she screamed to a comfortable cruising altitude. Navigation was dead easy; I had all the latest GPS and auto-heading facilities. In such a fast machine I was no sooner at my allotted altitude than I had to call Hamilton for landing instructions. The trip in *Cloudier I* would have taken a couple of hours, but *Cloudier III* could make the trip in just over half an hour.

By the time I had put *Cloudier III* to bed, arranged to pay the parking and storage, organised an engineer and finally took a taxi home, I was completely exhausted. I felt drained both emotionally and physically. A nice hot bath and bed – I hadn't been home in twenty-eight days.

As I entered the house, Griffin met me in the hall with a huge smile on his face. I looked up and couldn't help grinning myself.

'Good news?' I asked.

'Indeed, sir.' He handed me the mobile phone. 'Sir is greatly in demand. Welcome home, sir.'

'Hi, this is Reyner,' I said into the instrument.

'Ah, Mr Reyner, sir.'

'Paul, is that you?'

'Yes, sir. We've done it, we've done it.'

'What?'

'We used the same holes, sir, and we've done it. You should see the quickie.'

'Quickie? What are you on about, man?'

'There's masses of data, but a quick look on the portable shows more than we got on the master rendering last time. And I think we may have actually found your treasure.'

'What?' I said in excitement. 'You don't mean – no, you couldn't?'

'Yes, sir, we may well have found King John's treasure. We'll know better once we get home and do a proper rendering.'

Chapter 15

Our First Clue

Gran seemed to be in a somewhat sombre and melancholy mood. I found her in the lounge looking at an old photo album.

'You're quiet, Gran.'

'Yes, dear. I think my age is catching up with me. I've been a little off colour for a while now.'

'What you looking at?'

'Just old pictures, dear. Look, this is your granddad, shortly after we were married. He was a fine-looking man – a bit like you in many ways.'

I sat beside her and shared the volume. A mini tear trickled down the old girl's nose.

'You alright, Gran?'

'Yes, dear. I seem to spend a lot of time thinking of your grandfather. I suppose I'll be meeting him soon.'

Her words sent a cold shiver down my spine. 'Oh. Come on, Gran. We all love you; don't be sad.'

'He would have loved your children, William. Oh dear, why do I feel so sad?'

'Come on, Gran; you'll have me in tears in a minute. I'll tell you what, why don't I show you my new toy? You do know I bought a new airplane?'

'Yes, dear. Tinker toys do not excite me at all, not even ones of that magnitude.'

'You'll love his one. It's got everything: a toilet, a kitchen … even has a dining table. If you want, I can have a bed put in for you.'

She chuckled and closed the book. 'Perhaps, William, perhaps. Who knows what the future may bring. I hear your boys were successful in England.'

'Yeah, they're supposed to be on their way home. I'll tell you what, when they get here we'll all have a short holiday in Ottawa, the capital city.'

'I haven't been to Ottawa in many years; that might be quite nice, dear. I could take young William Tan to some of the wonderful museums there and show him the Houses of Parliament.'

'Yeah, see, Gran, there's always something bright on the horizon.'

Heaven only knows what the three musketeers were up to. I had expected them to burst through my front door all excited and exuberant at any moment, but no. An entire week passed before we heard from them again. This time they were, as they put it, 'Stranded at Pearson Airport.' I sent the chauffeur to collect them. Just after the car had left I had a terrible thought: what if those idiots were bringing all the geras and equipment with them?

Fortunately, everything turned out for the better – the boys were jubilant but unencumbered. John Magnus, MA, BA, the history expert, came to see me while the others invaded the garage. Even at a distance I could recognize his tall and slender frame and his thick crop of dark hair. Being very quietly spoken the man could not be heard until I reached him.

'Could I have a word with you, sir?' he asked politely.

'Sure, in my den.' I led the way.

We both entered and I closed the door. He looked very serious.

'Sir,' he said hesitantly.

'Go on then, take a seat. Is there a problem?' I walked round my desk and sat in the command chair like the lord of the manor.

'Thank you, sir.' He sat cautiously. 'Well, yes and no.'

'Yes and no, what?'

'Well, we do have a problem and we don't.'

I sighed. 'For crying out loud get on with it; I don't have all day.'

'Sir, I want out of the group.'

Wow! that was a stunning announcement. I glared at him in puzzlement.

'You do *what*?'

'I … well, sir. You see, I want out of the group.'

'Why?'

He looked as if he was about to break into tears. 'You see … well, it's … my father, you see.'

'No, I don't see. What about your father?'

'Someone has to look after him; he's old and lives alone.'

'So?'

'I need to go to him and help him.'

'Why?'

His eyes seemed to dart about, almost as if he expected someone else to butt into the conversation.

'Sir, I have to help him, you see.'

'No, I don't see. Where does he live now?'

For a moment he chewed his bottom lip and after a deep sigh he said, 'He's in a home in Ottawa.'

'A home in Ottawa?' I said, quite astonished. 'What the hell's he doing there?'

'We come from Ottawa, sir. I have to go to him.'

'If he's in a home, they'll look after him. Or is it that you can't afford the residency any longer?'

I thought he was going to burst into tears. 'No, sir. I mean yes, sir.'

'Yes, sir, no, sir, what? Just what's the trouble? Can't you trust me with the truth?'

He licked his lips nervously. 'I … well … Alright, I was given this note at the airport and … well …'

'Yes, go on; I won't bite you.'

'It said …' He stopped and fumbled in his pockets for a moment before fishing out this scrap of paper and handing it to me.

The note was short and to the point: Your father's life or the project. I read it a couple of times then looked at John Magnus.

'So what do you interpret it as?'

'A death threat, sir.'

'Hmm, you know I don't take kindly to threats of any kind. You've worked hard on this project and as far as I am concerned, you are under my protection. Is your father ill in any way?'

'Ill? What do you mean, sir?'

'Is he sick or infirm?'

'No.'

'Then why is he in a home?'

'I couldn't work and look after him, sir. Mom died several years ago. Dad's only seventy-six but, well he's a bit absentminded sometimes. He'll forget to eat, you see.'

'Is there any reason he couldn't live here?'

'I don't think he'd like it in the garage, sir.'

'No, no, I was thinking in the house as a resident guest. We have moderate protection here with the gateman and all the servants. What d'ya think?'

'I can't put you to all that trouble, sir.'

'Yes, you can and we need you – you're our history major, right?'

'I guess so, sir. But what would your good lady say?'

'Don't worry about things like that. This is an enormous house. I think we could easily put up one more guest.'

'But how should we get him from Ottawa?'

'Don't say anything to anyone. We could all go up there in my new plane – have a short holiday and bring

189

the old man back. No need to give anyone any reason or warning. Let's say, fly in the face of whoever wrote the note.'

His countenance changed as though someone had thrown a hidden switch.

'Right, sir. Will you want to see the rendering?'

'Sure. When can I see it?'

'Well, the boys are running the big boy now. I guess it should be ready in ... say ...' He looked at his watch for reinforcement. 'Oh, say two hours.'

'Okay, I'll be there.'

And be there I was. The three musketeers were crowded around the large monitor, all excitedly gabbling.

'Hi,' I said in a loud voice to make sure they knew I was there.

'Oh, sir,' Manningham said. 'Come look at this.'

Typical of these eggheads. The screen looked like someone had exploded on it. A great splodge of crimson with what looked like spaghetti liberally spread around.

'So what am I looking at?'

Paul Manningham being the geologist seemed to be the most excited of the bunch.

'Well, there,' he said, pointing, 'you can see the separation or stratification of the anticline right on the line of the diagenesis.'

'Sure, of course I can,' I said sarcastically. 'Now, would you like to speak in English?'

'Oh, well, I ... er, well, I get carried away. If you look, you can see where the ... the ... er ... The lower layer, if you like, has started the process of ... well, of turning into rock as a result of the pressure. Above it is the sedimentary ... the deposited silt, or sand, if you like. You see, it was all sea bed at one time. Well that's the bottom. We won't find anything under that and it's only 20 metres down.'

I shook my head. 'So that's all very interesting, but I thought you lot had found King John's treasure?'

'Oh, we have,' he said. 'Look, there. Come on, Dave, do your thing.'

David Carter began giving the machine instructions with the keyboard then the colours changed and there, right in the centre of the screen, was an artefact. I could only call it an artefact because it had no particular shape, but it definitely looked to be out of place.

'So what is it?' I asked.

David pointed with his left hand as his right pressed a few more keys.

'It's a cart or coach. Look at it. I'll turn it round a bit. See, now you can see it's a flatbed of a cart.'

'What about the wheels, I don't see any wheels?'

He smiled. 'John says that it probably broke up and the thin pieces of wood probably rotted away. We'll have to dig it up to be sure, but of course this is only a simple rendering. Maybe a full work-over will tell a different story.'

'Full work-over?' I quizzed.

David sort of grimaced. 'We just wanted to keep you up to date.'

'Full work-over?' I repeated.

'Well,' Dave said sort of shyly. 'It's now so complicated that it takes ... well, there are thirty chips and each with three shots.'

'So?'

'Well, it will take at least ... well, say, maybe forty-five to forty-eight hours.'

'Then get on with it. What's the point of half doing a job? Sometimes you guys don't show any initiative.'

'Yes, sir.'

'What about the treasure?' I said, craning in to get a closer look. 'Will it show any better if you do a proper rendering?'

'So look in the centre. There's stuff there. Something heavy; probably metal. I think it will be improved.'

I felt vindicated as the technical magic had worked – or at least with a little tweaking it would be useful.

Standing up straight and addressing them all, I said, 'Well, lads, we'll take a weekend holiday. I've decided we're all going to Ottawa to celebrate our success. You can leave this monster computer to do its thing while we relax.'

'Roger dee, sir,' Manningham said. 'When shall we go to Ottawa, then?'

'Oh, I don't know. I'll talk with everybody at dinner and make a decision on that. Okay?'

'Sure, sir. Thank you.'

My life seems to swing from boring to totally out of control. When the Brains Trust was in the UK things sort of moved gentle and slow, but on their return I have a dozen things to do all at once and all the time. I phoned my engineers to make sure my plane would be ready. Then I called my lawyers in Parry Sound, phoned Ottawa for a hotel reservation and arranged a flight path. After all that, I started on the family – wives, children and grandmothers have to be catered for. The house had to be organised for our departure, stay away and return. Then of course there was Newf and Morag to allow for, not to mention the three musketeers.

By the time we were ready to depart, the list looked more like a transatlantic flight than a mere weekend at the capitol. With Gran, Newf and Morag, Deloris and the baby, plus William Tan and Miss Whine, his nanny, John Magnus, David Carter and Paul Manningham, we had a plane full. Maybe I should have bought a larger version. The three musketeers took themselves to the airport in their old banger, while the chauffeur took Sally Whine, Deloris, Gran and the kids. I drove the SUV with Newf and Morag.

Everything worked out nicely and the journey to Mount Hope, or to give it is international name – C. Munro Airport, went without a hitch. The mechanics had taken care of everything and the plane sat there parked outside Hangar Two with the engines ticking over. I had of course flown her before and had actually put several hours in, but I felt like an opera singer on his very first public performance.

Tom, the chief mechanic, came to the car as I climbed out.

'Sir,' he said, grinning from ear to ear. 'You should have worn your captain's uniform.'

'You'll take care of the cars for me?'

'Sure,' he replied. 'No sweat. I've got your itinerary; if you change it, call me.'

'Thanks.'

I walked over to the plane and ushered my guests aboard. Gran seemed suitably impressed.

'Well, William, it's very small, but it is almost as comfortable as my apartment. It smells very nice, too.'

'Make yourself comfortable. There's a little kitchen just over there behind the cockpit. If you like, once we're airborne, you can make everyone a sandwich. There should be plenty of supplies.'

I waited for everyone to climb aboard, and then closed the port and beckoned Newf.

'Wha's up, Bill?'

'Nothing; you're the co-pilot.'

'What? I ain't no pilot.'

'All you've got to do is sit there and talk to me.'

'Oh, okay. If yous say so.'

I double-checked the exit door and then led the way to the flight deck.

'You sit there and don't touch anything.'

'Right ye are, Cap. Or should I say, aye aye, sir?'

'No, you shouldn't. Now that there is the intercom. Pick up the mic and press the button.'

'What for?'

'Tell the passengers to buckle up, we're on our way.'

'Aye aye, sir.' He picked up the mic and pressed the button. 'Now listen up, you lot,' he said. 'This here's the co-pilot gabbing. Seats in the upright position and buckle up, we's off to Ottawa.'

I thumbed through the flight checklist then checked the controls, temperature and all the necessary instruments. Everything looked kosher.

'*Cloudier III*, Reyner-1 to Hamilton control, permission to roll?'

'Control to Reyner-1, proceed to taxiway.'

Oh, man, this was the real thing. Moments later we were gently rolling along the peri-track to the take-off point. My heart pounded with excitement, but … well, it's only routine. Eventually, we were up there in the clouds on our way to Ottawa and hopefully an exciting and enjoyable weekend. David carter had brought one of his electronic gadgets with him. He said he wanted to test it in the field. Whatever it was, it looked like a small cell phone.

The flight was uneventful, but the service at Ottawa was great. They took my plane with one of those little tractor things and parked us on the concrete near the hangars. The chief tech said she'd be ready and fuelled whenever I wanted. A small bus had been arranged to take us and our luggage to the hotel in downtown Ottawa. It was all part of the service, but pay-as-you-go sort of thing, rather like a giant taxi.

The trip was multifaceted. Firstly we had to rescue John Magnus' father and secondly, I needed to know

194

more about François Quiberon – like who or what is he? Then of course there was Gran and the children. We had perfect weather and Newf wanted to be entirely independent – no crutches or wheelchairs.

I told John to arrange for his dad to be at the airport ready to move at six o'clock on Sunday night.

'And, John,' I said. 'No fuss. No need to say anything to the residential home other than that the old man's going on a holiday. Alright?'

'Sure.'

David Carter asked, 'When can we test my device?'

'What device?'

'The one I brought along for testing.'

I sighed. 'Listen, when I ask what device, I want to know what device, you got that?'

'Oh, well, it checks for radar.'

'Great – and what use is that?'

'It measures the sweep and the frequency.'

'Great, so what?'

'You see I'm working on the idea of radar echo copy. You see, if I can simulate the mother radar, I can fool it into thinking I'm not there.'

'You can say that again. From where I'm standing, you're mostly not all there. Why didn't you test it on our way in?'

He actually blushed. 'I thought that it might upset your instrumentation. But … well, well, if we took a special flight and I was in the cockpit …'

'Flight deck,' I interrupted.

'Yes, the flight deck, then, so, I could do a controlled test.'

'Alright. I'll think about it. Now, I'm off to do some research.'

After we were fully checked into the hotel I gave everyone their orders. The three musketeers were told to forget about technical stuff or any form of research

195

and just go and enjoy themselves. I even gave them some cash. God only knows how techno-critters enjoy themselves – probably by watching something being built or dismantled.

As David Carter wanted me to help him test his new invention, I deliberately ducked the Brains Trust, grabbing Newf on the way. We slipped out of the hotel, trying not to be noticed by anyone. My intention was to visit the library and learn about Quiberon, but … well as they say, "the plans of mice and men".'

As we quietly and calmly exited the building by the front door, someone approached me from behind and tapped me on the shoulder. Looking round, I was shocked, for standing there as large as life was LePort, looking as if he had just finished a marathon lemon-sucking session.

'Oh, Christ!' I exclaimed. 'What the hell do you want?'

'*Bonjour*,' he said. 'I am so glad to see you, too.'

'So what do you want? We're on holiday – not going anywhere near the Institute.'

He slipped his arm into mine and nonchalantly commenced walking.

'We are friends, no?'

'Exactly – no. So what do you want?'

He stopped walking and forced me round to face him.

'We have a problem, *comprenez-vous*?'

'If you're going to talk to me, then you'd better drop the Froggy stuff. I don't speaky de language.'

'Come, let us walk slowly and not make a congregation. You know I have been suspended from duty? Pressure has been applied to have you … how should I say? Taken care of.'

'Meaning what?'

'If I knew I'd break this deadlock but, alas, like you,

I am in the dark. I think we should work together. I have a few contacts and I feel it imperative to solve this … er, mystery before anyone else gets harmed.'

'Such as who?'

'Well, myself, yourself. We are dealing with shadows. They see us, we do not see them.'

I stopped walking and looked at the little detective. 'Are you really RCMP?'

'*Oui*, yes. Time is short; we must act and act together, yes?'

I shook my head. 'Like what? Without breaking into the Institute to see what they are really up to, there's nothing I can do.'

He nodded in agreement. 'Can you improve the picture you have of the woman?'

'No, that's it.'

'Hmm, so, somehow, they come and go. Could we secretly intercept a shipment and perhaps discover their workings?'

'No. A shipment of what?'

'Whatever comes and goes into and out of that place.'

'You don't have a clue, do you? I'll tell you what – have you ever been to the Institute?'

'No.'

'Okay. Then how about this – one of the nutcase geniuses who works for me wants to do a radar test. I'll do the test and at the same time fly you up to the Institute. We can't land, but you will get an idea of what we are up against. You can see the fortress that confronts us.'

He actually smiled. 'Excellent, when?'

'This afternoon. My plane can make the trip in no time flat – it's a jet.'

And so it was arranged. Newf wanted to come and fortunately, no one else was interested. David Carter was easy to find; he never went anywhere without his mobile phone, iPad and a hoard of other electronic devices. We arranged to meet at the airport at two in the afternoon, which would give me time to have a meal and for the boys to fuel-up and get the plane ready. Newf, Dave and myself took a taxi from the hotel to the airport. Mr LePort made his own arrangements and would meet us there. I really didn't like him or trust him.

Being a next to nothing run and not travelling in any air lanes, permission was easy; the only difficulty was arranging the return. As luck would have it there was light to no air traffic and we got the go-ahead. The taxi dropped us and we walked to the hangar where I expected to find *Cloudier III*, but when we arrived the hangar was bare.

'They have taken it to Dispersal Point 05,' said the mechanic.

'Is she ready to go?'

'*Oui.*'

When we eventually found Dispersal Point 05, LePort was already there leaning on the wing of the plane.

'Nice aircraft,' he said. 'Do you own it or rent it?'

'Own it. Come on; everyone in. Let's get this show on the road.'

'Must be nice?' LePort said. 'How the rich and famous play and live. I have a car, an old car.'

'Yeah,' Newf replied. 'Bill worked for it. 'e's solved more crimes than you've ever dreamed of an' if yous jerking 'is chain on this one, guess 'oo's gonna be the loser?'

Dave sat up front with me – the technology of the flight deck excited him like a child. His eyes gleamed and he wanted to fiddle with everything.

'Hands off. Just sit there and do your thing. If I tell

you to shut your toy down, do it and do it immediately. Is that clear?'

'Yes, sir.'

With throttles wide open, we rushed down the runway and gently climbed into the clear sky.

'Wow!' exclaimed Dave. 'They're using multiburst, omni-phase Doppler at really high frequency. Amazing.'

'Sure, whatever that might be.'

The flight was calm and easy and with a slight headwind, we reached the Institute in thirty-eight minutes. For a giggle, I flew in at less than 150 metres altitude. Dave was ecstatic with excitement.

'Wow! They have radar, here. It's low frequency, but it should have a good long range.'

LePort wandered onto the flight deck. 'I see what you mean about the isolation. I see they have a road down there – can you follow it and see where it leads?'

'Sure.' I gently climbed and changed course. I had wondered where the road leads myself. I knew that in one direction it led to where we set up camp on Lake Opinnagau.

It turned out that we were only 58 kilometres from the coast and low and behold, there in the shining sea sat a ship, flying the Turkish flag on the jackstaff, and beside her in the water sat a seaplane. Not far on the land were three trucks. The vehicles looked like military ones with large wheels and a high chassis – probably all-terrain vehicles.

'Smugglers. This has to be our first real clue,' I declared.

LePort smiled and produced a small monoscope from his pocket – the type golfers use. 'Indeed,' he said, grinning from ear to ear.

Chapter 16

Getting in Deeper

LePort was happy and quite enthused by what we had found up north. The prospect of the Institute being some form of smuggling agency tickled his sense of humour. Personally, I thought it didn't add up – for instance, what would they need doctors for? Who were all those women pretending to be pregnant? Why were there two dead females? Where would they sell whatever they smuggled? Turkey would suggest opium and that would be easy to move, but where to?

As LePort climbed from my plane in Ottawa I said, 'Should be easy for you to have the coastguards board that ship and search it.'

'Hmm, perhaps.' Without a so much as bye your leave, he wandered off, hopefully never to be seen again.

Walking over to the main building from the dispersal, Newf came up with an excellent idea.

'Bill.'

'What?'

'I fort o' sommat.'

'Marvellous, perhaps you should sit and give that lonely little brain cell a rest.'

'Yeah, very funny. This Qui-er-oon geezer – if 'e goes up norf, 'ow's 'e get there?'

'You mean Quiberon?'

'Yeah, that's the geezer.'

I stopped walking. 'You're right, Newf. If he actually does go to the Institute, he must fly – there aren't any roads. You're brilliant. He must fly from here.'

'I ain't just a pretty face.'

Already, my brain was in fast forward. If Quiberon flew from Ottawa, one of the mechanics would more than likely have heard about it and know who he flies with. I changed direction and walked back to the dispersal. The tow driver was still there talking to a marshal.

'Hi,' I greeted with a big smile. 'Are you the man who looks after my plane?'

'I towed it,' he said, leaning over the side of his tractor.

'Oh, right. Great job. I love people who do a good job. Am I allowed to tip for excellent service rendered?'

He smiled and said something in French to the other man then said, 'Sure.'

I pulled out a twenty and handed it to the driver. 'Buy yourself and your buddy a drink, but only after you've moved my plane.'

He took the joke and the money then laughed.

'I hear a friend of mine often flies from here, François Quiberon. Yah know him?'

The driver laughed and then clearing his throat, said, 'Sure, that Parliament fellow. Yeah, he flies with Warren Air, a charter company. They've only got three planes and I guess mostly government men use them. They park in that hangar over there.'

'You all right, Newf?'

'Yeah, why?'

'Okay, we'll take a walk over to the hangar if you're feeling up to it.'

'What about me?' Dave asked.

'Well, you're your own man. You decide.'

'Okay, I'll tag along.'

On reaching the hangar, I asked a mechanic where I could find Warren Air. He pointed to a door in the side

201

of the building, grunted something and then continued his work. We walked over and sure enough, on the door in gold letters was the name we were looking for. I pushed it open and found a girl sitting at a regular office-type desk.

'*Bonjour*,' she said and smiled sweetly.

'Hi,' I said. 'Do you speak English?'

'Of course.'

'Oh, right, we want to fly to the Cormorant Institute.'

'I am sorry, sir. They do not have a runway. You either have to go in the winter or take a floatplane.'

'Oh, right,' I said, pretending to be ignorant. 'Where would we get a floatplane?'

'I'm sorry, sir, perhaps you should consult the Yellow Pages.'

'Yes, thanks very much.' I grabbed the lads and led them out.

'Well that were a waste of time,' Newf said as I closed the door.

'No it wasn't. Notice she didn't even blink when I mentioned the Institute and she knew they only flew off a frozen lake. Like who else would even have heard of the place?'

'So where we gonna get a floatplane?'

'Nowhere, you twerp. We've learned all we need for the time being.'

'Speakin' o' twerps, when we gonna dig up old King John, then?'

'When I've studied the options and the new rendering. Now shut up.'

John Magnus had apparently dropped off the map – he was nowhere to be seen all day Sunday. I was quite worried about him, but as the taxi dropped the rest of us off at the airport, there he stood with another gentleman. Edward John Magnus was tall and slender;

he stood bolt upright and looked quite stern and young for a 76 year old.

'This is my dad,' said John as I approached.

'Hi,' I replied. 'You do know what's going on?'

The tall gentleman spoke with a commanding and clear voice. 'Presumably, I am being abducted.'

'Yes but not by force and it's for your own good.'

'We haven't been introduced,' Gran said, muscling in.

'Oh! Sure. This is my Gran, Zelda Hubert. Gran, this is Edward Magnus, John's dad.'

'How do you do, sir,' she said and put out her hand.

I expected him to shake it but instead he gently took it and kissed the back of it.

'*Enchanté, madame*,' he said, beaming from ear to ear.

'For crying out loud, does everyone speak French around here?'

Gran glared at me. 'Manners, dear.'

The old man was well educated and well travelled; this created an instant bond between him and Gran. I think she took a shine to him. They sat together on the plane and practically ignored everyone else as they giggled and laughed at each other's tales of adventure.

The flight home was totally uneventful and comfortably short. Apart from his funny way of talking, Edward fitted in like one of the family. When I say funny way – well, he would stand rather like Napoleon with one hand in his jacket and speak as if he were addressing an audience. His words were always crystal clear and sometimes accompanied with definitions.

'Which is my room, abode, *mon chambre chez un particulier*?' he asked when we arrived home.

Gran smiled and took his hand. 'Come with me, dear sir. I'll put Mr Magnus in the blue room, William.'

'Sure, whatever, Gran.'

I wandered out to the garage to see what the gang were up to. As usual, they were all crowded around a monitor and gabbling on about scientific stuff.

'So,' I announced.

'Oh, hi, Bill,' said Manningham. 'We were just taking another look at the King John test – our big boy's done a fine job.'

I wandered over to the display. 'So you guys reckon you've found it?'

Paul pointed to the screen. 'There – you can see it quite clearly now the machine has performed a complete rendering. Even with this power, it took almost forty-sixty hours to get the real thing.'

I looked at the screen. It certainly looked different to the first scan I saw. The picture had more natural colours and you could clearly see the sedimentary deposits. A strange-shaped black thing sort of splodged itself on the screen. It had no recognisable shape.

'It looks like a pile of garbage to me. I don't see any horses or wheels.'

Paul Laughed. 'No, after almost 1,000 years under salt water you wouldn't. I think it's a coach, or perhaps a wagon. If you look closely … Dave, rotate it a bit so we can see all sides. Ah! there, look. You see, it's longer than it is wide.'

'Well,' I grumbled. 'Sorry I can't get enthused but, so, as I said, it looks like a pile of garbage that's longer than it is wide.'

'We won't know until we actually dig it up,' Paul said, grinning like a Cheshire cat. 'But look there … Magnify it, Dave. See, there's a load of unusual deposits there and look at that form – wouldn't you say that looks suspiciously like a vessel of some kind?'

'Wow! I think you're right.'

'So shall we go dig it up?'

I thought about it for a second or two. 'Ah, you see,

there are all sorts of legal difficulties. I have put my lawyers on the case. If it is King John's treasure, the Crown will be involved and then there is the owner of the land. Don't worry about it, boys; I've got it all in hand. As soon as we get the go-ahead, we'll crack out the shovels.'

'What about the monetary return?' Paul asked.

'Hmm, well, after you pay me back my investment, we'll go even-steven and I'll forget about the rent of this place and the food. Now, I want you to worry about the firing up north.'

'Oh, really? You want to go ahead with another firing up there?'

'Yes, and at the same time I want to have another look at the Institute.'

For once I was up early enough to join everyone at breakfast. I couldn't believe the crowd – you'd think we were running a hostel for out-of-work eggheads or something. The conversation was, as expected, at least half a metre over my head, but Gran seemed to be enjoying the talk.

'Morning,' I said, sort of announcing my presence.

'Mornin', Bill,' Newf replied. ''ave a good nap, did yah?'

'Yes, thank you.' I took my seat and smiled at Deloris and then at Gran. 'Where's the children?'

Deloris answered.

'William is with his tutor and at this moment Christi is asleep. She had a very rough night, and I also. Though I did notice that nothing seems to wake you.'

'Sorry, love.'

'Edward has an interesting theory, William,' Gran said, grinning and with eyes sparkling.

'Edward who?'

'Don't worry,' Newf said. ''is brain usually wakes up around noon.'

'Yeah yeah, very funny. So what's this interesting theory?'

Edward Magnus coughed to clear his throat then, in a commanding voice, said, 'You appear to be suffering under some misconception concerning the Cormorant Institute.'

'No, I'm not suffering; just a little perturbed, that's all.'

'I comprehend and I do believe you have encountered a copycat conspiracy. A profitable and illegal conspiracy modelled on the misguided adventures of William Peach Young.'

I looked at him and silently shook my head sadly. 'So who the hell's he?'

'William, dear, please modify your language and show some respect for your elders.'

'Yes, Gran, so who's this Peach fellow?'

Edward cleared his throat again, smiled all-knowingly and began, 'William Peach Young and his wife Lila Gladys Young, operated the Ideal Maternity Home – ideal in name only, for the two were in fact thieves and murderers of the most despicable variety and operated a charnel house for profit.'

'Yeah, sure. But what the heck have those two got to do with the Institute?'

'Young ladies were enticed to the Ideal Maternity Home through concise and insightful advertising. Any unmarried and gestating female was welcomed with open arms. The net result being that the Youngs would sell the progeny and extort money from the mother in the form of blackmail. If the child was worthless, being low in intellect or disfigured, it would be starved to death and disposed of.'

I stared at him for a moment. 'You *are* kidding, aren't you?'

'Distasteful as it may seem, I am not. The Butterbox

Babies is a well-known case.'

'Butterbox, what's that mean?'

'The babies were often disposed of by interring them using a butter box as a makeshift coffin.'

'Coffin?' I echoed as the memory of the rendering came to mind. There were things under the Institute. 'So you figure they're selling babies?'

'Naturally. Perhaps they are generating them to order, using modern science and genetics. Perhaps they have a niche market that requires their essential expertise.'

'Wouldn't be profitable, would it?' Then I remembered what Jane said. 'I can't see it. How would they move the babies without anyone knowing? In this country, you have to register births.'

He smiled a sort of sickly smile. 'Only if you intend the progeny to live here. What if the destination should be some other country?'

'Yeah, you're right.'

'Oh! crikey,' groaned Newf. 'Remember, Bill, Doc Worthington? What if them buggers is doing the same as 'im you know, running a spare-parts-to-order outfit?'

I looked at Edward. 'If such an affair is going on, that would explain the secrecy. I know for sure they have pregnant women there – I've seen some.'

'My boy, your task is simple: should they be executing nefarious deeds, you must stop them. First, you must discover their shipping methods and find a way to legally intercept it.'

'Shipping – you're right. We saw a Turkish ship just off the coast where the Institute is. I'll bet that's how they do it.'

'What abart Jenny Stilton? she weren't on no Turkish ship.'

'No,' I agreed, 'but I'll bet she was trying to make an escape. Or maybe Dr Bromley really was trying to help her.'

Newf grinned all over his face as a thought struck him. 'I just figured it art. I'll put money on it that the good doctor weren't 'elpin' 'er. I reckon 'e was delivering a body part to the 'ospital in Owen Sound. That's why 'e was in such a 'urry.'

Newf had a very good point. I decided to call LePort. If anyone could unearth the doctor's movements, he could. Afterwards, I wandered off to my den and fished out LePort's calling card. Although the man was a menace, it seemed he was in as much trouble as we were. Fortunately, he always carried his mobile.

'*Bonjour, je suis* LePort.'

'Hi, this is Bill Reyner.'

'Ah! Monsieur Reyner, to what do I owe this pleasure?'

'Yeah, well, I've been thinking. Could you find out where Dr John Bromley went the day before Jenny Stilton was killed?'

'Why?'

'You do know who I'm talking about?'

'*Oui*, yes, but why is it important?'

'Well, Newf, that is Mr East, has a theory. Well, anyway, he thinks the Institute is dealing in body parts.'

LePort laughed and then said, 'It is quite possible, but how will that help?'

'Just find out where the good doctor went after he landed in Georgian Bay.'

'Landed? Please explain, landed.'

'We think he flew from the Institute to Georgian Bay, probably carrying a body part for delivery to a hospital in the area.'

'Flew? How is this possible?'

'He had an aeroplane, a floatplane, parked in the bay. We think Jenny Stilton stowed away on-board and somehow finished up in his boat, which we think was on the shore and not in the water. Anyhow, can you find out or not?'

'*Oui*, yes, of course. I will contact you, yes?'

'Yes, great, thanks. I'll keep you informed.'

'*Au revoir*, Monsieur Reyner.'

'Yeah, sure, bye.' I hung up. The man's a twit – not surprising he got fired.

I called my lawyer in Parry Sound before eventually wandering out to the garage where the gang were doing whatever brainiacs do. As usual, I found them huddled around a monitor.

'Ah, Bill, sir. We were wondering when we could go dig up King John,' Paul Manningham asked and grinned as if he knew something I didn't.

'Dig *him* up?'

'Well, the treasure.'

'Oh, that. I talked to my lawyer about it. He says there's a Limey professor who says he could organise a dig if we tell him where to make the hole.'

'But that's our secret, isn't it?'

'Sure. But as soon as we stick a shovel in the ground, everyone's going to know the exact spot. My lawyer said we should register with the Crown and then allow the professionals to do the work. Like, are any of us archaeologists?'

'I'm a geologist.'

'I've been on digs,' John Magnus said, butting into the conversation.

'Okay. I want to go back up north and blow another thirty geras – with your newfound expertise, you can map the underground all around the Institute for me.'

Paul scratched his chin thoughtfully for a moment.

'Is there any point?'

'Yes, there is. Firstly, I want to show them buggers at the Institute that they can't frighten me or give me orders. Secondly, I want to know exactly what's under that building. Remember on the first shot we saw something underneath?'

He nodded. 'Right, I'll arrange everything. Do you still want to use Johnny Horner and his helicopter?'

'Sure, so when?'

'Best go when the snow starts. We can get better reflectivity if the ground's frozen. We know where all the holes are and only need to make them a little deeper.'

I sighed. 'Right, the year is rapidly coming to an end – let's make it as soon as possible.'

'Can I go to England and supervise?' Magnus asked.

'Sure, you're the history expert. I figure it would be a good idea if you represent us. I'll call my lawyer and get everything organised. You alright to fly commercial?'

'Oh, sure. When?'

'As soon as I can get it all arranged.'

My main point of interest was the Institute – I just couldn't wait to start sorting them out. No one knocks people off and lays the blame at my doorstep without a damn good fight.

Nothing works out the way you'd expect it to. Gran stuck her oar in and got everything moving. She organised the trip to England for John Magnus and his dad, Edward Magnus, and would you believe, herself as well.

'What do you mean you're going to England, Gran? We need you here.'

'Nonsense, William. I shall proceed to England with John and his father. Then, when John is comfortable with the arrangements in Norfolk, I thought Edward and I would fly to Cromlet.'

'You're not soft on the guy, are you, Gran?'

'Even if I were, it is no concern of yours, William. Now, please be a good boy and play detective while I take a small and well-deserved holiday.'

'You just came back from one.'

'I was looking after your offspring – it was a working holiday. This time, I expect to take it nice and easy. Now, if you have no further objections, I shall complete the arrangements.'

'Yes, Gran. So when will you be coming home again?'

'When I am good and ready, William.'

Like wow! Gran certainly put me in my place. Generally she's a real pussycat, but something seemed to have got under her skin. Not to aggravate the situation, I let her get on with whatever she wanted while I made the arrangements for Mr C. Corner to ferry all our stuff to the great white north.

By the time Gran and the two Magnus members of our ever-growing family had arranged everything and actually left for Toronto Airport, I was ready. Johnny said it was already snowing up around Lake Opinnagau and as long as there were no high winds, he could fly in just about any weather.

This time we were properly prepared. I had electric underwear – great invention; they tell me it was invented for space exploration. We also took the English anti-tamper devices so that no one human or otherwise can interfere with a gera once it's been set. We didn't want anyone else getting killed and us getting the blame.

The November weather in Hamilton was cool but nowhere close to snow. In Opinnagau, we arrived during a blizzard. Johnny had difficulty putting the machine down safely, but thanks to GPS we were able to avoid landing on the lake and falling through the ice. The hut was a good 200 metres from where we finally landed. Johnny took off almost immediately, leaving us stranded in a snowbound wilderness.

Eventually, we huddled in the hut and Newf started the generator so we could have heat and light.

'When can we begin drilling?' I asked Manningham.

He breathed out like a whale surfacing. 'Well, the snow makes things difficult. Fortunately, it's not all that cold yet. As long as our GPS devices work, I see no problem. We could start right away. We don't have to worry much about the light, as it won't get much darker than it already is; the snow will brighten up the place.'

'Okay, let's get this show on the road.'

With all the bad weather – not really unexpected – we had enormous difficulties. With thirty holes to deepen, it took one day per hole –mainly because one of the two drilling rigs died and we wasted a lot of time, in vain, trying to get it going before we abandoned it.

'Oh, heads up,' I demanded as we all crowded around eating our canned supper in the shack. 'We've got the bombs planted, so I vote we fire as soon as possible, collect the chips and abandon this site until spring.'

Manningham shrugged his shoulders. 'What about the equipment?'

'I don't think anyone's going to steal it. I figure we can grab the chips, go home and let big boy do his thing while we celebrate Christmas.'

A chorus of cheers rang out.

Chapter 17

Beyond Belief

As we all huddled in the shack hiding from the tempestuous weather outside, Paul did a remote signal test.

'Standby,' he said. 'In three, two, one .... Oh, crap.'

'Now what?'

'There seems to be a problem with number sixteen.'

I exhaled. 'Yeah, that's "oh crap" alright. It's the one closest to the Institution. I don't suppose they've buggered around with another one?'

'Me an' you'll go, Bill,' Newf volunteered.

'What if it needs servicing?'

'We'll take two machines,' Paul said. 'I'll take Dave; he's the electronics expert, anyhow.'

I took a peek outside – the wind was howling and rapidly approaching gale force.

'Maybe we should wait this storm out.'

Paul shook his head. 'First easing up, Johnny'll show up and it'll be time to get the hell out of here.'

'Alright. Everybody carry a GPS; I don't want anyone going missing. I want everyone to carry a radio as well, plus an aluminium survival blanket. Agreed?'

They nodded in full acceptance of the rules. I didn't like it – somehow, this smelled of a trap. Within half an hour we were ready. The snowmobiles were fuelled and ready to go. Newf rode pillion on my machine while Paul and Dave took the second machine.

The wind howled almost continuously, making talking difficult. As we sped up towards the rise the side wind buffeted us, making progress somewhat slower than I had expected. I kept the speed fairly slow, as it was impossible to see more than a few metres ahead. In only minutes, I lost Paul and Dave. They disappeared into the whiteness ahead of us. Only ten minutes into the trip, I was lost and had to stop and consult the GPS. Something told me this was not a grand idea. I began to have visions of four thoroughly frozen and dead bodies being found some time in the spring.

'Newf, this is impossible. I can't drive and look at the GPS at the same time. You navigate. Tap me on the right shoulder to go right, the left to go left and the middle of my back to go straight. You got that?'

'Sure, I ain't stupid. Would you like me to walk a'ead wiv a red flag?'

'Shut up and stop wasting breath. Here's the GPS, now get navigating.'

Though not the perfect system, it worked. I had to drive slowly owing to visibility and Newf tapped me every now and again, correcting my course. In just over fifty minutes we arrived at the troublesome gera. I stopped and turned off the engine. All I could hear was the wind – Paul and Dave were nowhere in sight or sound.

The Institute, though only 100 metres away, was totally invisible. I looked for tracks but with that wind, tracks wouldn't last more than a few minutes.

From what I could tell, the gera looked alright. There was no obvious sign of tampering. Reasonable, I figured, as only a lunatic would venture out in this weather. With all the clothing, fur and goggles, finding anyone would be a miracle. But as I stood there wondering what to do, a snowmobile emerged out of the whiteness. Its headlight blinded us for a moment. Paul and Dave had arrived.

'What kept you?' I yelled over the wind.

'We hit a ditch the other side of the Institute and

stalled the engine. Have you checked the gera?' Paul asked.

'No, didn't want to open it. I haven't a clue what I'd be looking for.'

As best we could, using our bodies and an aluminium blanket, we shielded the wind and snow off Dave as he opened the device and checked for problems. It seemed to take forever. Just standing there and being buffeted by the freezing air seemed exhausting and totally tiresome. I thought he would never finish tinkering.

'Okay, I've found the problem.'

'Can you fix it?'

'Done already. Let's get back to the shack.'

'Oh, what a relief.'

At this rate and in this weather I figured it would take a week to collect the chips after the firing. In that weather you tend to lose track of day and night, but we eventually made it back to the shack. Tiredness prevails all the time – every now and again someone would drop off. I can now understand how Ernie Shackleton felt when his Antarctic expedition went wrong. Just looking at the miserable landscape outside – the little that was visible – was enough to make a hermit develop cabin fever.

'Aren't you ready yet?' I said, raising my voice.

Dave Carter checked his electronic toys and grinned at me.

'Yes, you wanna push the start?'

'No, for Christ's sake. Press it and let's get this over and done with.'

With an ear-to-ear grin, he pressed the button. Instantly, there was a bang outside. My heart sank as I thought it had failed. Then a second bang.

'Don't worry,' Dave said. 'They go every four seconds, so it'll take just under six minutes to complete.'

It was certainly weird, even with that wind – I guess you could more feel it rather than hear it as the explosions slowly crept round that huge circle three times.

'How long is it going to take to collect the cards?' I asked, feeling somewhat impatient.

'You go one way and we'll go the other. I figure in this weather it's going to take maybe three or even four hours,' Dave said almost shyly.

'Okay, I'll see if I can raise Johnny and get him here to pick us up ASAP.'

Although Mr Cedric Corner had visited us every other day for the past month, he hadn't shown for the last three days. We had enough supplies to last a week without rationing, but the fact he hadn't shown or called worried me. I remember what happened to Captain Scott and they didn't even have helicopters. The problem being that my radio could not reach Sault Ste Marie unless the helicopter was flying high. On or about my third call I got an answer from a third party.

'Hi,' I said. 'This is William Reyner. We are stranded up at Lake Opinnagau. I'm trying to contact Sault Ste Marie.'

'Oh, roger that. This is the Northern RCMP detachment at Moose Factory. Give me your message and I'll relay it.'

I gave him the name and address of where they could probably find Johnny and hoped that they actually would find him. Apparently, they had telephone lines or maybe satellite and made contact with Soo Airport only moments later. I figured we would wait for a call from Johnny before we set out to retrieve all the gera chips.

Eventually, the radio sprang to life – Johnny called in.

'Where the hell are you?' I asked, feeling a little peeved.

'Had a spot of engine trouble; everything's okay now. My ETA, three and a half hours. Chin-up, I've got you all a present.'

Dave's estimate of three or four hours to collect the chips was off. After almost five freezing hours we all met at the Institute. Although the wind had let up and the snow had stopped falling, the fresh light covering made progress difficult. Every now and again we'd drop into a snowdrift a metre or so deep. Twice I stalled the engine, but the headlights of the other snowmobile made us feel less than lonely. When we eventually reached base camp, the beautiful helicopter stood there looking like the angel of salvation. Johnny was in the shack making coffee.

'We're done,' I yelled excitedly. 'Where the hell have you been?'

Johnny grinned. 'Sorry, Bill, but you haven't paid my bills. The old bird needed her book A and they wouldn't do it until I paid the fuel and landing fees.'

'The bills have all been paid. They have an open account, what are you talking about?'

'Sorry, but I had to get a bank loan.'

'What?'

'Yup, you're lucky I know you. Other companies would probably have left you here – you could say with your frozen assets.'

'Don't worry; I'll sort it all out. There has to be a mix-up somewhere.'

'No mix-up,' Newf said. 'I'll bet yah it's interference. Someone don't like you an' someone's got the push to cause trouble.'

As soon as we arrived in Hamilton I called my lawyers in Parry Sound and put them on the "lack of payment" case. The boys, of course, went to the garage to play with their expensive toys. Deloris acted like a spoiled schoolgirl.

'So where have you been?'

'Where have I been? You know where I've been. I've been freezing my ass off in the snow up north.'

'You have responsibilities here – you have children. If you hadn't noticed, you also have a wife.'

'Okay, okay, I'm sorry, but the weather was bad and Johnny had aircraft troubles. I promise it won't happen again.'

She stormed out of the room in a huff. Women! Man! are they ever difficult to deal with. I was about to leave and join the boffins, when Johnny walked quietly into the room.

'Excuse me, sir.'

'What?'

'I got you a present; well, two, actually.'

'Oh yeah. What?'

'First, I got you a case of genuine Champagne straight from the Champagne Valley in France.'

'A case, a whole case?'

'Yeah.'

'And the second?'

'You'll have to wait to see that.'

'Okay,' I said. 'And why?'

'Well … a sort of a thank you gift or a Christmas present, if you like.'

'Well I don't know what to say, except thank you; you shouldn't have.'

'I also got news.'

'News?'

'Yeah. John Magnus phoned – you know, from England.'

'And?'

'Well, I guess it's good news and bad news.'

'Oh, come on, Johnny, stop farting about. If you've

got something to say then say it.'

'Well,' he said and scratched the tip of his nose. 'You know that treasure, the King John thing?'

'Yeah.'

'Well the good news is, they dug down and actually found something.'

'And?'

'Well, the bad news is it ain't royal.'

'What do you mean?'

'Magnus said it's turned out to be a Viking raider.'

'So it's bloody worthless, then?'

'Not quite, sir. Magnus said it has great historical value and it looks like it was carrying loot.'

'Loot? What loot?'

He grinned. 'You see, it seems the Vikings were anti-Christian and raided the churches for gold. Apparently, this boat is loaded with the stuff they took from local churches.'

This of course changed my mood. It looked like the experiment was not a total waste of time and money.

'Okay,' I said with jubilation, 'we'll have a bang-up Christmas and the party's on me.'

I took to my new job with enthusiasm. This Christmas was going to be one to remember, even if Gran wasn't going to be with us. I called the Canadian and asked Veronica, my manager, to arrange for the place to be empty, or as empty as possible, for the Christmas week. I told her that she and the staff were welcome to our slap-up Christmas party and I had guests needing rooms.

Feeling great and a little like Santa Claus, I waltzed out to the garage to give the whole gang the good tidings. Johnny met me in the hall.

'Oh, sir, Mr Reyner, sir.'

'Yeah, you still here?'

'Yeah, sure. I've got your present in the workshop,

if you'd like to come and have a look?'

'Workshop? What workshop?'

'The garage.'

'Oh, okay; that's where I was going, anyhow. I'm throwing a party Christmas week. You're invited and there'll be a fully paid hotel room for you and your wife. It's going to be Christmas and a victory celebration all at once.'

'What about my machine?'

'Machine? Oh, you mean the helicopter. Bring her along as well, if you like; there's plenty of landing space in the parking lot. In fact, I think that would be great we could fly there instead of drive. So what's this present?'

'It's in here,' he said, opening the door for me.

Just inside the garage, or laboratory or whatever the lads called it, stood this enormous packing case.

'So what is it?' I asked, staring at the thing.

He chuckled. 'It's 144 bottles of Newfoundland Screech.'

'Screech? What's that?'

'What you a true blue and born Canadian and you don't know what Screech is?'

'Well … I've probably heard of it but, well … I'm not a Newfoundlander.'

Johnny shook his head in disgust. 'I was born in St John's and I thought everyone in the world knew about Newfie Screech.'

'Okay, explain me to it.'

He laughed. 'It's rum. Supposed to have been discovered accidentally when they used to buy rum shipped in fish barrels. Now of course it's official and it's about 40 per cent alcohol.'

'Wow! You bought me 144 bottles?'

'A gross – and no, I didn't buy them.'

'Gross?'

'That's old French for 144.'

'Well, thanks. We can certainly do with that at the Canadian, if it really is Canadian.'

'Through and through.'

Although somewhere back in the depths of my mind I had heard of Newfoundland Screech, I surely was not familiar with it.

When we entered the work area of the garage, the boys were crowded around one of the monitors.

'So what have you got?' I asked.

David answered in his quiet and timid way.

'We, er … well, that's the Institute. It's only a quick rendering – the big boy will take a couple of days to give us the details – but … well … I think you should have a look at this.'

The screen looked a familiar shade of red canned spaghetti with worms and splodges liberally scattered about.

'Oh, yeah, that's great. What is it – a Picasso?'

'No, that's the Institute. Look there under the main building.'

I glared at the screen and could only see spaghetti.

'No, I don't see it.'

He sighed as if I bored him. 'Well I'll explain. That is the main structure and that is the basement. Just a minute and I'll rotate the picture. Oh, wow! It's not under the building, it's under the back quadrangle.'

'So what is it?'

'It looks like … yah know … I should say a couple of dozen boxes. Holy mackerel! They're coffins, I think.'

I couldn't see it.

'Well get your … or should I say our, expensive machine to render it properly so we can all see what the hell it is.'

Deloris was not enthused when she discovered my

Christmas plans. Almost instantly she took offence.

With her hands on her hips, she said, 'And who gave you the right to decide our Christmas?'

'Our?'

'Yes. The children and Miss Whine.'

'Oh, well Sally can do as she likes. I'm just throwing a bash-up for the lads and staff. I thought if it were at the Canadian, neither you nor Gran or any of our household staff would have to work during the hols. And besides that, if anyone wants to get pi … drunk, they can sleep it off at the hotel. Do you know what Screech is?'

She looked at me as if I'd slapped her with a wet kipper.

'Screech? Screech? Just what on earth does that have to do with anything?'

'Johnny bought you a present,' I lied. 'About 200 pounds or around 100 kilos of the stuff.'

I guess she must have known something I didn't, for suddenly she hugged me and kissed me.

'You can have your Christmas wherever you wish, my darling.'

'But?'

'But nothing. I'd love to go back to the old hotel – just for a visit, mind. The houses have been rented and so have the cottages.'

'We'll stay in the Reyner Suite.'

She grinned. 'Very well. Oh, by the way, Screech is sweet rum.'

The Brains Trust were like children – I'm not sure whether it was the rendering process or the thought of the Christmas event I was planning, but slowly they rose to the boil. It's hard to believe grown men could act like children.

I called the Canadian and had them pick up the Screech; it was far too heavy even for me to shift it. A few days before the party Paul came running to me all excited. I mean for a man around fifty he acted like a child.

'Oh, Mr Reyner, sir. You gotta come quick.'

'That's Bill, and I do believe I don't *have* to do anything.'

'Yes, you do. You should see what Dave's dug up.'

'Dug up?'

'Well, it's on the screen. Come on, quick.'

I followed; he acted like an excited puppy dashing off then returning to make sure I was following. When I entered the garage they were all there, including my newest follower Johnny Horner. It sounded more like a rave-up than a science meeting.

'So what's going on?' I yelled.

Dave sheer bubbled over with enthusiasm.

'Look at that, Bill, look at that!'

I squeezed in and peered at the huge screen. 'So what am I looking at?' All I could see was something that looked like an iceberg with what looked like meat skewers stabbed through it in vertical lines.

Paul said, 'Let me explain. See that huge anticline, it –'

'Anti-what?' I interrupted.

'Oh, never mind. Look, it's a fold in the rock formation caused through immense tectonic pressure.'

'I haven't got a clue what you're talking about, could you put it into English?'

'Sure, in brief.' He sighed and slowed his words down a couple of notches. 'That's quartz.'

'Great, I always get excited over a load of quartz. Maybe we could mine it and sell it to make watches.'

He shook his head sadly. 'Mr Reyner, do you know how gold is formed?'

'No.'

'Well I'll not bother with its entire history, but

mostly gold is down there with the magma white-hot and liquid. Under certain conditions it gets squeezed and squirts up through fissures – what you might call a vein.'

'Yeah, so?'

'So what you're looking at is what all prospectors pray for – it's the mother lode.'

'Mother lode? You mean … you mean … nah.'

'Yes, those vertical black lines are gold rivers that solidified on their way up from the magma. I'd guess there is literally tons – metric tons – of the stuff just sitting there waiting for some genius like me to get a shovel to it.'

The lads, including Newf, started whooping and hollering like a bunch of raving savages. I just stood there glaring at the screen, wondering what kind of genie lay in that bottle and what would happen if and when we uncork it.

'Alright, quieten down, you idiots. It's a problem.'

'Problem!' exclaimed Dave. 'Problem, my ass. We're rich beyond belief. There must be enough there to make every one of us richer than Bill Gates and still be enough over to pay the national debt.'

'Don't count your horses before they hatch,' I growled.

'Horses don't 'atch,' Newf said calmly.

'Whatever. We must keep this top secret. Do you hear? Absolutely not a single word to *anyone*. Should this get out, it'll make the 49ers look like two and a halfers. Gold fever will sweep the country. Holy crap! not a word to anyone.'

My brain was beginning to swim as in my mind's eye I could see the disaster that would follow such an announcement.

'Come on,' Dave said. 'All we gotta do is register a claim; it's standard practice.'

'I don't care. Secrecy is top dog. I'll call my lawyers in Parry Sound right now and get them to work on the project. I have to know the exact coordinates of this gold field, area and depth. Can you give me that information?'

Paul smiled. 'Sure, when?'

'Now, the sooner the better. Write it down, now, and I'll get the ball rolling immediately.'

'What if someone 'as our phone tapped?' Newf asked.

'Okay, I'll phone and tell the lawyer to expect us in person. Johnny, is your machine fuelled up?'

'Yeah.'

'Okay, let's say half an hour and we'll be on our way up to Parry Sound.'

'What about the other?' Paul asked.

'What other?'

'I'll show you.' He sat back on his chair and fiddled with the keyboard and the picture changed. 'Look, see – that's the Institute, just as you wanted. I've cleaned up the rendering and selected more favourable colours.'

'So?'

'Well that's the basement. As you can see, there are things buried under it and that is the patio or garden. There are more than a dozen small coffins.'

I looked at the screen and a cold shudder ran down my spine. Sure enough, there were all these objects that looked exactly like coffins and there were even shadowy outlines of bodies in them.

'Holy crap!' I eventually exclaimed. 'Oh, Jesus! What are we going to do about that?'

'Call that twit Froggy,' Newf suggested.

'Right, I'll call LePort immediately after the lawyer.'

A multiple dilemma flooded my brain. If I call LePort he might put the dampers on us leaving and I had to get that land claim registered before the shit hit the fan, so to speak. The solution was simple: I would call LePort from Owen Sound. The most important thing would be to get that claim registered. Then I wondered when civil servants knock off for Christmas.

Chapter 18

Holidays

I love it when there's action and having Johnny and his machine in the yard turned out to be most opportune. I phoned Purvis & Pringle Law Partners up in Parry Sound. I don't think the old buggers have any other clients but as Purvis lives in the huge house they use as law offices, he answered the phone.

'Ah, Mr Purvis, this is Bill Reyner. I have something very important to tell you but it will have to be in person. Will you be in this afternoon?'

'Afternoon? Why, yes, I suppose so. What could be so important?'

'I can't discuss it over the phone. We'll be there at around three.'

'Very well.'

I hung up and felt proud of myself for such efficiency – now all I needed was the land coordinates and a pilot.

'You coming with us, Newf?'

'Like you can stop me.'

'What about Morag?'

'What about 'er?'

'Does she want to come, you idiot?'

He shook his head. ''er and yours old lady are in cahoots; they's plannin' your merry Christmas do, ain't they.'

'Okay, go tell Johnny to be ready to go at one this afternoon. Oh, yeah, and tell the eggheads I need the land position of the gold.'

'What yours last servant die of?'

'A bullet in the brain, now get going.'

I seemed to be surrounded by idiots – the discovery of the century and everyone's all a dither. Immediately after lunch I bowed out with the excuse I had an important legal matter to discuss with Purvis. Surprisingly, I didn't get any arguments. Both Deloris and Morag smiled sweetly and said almost in chorus, 'Have a good journey.'

Outside I could hear the turbines running on Johnny's machine.

'You ready to go?' I yelled.

'Hop in, mate.'

Newf and I climbed aboard and closed the door. I sat beside the pilot.

'You know where we're going?'

'No?'

'We're going to Parry Sound.'

He nodded and grinned then twiddled a couple of switches and the rotors began to rotate.

'So where's Parry Sound?' he asked.

'Oh boy, take the 401 to the 400 off ramp then follow the 400 north.'

'It's a helicopter, not a car.'

'You can still follow roads, can't you?'

'Do you have coordinates?'

Newf poked his head in through the hatch.

'It's abart 80 degrees west by 45 north.'

We started rising like an express elevator. In moments we were on our way north.

'So how come you know such things, Newf?'

'I's told yah, I ain't just a pretty face.'

Johnny stayed with his machine after we landed right in the middle of the harbour car park. Newf and I called a taxi and proceeded to Purvis' place up by the courthouse. The old man ushered us into the house. Usually he had a young girl to do all the menial stuff.

'On your own?' I asked.

Purvis smiled. 'So what seems to be so important that you have come in person?' he asked and led us into his office on the ground floor.

Newf and I made ourselves at home while Purvis walked round the desk and sat in the command chair.

'I've, that is we've discovered the mother lode of gold. It's on government land and is probably worth billions.'

The old man nodded. 'And for this you have to come in person?'

'Yeah. I couldn't phone the location because someone might be listening in. I want you to make a claim for me so that we can legally extract the ore.'

Purvis blinked furiously for a few moments – you could almost see the cogs turning in his head.

'And how exactly do you expect me to perform this?'

'I don't know. You're the lawyer, you figure it out.'

'The government offices are closed for the holidays, they –' He stopped as a light come on in his head. 'Very well, I can assure your claim, but I cannot assure the government will permit it.'

'It's gold, more gold than you can ever imagine, they'll agree.'

'Very well. First, we must create a company. I shall put you as Chief Executive Officer –'

'No. We, that is I, have an enemy in Parliament who might put the dampers on it. Make someone else chief. Here's a list of the partners; they can be the board of directors. These three owe me a couple of million dollars. Write something into the agreement that they have to pay me back. Okay?'

'Certainly. And where is this deposit to be found?'

I handed him the paper with the coordinates on it.

'You will execute this with the utmost secrecy?'

'Certainly, my boy. Now, I'll prepare everything. If

you give me an hour or two, I can get the necessary papers for you to sign. Then I can get, as they say, this ball of wax rolling.'

Newf and I took a taxi, picked up Johnny and then went for a meal and a drink. Later, we went back to Purvis and signed the appropriate papers. Somehow, it was a great relief to know that competent hands were at work. The old boys had never let me down in the past; I figured they'd do this right even if it was a bad time of the year to be making land claims. Next on the agenda would be Christmas and Deloris would kill me if that didn't go right.

It felt strange going back to the old Canadian, especially without Gran. We made a grand entrance in Johnny's helicopter. I had to admit, it was the first time in my life I had gone to a Christmas party in such a grand style. Deloris seemed to enjoy the royal treatment and the young William Tan had an absolute ball.

Apparently, there were still two guests in the hotel as they were more or less permanent fixtures. Veronica had done an excellent job of organisation. This time there would be no boat trips or icebreakers, only indoor activities; although Santa Claus would be visiting. I noticed that the main drink for the party was Newfoundland Screech.

It was during the festivities on the very next day – Christmas Eve – that I went to my room on the second floor. It was there in the Reyner Suite that I had an unexpected encounter. Both Newf and I excused ourselves and headed upstairs – he wanted something from his room and I needed to change my shirt, having spilled some blancmange on it.

I went into our room and closed the door and there, sitting on my bed, was this lad who broke into the house a while ago.

'What the hell are you doing here?' I growled and

prepared for a fight.

'Don't get excited, Mr Reyner. I'm here in peace.'

'In peace? In peace? I thought you had been locked up for the last intrusion?'

He stood up and I backed away.

'I'm not armed, honest. All I want is a talk,' he said.

'So talk and be quick.'

'That French cop said you were one of the good guys, that's why I'm here.'

I backed up even further and opened the door. 'You stay where you are, boy.' Then I yelled at the top of my voice. 'Newf, Newf, get your ass here at once.' Hopefully he would hear, as he was only just in the next room. I turned to the lad. 'When Newf gets here, your number is up, so talk while there's a chance.'

'I came for your help, Mr Reyner. I need you to help me rescue my sister.'

'What?'

'She's a prisoner at the Cormorant Institute.'

I blinked a few times as the door banged into the back of me.

'Oh, sorry, Bill. What's all the fuss?' Newf said, entering the room.

'We got visitors.'

Newf looked round. 'So where's the uvers?'

'What others, you pillock?'

'You said visitors.'

'Oh, Christ! It's him, the boy who broke into the house.'

Newf looked at him. 'So what you want, boy?'

'I came for your help. My sister is being held against her will at the Institute.'

'How do you know that?' I asked.

'I got a letter from her; it's all wrong.'

'All wrong? What do you mean?'

He pulled an expression as though he was in pain.

'She wrote to me to tell me all was okay, but I know it's all wrong.'

'Why?'

'She always calls me Pip, but this time she said, "Dear Josh," and she signed it, "Your loving sister."'

'And you find that suspicious – how?'

'She always signs off, "Love you, sweetie, Sis." So I know she was forced to write the letter or someone else wrote it.'

'You seem to have a very suspicious nature. Why would you think it's a fake? Was it typed or handwritten?'

'Handwritten. But, you see anyone could copy her writing. And LePort said you were one of the good guys. I figured you weren't looking into this place for fun – you must know something I don't. I need your help or if you like, I can help you. Either way, we can work together.'

I sighed loudly. 'What d'yah think, Newf?'

'Could be tellin' the troof.'

'Alright, boy. Tell me about you and your sister.'

'Well, my name is Joshua Tyler. My father owns the Brown Book Connection. He prints books for anyone who wants them; sort of a ghost company, you see. He's got plants in seven countries.'

'The BBC?' quizzed Newf.

'Yeah, and well, it all stems from the inheritance.'

I sighed. 'Is this going to take a long time?'

He shrugged. 'Please listen; you can easily check my story.'

'Go on, then.'

'Well, Granddad started the company and he left an inheritance for both me and Sis. See, it has rules. Neither of us can inherit until we're twenty-one and married. It also stipulates that we can't inherit if we're not pure.'

'Not pure? What the hell does that mean?'

'Well, we can't be married nor have any children when we reach twenty-one. See, Granddad figures we have to become adults before starting a family.'

'Go on.'

'Well, Delilah got herself pregnant, see. Now she can't inherit.'

'So how much is the inheritance?'

'It's about a ten million in North American terms.'

'Each?'

'Yeah. So she had to get rid of the kid, before anyone found out. She saw this ad in the paper and answered it. Next thing, she's on her way to the Institute. I wouldn't have twigged, but the quack who did everything for her was Dr John Bromley.'

I nodded in silent agreement.

'So will you help me?'

I couldn't make up my mind if this was a wind-up or not.

'How do I know I can trust you, kid?'

'You don't, but think about it, what have I got to gain? My sister's in danger, that Froggy cop won't help and I know you are an honest man.'

I had to scratch my chin and think for a moment.

'Well I don't know. Just what do you expect from me?'

''e wants your bleedin' 'elp,' Newf said in a growling voice.

'Help to do what, exactly?'

'Cor, Bill, 'is sister's in the same shit that Jenny Stilton were in afore she got topped. I fort you was a knight in shiny armour. Ain't you got no chivalry left in yah?'

'Chivalry, my foot. What if this little turd is just leading us into a trap?'

'Nah, 'e's on our side. 'ow could it be a trap?'

233

I breathed out audibly, showing my discontent.

'I don't trust burglars or people who point a gun at me. So if I should decide to comply, what exactly do you think I will do for you?'

The lad smiled. 'Great! I know when François Quiberon is going to the Institute.'

'So?'

'So, Mr Reyner, he's something big. I figure he's the money man or even the brains behind it all.'

'Well I know he's the one who's been trying to put the brakes on my project up north. I still don't see quite how knowing when he's going to the Institute would help our quest for information.'

The kid grinned again. 'I thought I'd capture him, see. Then I could torture him for information and maybe get my sister out by threatening his family.'

'Man, you think big for someone so little. To start with, you'd have the RCMP down on you like a ton of bricks. Threatening or even interfering with a Member of Parliament is akin to treason and would get you a permanent room at taxpayer's expense in Hotel Kingston, courtesy of Her Majesty, the Queen.'

'Well I figured I'd stow away on his plane, then take him once he reaches the north. Who would know?'

'Have you ever been up there and seen the weather?'

'No.'

'Thought not. You're crazy; it couldn't be done.'

Newf grinned like the proverbial Cheshire cat.

'I fink it's a great idea.'

'Yeah, so you would. You're as mad as he is.'

'Nah, Bill. Fink abart it. If we's grab the old bastard up there in the snow, 'oo would know?'

'To start with, you dink, the Institute would know and before you could say "How's your father", the place would be crawling with redcoats.'

'In fur parkas,' Newf added. 'Nah, Bill, me ol' mate. Yous got the wrong end of the stick, as usual.'

I sighed. 'Alright, Einstein, explain how we could give the RCMP the slip in a snow-filled wonderland.'

'Easy. Get Johnny to land on a frozen lake kilometres from Lake Opinn-whatsit. Let me know the coordinates, see. Then me and the young fellah 'ere, we'll stow aboard Frank whatever's plane and 'ijack it. We'll land on the lake where Johnny is an' there you are, we's got one smarmy prisoner ready for the pounding wiv yours fists.'

'And what stops the RCMP from riding over the hill and arresting the lot of us?'

'Fink abart it, Bill. We'll call in wiv engine trouble an' give 'em the wrong position. They'll all bugger off searching neverendin' snowdrifts.'

I scratched my head, deep in thought. The idea is mad enough to work.

'Why you and Joshua stow away?'

'Cuz it's 'is idea.'

'And you?'

'I like the idea and 'sides, I fort of it.'

'If I didn't know you were an idiot, I'd think you were a fool. I'll do the stowing away.'

'Why?'

'Because I could fly the plane.'

'So can the pilot.'

'Yes, but what if you hijack the pilot and then I'll pretend to be the substitute? No one will know the difference. No one gets hurt and stowing away becomes unnecessary.'

'What abart the pilot?'

I had to think on that for a moment.

'Well, we could take him to the secret location separately and just hold him for a day or two.'

''ow?'

'Shut up, Newf, and let me think.'

If only Gran was home, she would know how to conduct an operation like this. I needed to think about it. Maybe Newf was right; it might be better just to hijack the plane. Of course, then we'd be open to piracy, hijacking and assaulting a government official. Oh boy, well, as Gran would say, in for a penny, in for a pound.

Josh suddenly piped up. 'I could be your eyes and ears in Ottawa.'

'Meaning what, exactly?'

'Well, I could keep track of François Quiberon and inform you when he's going to visit the Institute.'

'So what's his connection to that place, anyway?'

'Don't know. So should I?'

I shook my head. This lad seemed too eager – is he trustworthy? Or is he just a spy from the Cormorant bunch, to inform on us?

'Alright, you can be our Ottawa connection. Keep your head down and don't give anything away to the enemy.'

'And you'll move?' he said.

'Move? What do you mean, move?'

'You'll make a move against the bunch at the Institute. I have to get my sister out.'

'Oh! Sure, but not till the new year. My boys need a holiday and my lawyer is working on another angle. Let's leave everything until January. So how did you get here, anyway?'

'Train.'

'Trains don't run to the Canadian.'

'Oh,' he giggled. 'I came from Ottawa on a train. They said at your house you were all here, so I called a taxi.'

I let Joshua stay for the Christmas festivities; we even found a small room on the top floor for him.

After the slap-up Christmas do we all returned to Raven House, except Josh; he went back to Ottawa. Somehow, it seemed calm and sedate after all the raucous partying at the Canadian. Gran surely took her time. I phoned on 5 January and she said she would probably come home in the next week or so.

I wanted to get the ball rolling again. Newf wanted to have another firing in England to see if we could locate King John's treasure and not another Viking ship. We had no news from the dig in Norfolk, no news from the Institute and no news from my lawyers about our land claim.

Just a couple of days later round mid afternoon I was in my den mooning about the unfinished projects when Griffin walked in.

'Excuse me, sir, but madam would like a word with you.'

'Where is she?'

'In the drawing room, sir.'

'Okay, thanks, Griffin.' I walked over to the drawing room to see what Deloris wanted. Man! what a shock. As I entered there was Gran sitting all prim and proper in one of the easy chairs by the roaring fire and sipping on a sherry. Somehow, she looked younger than the last time I saw her.

'Gran!' I exclaimed in total astonishment.

'William, come and sit with me.'

'Wow! Gran, like when did you get home?'

'Over an hour ago, William. Now, come and sit with me – I have something very important to tell you.'

Somewhat shocked and surprised, I walked over and sat on one of the wing chairs near her.

'So why the surprise and secrecy?'

'No surprise, William. You were sleeping in your den. Now, I have an announcement to make.'

'Yeah, so?'

237

'So, dear William, I have decided to live at the Canadian with my husband or possibly at Cromlet.'

For a moment I sat there with my mouth open and my eyes wide. I thought my ears were playing tricks.

'For goodness sake, William, you look like some kind of idiot.

'Idiot? Yeah, you said your husband? You don't have a husband.'

'Yes, dear. If you listen closely you may comprehend what I say.'

'But you don't have a husband. Granddad died long ago.'

'Well, now you have a new granddad.'

'I do?'

'For goodness sake, William, pull yourself together. You are acting rather foolishly.'

'But, but … well, but … Like … how?'

'Goodness me, William. Pull yourself together. Edward John Magnus and I married at Gretna Green shortly after Christmas. I am now Mrs Magnus.'

If I hadn't been sitting I would have fallen down. Words defied me.

'Possibly, I will move into my old suite and when one of the houses is unoccupied, I think I may move in there.'

'With your husband?'

'Of course, William. For heaven's sake, pull yourself together.'

'Yeah, sure. Yeah! But … Wow!

Chapter 19

Digging Even Deeper

I found it very hard to believe that Gran had married that lanky twit from Ottawa. The first thing on my mind was to phone John Magnus and complain about his father's actions – the problem being the time difference between England and Canada. I managed to phone him just before our lunch, making the time in England about five in the evening. Fortunately, he carried a mobile with him.

'Hi, John, this is Bill Reyner.'

'Oh, yes, sir. Isn't it great?'

'What is?'

'Well, we've reached the boat. They tunnelled to it from a vertical pit. Any time now we should reach the heart of it.'

'Great. Did you know your father got married?'

'Sure, he married my mother.'

'No. I mean recently.'

'Recently? I don't think so.'

'Hmm, well, you're in for a shock. He married my grandmother up in Scotland.'

'Oh, crap, I guess I must be your great-uncle, then.'

'Is that all you have to say about it?'

'Sure. He's his own man; not really my business. Now, about the Viking ship – will you be coming over for the ceremony?'

'Ceremony, what ceremony?'

'Well, the college is going to have a big do, when we get this thing excavated.'

'No. I don't know. I'd not thought about it. Why all the fuss, anyway? I thought all we wanted was the gold, if there is any.'

'Oh, there's gold, alright. All sorts of stuff stolen from the churches along the coast.'

'Great, then we'll be rich, then?'

'No, not really. I gave it to the Norwich Museum in your name; that's what all the fuss is about.'

I was shocked, stunned. All that expense and then give it all to a bloody museum – I'm surrounded by idiots and traitors. I sighed very loudly.

'Alright, phone me with the details when you're ready.'

I put the phone down and stood paralysed for a moment. It felt as though I had lost control of things. Everywhere there was negative activity and all beyond my reach. At least at lunch I would be able to talk to Gran. Everyone was seated when I entered the dining room.

'Gran, I need to talk with you.'

She smiled. 'I'm sure there is nothing stopping you, dear.'

'I was wondering about this Institute thing. I can't figure it out. I thought we'd hijack François Quiberon's plane and see if we can't beat some truth out of him.'

She looked at me as if I had suggested murdering the queen or something like.

'Are you mad, William? You cannot go around hijacking anyone or thing. What kind of stupidity have you been up to in my absence?'

'None, Gran. I was just asking.'

'Why would you desire to hijack this man?'

'He's a government official; elected, I think. Anyhow, he's pretty deep into the Institute and he's the one who's been putting the dampers on my project up north.'

'And this warrants criminal action?'

'I was just asking your opinion, Gran.'

'Then use stealth, intellect and do not intentionally break the law.'

I was beginning to feel a little hot under the collar and decided to turn the tables by going on the offensive.

'So what about this new fellow of yours? I suppose you'll be sharing your wealth with him?'

'William, dear, you do jump to conclusions. I decided to leave Cromlet to North and Morag.'

'What? Like, what?'

'Oh, William, please calm down and pull yourself together. I've arranged to leave my share in the Canadian to you.'

'Oh, great.'

'And the rest of my estate will be divided equally between my two great-grandchildren upon their reaching the age of twenty-one.'

'Then what about your new husband? Where is he, by the way?'

'He's sleeping in.' She smiled. 'Should he outlive me, there is no difficulty; he is independently rich. Now, be a good boy and don't bother me with these annoying trivialities. Oh, yes, and for your information, it was Edward's idea to leave him nothing.'

I nodded in agreement but felt about 7 centimetres tall.

'So ... so ... well, what do you think I should do about the Institute?'

'Well, if anyone asks me,' Newf said with a grin, 'I fink we should break into the place an' bust a few faces.'

'North, dear, I think stealth and not brute force may prove more helpful,' Gran said, grinning like a Cheshire cat. 'Why don't you and William do as you used to do?'

'Which is?' I asked.

'Carefully and stealthily enter the building in the dead of night and find evidence of a damning nature. The worst that could happen is you get arrested for breaking and entering. No one gets harmed, if you see what I mean. Plan the foray with military precision; execute the adventure with accuracy and careful forethought.'

'I reckon she's right, Bill. Just like the old days. We could use our blacks.'

'We haven't got any blacks.'

'Could get some.'

'Okay, meet me in the science den and we'll talk it over.'

'Science den? Where's 'at?'

'The garage.'

After lunch, Newf and I wandered over to the garage. The two brainiacs we as usual gabbling in techno-jargon and staring at a non-comprehensible picture on one of the monitors.

'Oh, Bill,' Dave said, pulling his face away from the screen.

'Don't you guys ever get tired of looking at that crap?'

'Well, no; there's always something new to see.'

I shook my head in disgust. 'I need your help to plan the perfect burglary.'

'I can't assist,' Paul said. 'I don't do anything illegal.'

Again I shook my head and plopped down in a nearby chair.

'Listen. I'm going to break into the Institute and see if I can find any damning information, any clues as to what they get up to in there. What I want you guys to do is help me come up with a plan of entry.'

Dave Carter said, 'Entry without their knowledge will be difficult – they have radar; they'll know we're there.'

'Exactly, that's why I need you guys to help me. Can you build something that will confuse their radar or something like?'

Dave smiled as now I'd set him a technical challenge.

'Well I'll think about it. But you know, if Johnny flies away, they'll not know how many people are left behind.'

'Oh, why's that?'

'Because of the hill between the Institute and our landing site. Radar is line of sight. Therefore, we can land – they'll know that – but they won't know how many people are left on the ground. I figure we could get almost to the top of the hill then walk the rest of the way. I suspect their radar won't be accurate enough to see a human.'

'Hmm, is that the best you can come up with?'

Paul sat on the monitor bench. 'It's simple. You could drive up to the Institute on a snowmobile and then if the vehicle were to leave, they wouldn't realise that someone was left behind. They would assume everyone left the way they came.'

'Now that's a good idea. Great. Ah, but what about the regress? How would we get back?'

Dave tapped himself on the head. 'Easy, easy as punch,' he said, getting enthused with the idea. 'If we take three snowmobiles – one on tow, two people each on the leading machines – as soon as we are under their radar range, hide one snowmobile, leave two people and the other machines will boldly circle just to get noticed and then leave. When you want to make your getaway you'll have a machine to do it on.'

'Now you guys are earning your keep. Great! So how will I get over the wall?'

Paul scratched his chin for a moment then said, 'The

radar can't see things close up because it's on top of the building. Close to the Institute, they won't see you. As for getting over the wall, I saw an advert on the Internet for a folding ladder, that would do.'

'A folding ladder?' I quizzed.

'Yeah, it's about 2-metres long and it unfolds and locks. I think it was something like four sections and opens up to about 6 or 7 metres long.'

'How heavy is it?'

He shrugged. 'Well, in the ad it showed a guy carrying it with one hand.'

'Okay, guys, look at it this way. I'm going to break into the Institute at night. I shall –'

'We,' interrupted Newf.

'Yeah, okay, we are going to break into the Institute at night. We'll be looking for evidence to sink their organisation and at the same time we'll try to rescue Josh's sister.'

''oo's Josh?'

'The lad who broke into our house. Now come on, boys, we've things to buy and plans to make.'

'We need to take a core for assay,' Paul said.

'What's that for?'

'We need to prove we've found gold and not just pyrites. The drills are still up there, probably buried under the snow, but we can dig one out and take a core sample, then we'd know for sure if we've found gold.'

'I thought you guys were sure?' I said in surprise.

'Yes, well, yes … we sort of do, but if we want anyone to invest in the mine then we'll need conventional proof.'

'Okay, that's the reason we're going on this trip, then. I'll leave it all to you to organise, Paul, but remember, secrecy is uppermost. We don't want to tell the world and start another Klondike Gold Rush in Ontario, if you see what I mean. Come on, Newf,

244

we've got work to do.'

Newf and I left the garage and walked back into the house.

'It's a pity abart the king's treasure, ain't it?'

'What?'

'Well, young John Magnus handin' it all over to the school an' all that.'

'School. What school?'

'Yah know, them that's organised the digin'.'

'You knew about it?'

'Well 'course I dose.'

'Hmm, I thought it was the museum?'

'It is, but them university geezers is the ones runnin' it all.'

'So you knew all about it?'

'Well o' course I did. If yous kept yours ear'ole to the grindstone, you'd o' known an' all.'

'That's the nose, not the ear.'

Newf stopped walking and glared at me. 'Crikey, Bill, that's why yous always in the dark. You can't 'ear nofin' froo yours nose.'

It's like talking to an elastic band.

'Newf, you're an idiot. Lucky for you, I understand you. Anyone else would have you certified. The saying is "keep your ear to the ground", or "keep your nose to the grindstone".'

'I still say you can't 'ear nofin' froo yours nose.'

Arguing with Newf is at times akin to arguing with a monkey.

'Alright, have it your way. Now, we have to plan for a night-time incursion into the Institute. Are you up to it?'

'Well o' course I am. I ain't gonna be left art o' this 'un.'

The only thing that I did not look forward to was the stinking weather up there at this time of the year.

Nothing would be left to chance; this excursion will be executed like a military operation – each and every man knowing his exact job. I decided that this time, Joshua Tyler would be left out of the loop. If he was on our side, then he could rest, but if he were on the enemy's side, well … he wouldn't know what was happening until it was too late to interfere.

So that the women were also left out of the loop, we made the garage the headquarters. Here, we would carefully make our plans and leave nothing to chance. I would have liked to have allowed LePort into it, but … well, who knows if he is trustable under these circumstances.

Young Johnny arrived in his great bird late evening around mid January. Talk about cold – I was beginning to have second thoughts about going up north in this sub-zero weather. Nonetheless, we set out early on the following morning. Hopefully, we had forgotten nothing. The Institute was about to meet its match and with luck, come crashing down about their cocky ears.

'I don't have ground support,' Johnny said over the intercom. 'I'll drop you guys and your equipment then head for the Sioux. I'll be back in exactly forty-eight hours.'

Needless to say, the lake was frozen hard enough for a 747 to land on it. Johnny waited long enough for us to unload and check the cabin. Everything looked A-okay and he left us marooned for the next two days.

'I'll get to the drilling site and extract a sample core,' Paul said with enthusiasm.

Personally, my excitement drains as the temperature goes down and here the temperature is as low as it can go. This time we had three snowmobiles and a load of extras the science boys wanted to play with. While Paul and Dave were out digging for gold, Newf and I prepared for our raid on the fortress Cormorant. The plan was to enter, search and leave without being detected. Should anything go wrong, we did not have a plan "B".

The daylight up at Lake Opinnagau is more like twilight; it never actually gets dark because of the snow. With a clear sky the moonlight is almost as good as sunlight. Visibility gets bad if it snows or blows hard. The wind will pick up loose snow and make both progress and visibility almost zero. So far we were having mild winds with a cloudless but excessively cold day.

By midnight, Curly and Moe had finished their set-up and had drilled a good way down to the pot of gold. They came back to the shack as ordered.

'Paul will take one sled and I'll take the other,' Dave announced. 'I have a radar detector here and I'll know if they are watching us and when we are in underneath their viewing area. Bill, you ride with me. We'll make it look as if we are checking the geras.'

'There ain't no geras out there,' Newf pointed out.

'We know that, but they will not. Paul will take North and tow the spare mobile. We'll put the ladder on the spare and sheet it down with this aluminium blanket.'

I shook my head. 'The blanket will show up like a mountain on their radar, they'll be sure to notice something.'

Dave laughed. 'Nah, you see, the blanket will present a smooth surface and low profile. To them it will look like a shadow. Besides, I'll put this on the front.' He lifted up what looked like a metal pyramid.

'What the hell's that for?'

Again he laughed. 'Mounted on the front of the vehicle and facing the radar scanner, it will throw a radar image ten times its actual size. They use things like this on airfields as markers, so the radar operator can see where the runway is. When Paul leaves the area, we'll put it on the back to give them a humongous reflection. They won't realise we've left one machine behind and in their dark zone.'

'What about me and Newf?'

'You two guys will get off in their zone of darkness and that's where we'll leave the spare snowmobile. You can drive it up to the Institute, do your thing and use it for a getaway.'

'How will I know they can't see me on the radar?'

'Easy, their scanner is on the roof – they won't be able to see anything close up. I'll tell you when we get there.'

Newf and I went into the shack and changed into our blacks and then put our fur parkas on over the top. Somehow I felt old – this outing held no excitement for me, just dread. As soon as we were ready, both of us walked out into the cold snow. Dave and Paul had the machines ready and we boarded. Talking is difficult with all that clothing on and the noise of the wind and the engines.

In moments we were roaring across the silent countryside towards the hill that hid the Institute from our view. As soon as we were over the rise, Paul followed our old route in a circular direction as if we were inspecting the geras. He stopped and examined his instrument.

'The radar is on,' he said. 'I can detect the waves. Don't worry – we'll head out to the gera nearest the Institute and pass under their scan range.'

Without warning, he gunned the throttle and continued the journey. Dave and the spare unit followed close on our tail. Eventually, Paul stopped again.

'This is it; they can't see us. Now be quick. I'll continue the inspection to make them think all is okay.

You must head directly to the building and park as close as you can.'

As soon as I was off, Paul continued his journey. Quickly, we unhitched the third machine and Dave left us. I ripped the aluminium blanket off and after bundling it up, gave it to Newf.

'Come on, get on the machine and we're off.'

'What abart the blanket?'

'Carry it.'

'Well what abart the ladder?'

'For crying out loud, Newf. I'll drive, you carry the junk.'

'It ain't possible.'

'Okay, okay. You drive the machine over to the wall and I'll carry the bloody ladder. Now, can we get going before they start celebrating Easter?'

'Alright, keep yours shirt on.'

It was only 60 metres or so in deep snow to the Institute's nearest wall. The ladder wasn't heavy but the going was hard. Eventually, I met Newf at the wall.

'I guess it's all the same. We may as well climb up here.'

'What abart the radar?'

'My expert informs me that the radar can't see things close up. Besides, the scanner is in that dome right at the top of the building. Are you ready?'

'Yeah.'

'You gonna be alright on the ladder?'

'Yeah.'

Unfolding the ladder and locking it into position whilst standing knee-deep in snow and wearing huge fur gloves turned out to be the feat of the month. At great and noisy length, we managed to get the thing extended between us and together we leaned it up against the wall.

'I'll go first.'

Climbing the ladder turned out to be almost as difficult as opening it. With snow caked on my boots and all the furs and wrapping, it became difficult to balance *and* climb. Carefully and very slowly, I made my way to the top. The wall turned out to be at least a metre wide at the top and rather slippery. I found it both safer and easier to lay down while Newf made his way up.

'It's bloody slippery, Newf. Be careful or you may just find a quick way down.'

He wriggled to the top and lay with his head near mine.

'I'll 'elp yah bring the ladder up.'

Carefully, we dragged the ladder up and slipped it over the top into the garden area. I had expected the main building to fill the compound, but here we were at the garden end of the enclosure with the main building some 20 metres away. The place looked well illuminated, with most windows on the ground floor lit up. The second floor was partially in darkness and the upper floors had no windows, at least none I could see. Placing the ladder in a safe, descent position was near to impossible from the top of the wall.

'Don't worry, Bill. I'll 'old it steady while yous shin darn.'

'I'm stronger than you. I'll do the holding, you do the shinning.'

Without another word, Newf slipped his feet over the wall and mounted the ladder. I held it from falling over. When he reached the bottom he stepped it out from the wall in a safe position and I descended.

'Well, here we are. Now what, Newf?'

'Find a door an' I'll open it.'

We quietly found a door that was obviously in use as someone had cleared the snow both from it and the garden path. Newf removed his gloves and using his special tools, released the lock in less than a minute. The doorway was rather like the entrance to a church, having a vestibule complete with a plank either side as a seat.

'Nar what, Bill?'

'We can't move or hide too well with all this clobber on. Let's leave the parkas, boots and gloves in this vestibule. They'll be safe till we return.'

The 20-below weather acted upon us the moment the parka was unzipped. Even before I divested myself of all the fur and footwear, my teeth began chattering. As quickly as possible, we squeezed in through the door and closed the frigid weather out. We were at the end of a very long hallway with at least half a dozen doors on either side of it extending into the distance.

Creeping about like a pair of black-encased idiots, we tried to explore the building. At the end of the long corridor we found a junction. Newf opened a door and discovered an office-like room. We entered and began searching for any kind of evidence.

'Queer that all the lights is on at this time of the night,' Newf said as he rifled through a filing cabinet.

'True. Hurry up; this place gives me the creeps.'

'Ah, look what I found.'

I walked over to him and he handed me a bundle of maps.

'Maps, who wants bloody maps?'

'Look an' see what they is of.'

The maps were in fact guides to the entire building. Why would they want bundles of maps? Quickly, I ascertained where we were and there on the map it showed that just up the next corridor is the operating room.

'Look at that, Newf. Let's take a look at the operating room.'

Stealthily, we exited the office and walked only

three doors down to a room marked "Theatre" and opened the door. Here, too, all the lights were on.

'Crikey!' exclaimed Newf. 'I 'ope I never 'ave a operation in this place.'

My eyes grew in size as I surveyed the contents. A huge bandsaw, a table saw, various and sundry handsaws and knives.

'It looks more like a giant butcher's shop.'

'Did you bring a camera?'

'No, let's get the hell out of here.'

'What abart the broad?'

I thought for a moment.

'Never mind her; we don't have clothing for passengers, anyway. Maybe next time.'

Chapter 20

A Bad Move

Escaping from the Institute was simplicity itself and we didn't even bother to look for Josh's sister and never encountered a living soul. However, trying to make it back to the camp was another story. I drove and Newf sat on the back, but there was no room for the ladder. Obviously, our plans were not as perfect as we had thought. Eventually we compromised, with the ladder sticking out like aeroplane wings lodged firmly between Newf and myself. I had to be careful not to encounter any undergrowth or snowdrifts taller than us.

Back at camp the place was deserted. I parked the machine and walked to the cabin – it was locked.

'So where's them buggers bogged off to?' Newf asked.

'Probably the drilling site. You got a key?'

'Nah, you?'

'Of course not. We'll have to go look-see what they are up to.'

'You know where?'

I shook my head. 'No, but we can follow the tracks, with a bit of luck.'

I folded the ladder properly and stowed it beside the shack, then the pair of us climbed on the snowmobile and sped off following the tracks from the camp. At first, I accidentally followed the wrong trail and found myself going back to the Institute, but after a couple of zigzags we were on the right course.

After only a few minutes we could see the horizon lit up where the boys were working. They had a generator and drilling rig. Lights had been spread around to allow them loads of working illumination.

Even with my parka on and nice woolly earmuffs, the noise of the rig was near to deafening. I tapped Paul on the shoulder to attract his attention. He shut the motor down to an idle.

'How's it going?' I asked.

He grinned through his fur-lined hat with his face all rosy and his eyes watering.

'Great, I got one core. Don't know if it's a gold bearer. Just making a second; should be through in about half an hour or so. Can't stop long; we keep getting trouble with the water freezing.'

'Didn't you use antifreeze?'

'Sure, but at this temperature it gets diluted with effluent and then it freezes up and causes problems.'

'So who's got the key to the hut?'

He pointed to Dave, who was crouched with a laptop on his knee. I only made three steps, when the engine of the rig roared and the drilling recommenced. I tapped Dave; he looked up.

'I need the key to the shack,' I shouted at the top of my voice.

He gently shook his head and looked blank.

I leaned into his ear and shouted, 'I need the bloody key.'

With a grin, he struggled with his parka for a moment then handed me the key to the hut. There was no point in hanging around as conversation was impossible. I jumped on the snowmobile and once again, with Newf on the back, sped off into the frozen landscape.

I think the sun was rising as we reached camp, but up in snow country it's difficult to tell. Even at midday, it's barely above the horizon. It seemed a relief to get into shelter away from the freezing air. But there was no heat in the hut, only shade from the wind.

'Newf, go start the generator; I'll get the coffee on. Oh, crap! all the water is frozen.'

Newf went back outside while I dumped a small quantity of ice into a saucepan and turned the electric heater and stove on, in anticipation of the generator starting. At length, Newf returned.

'We's only got abart ten hours of fuel for the diesel.'

I consulted my watch then began peeling off my many layers of clothing.

'Johnny'll be back in eighteen hours. I guess we'll have to economise. So what do you think?'

'Abart what?'

'The Institute.'

He pulled one of the maps from his inner pocket.

'This'll help us on our next excursion.'

'What do you mean, next excursion?'

'Well, when we goes again to get the broad art.'

'I can't see any point in it. They have everything well hidden from outsiders; I don't think we'd find her.'

'What abart the butcher's shop?'

'What d'yah mean?'

'Well, it smacks of the TOD. You don't fink they supply restaurants, does yah?'

'You have a nice way of turning a person's stomach, Newf. The Temple of Dominance was a religious order that snacked on the occasional virgin; I can't see much profit in it, can you?'

'Why's there 'ave to be a profit in it?'

'Doctors and the like, nah, there has to be big money involved. Besides, Jane said they were a baby factory and we have seen evidence of that.'

'So if we ain't goin' back, what you reckon we should do?'

'I don't know. Somehow, we have to find evidence

of wrong-doing. Then the RCMP will take over. LePort seems keen to get his hands on them.'

'Well I reckon we should go over there, knock on the door then knock on a few 'eads. Piddlin' around ain't gonna get us nowhere.'

'Yeah, sure. Well, before we upset too many people in high places, I want to know how Curly and Moe are doing.'

'Curly and Moe?'

'Yeah, Larry's still in England.'

'Oh, yous mean the science boys. Well, what abart Joshua?'

'What about him?'

'Well, I like 'is idea of snaffling that Ministry feller.'

'We'll see. First, I'd like to get out of this frozen hell; it's like living in a refrigerator.'

Probably because of all the exertion out there in the cold, the cabin, and in particular my bed, seemed cosy and comfy; within minutes of closing my eyes, I nodded off. The next thing I knew, Paul and Dave were back making a terrible racket.

'What the hell's going on?' I yelled.

Paul grinned. 'Someone has to feed the generator or we'll all freeze to death.'

'What?'

'There's extra fuel in these cans. I covered them with that canvas so that it didn't smell so bad.'

When all the fuss was over and the men returned from refuelling, I had questions.

'So what happened at the rig?'

'We've struck it rich,' Paul said, holding up what looked like a rather dirty salami sausage.

'So what is it?'

I climbed off the bed to take a closer look at this object that everyone was so excited about.

'It's a core; this is the second and deepest one. We hit the baby right on the head.'

'So it's gold?' I asked.

'No, but look here, that smear, that's gold, and that's pyrite, and that, believe it or not, is silver.'

'So what have we found?'

'The jackpot. We'll have to have this assayed, but I would guess from experience there's a very rich gold vein right where we figured.'

'So what about the silver?'

'You often find gold and silver in close proximity, but who the hell cares – this gold vein will be worth millions. The only drag is it's deep; it's gonna take a fortune to reach it.'

'So do I get back all the money you guys owe me?'

Dave laughed and shook his head. 'You can sell the claim for hundreds of millions. Anyone, even the Canadian Government, will be delighted at what we've found.'

'What about the Institute? They won't be very pleased at a mining company moving into their backyard.'

'Who the hell cares about them – this is money and money talks. Big money talks even louder. I know at least three companies that would buy this claim for cash.'

'Okay,' I sighed. 'We can't put the cart before the horse. I don't even know if we have a claim yet. This must remain our secret until all the legal stuff is on paper and signed by people in authority. If the Institute gets wind of it, they'll say they had the first claim and that twit minister will back them up to the hilt.'

'I vote we go bash 'is head in first, put 'im art o' the runnin',' Newf said.

I fell back onto the bed; somehow, I knew this would all end in a disaster. Already, I had literally spent millions and the Institute seemed as impenetrable as it had the first day we heard about the place.

'Alright,' I said, raising my voice. 'We'll keep this secret until my lawyer says we're safe. In the meantime, we should see if we can't sink the Institute once and for all.'

'What abart the ships?' Newf said, grinning like a monkey with a new toy.

'What bloody ships?'

'Remember, Bill, when we's flew over the Institute wiv that cop on-board – we found a ship.'

I sat up. 'You're right. There was a ship. Now the place will be frozen solid and deserted. That's great. When Johnny gets back, we'll take a little detour and see if there is any evidence over there by the ocean.'

'What abart polar bears?'

'What about them?'

'You got a gun?'

'No.'

Newf looked quite perturbed. 'I ain't gonna feed no bears on healthy Newf flesh. If you ain't got no gun, I fink we should give it a pass.'

'Don't be such a nancy,' I said.

Eventually, Johnny turned up in his helicopter. By the time he'd made a landing, we were all ready to go. I locked the shack and we headed out into the white wilderness towards the machine. Its rotors were still turning when I jumped in beside Johnny.

'Fire up, we're leaving.'

'What, no coffee?' he said jokingly.

'No, I want you to follow the road from the Institute east until we reach the coast, then land.'

'We'll have to call in Ottawa on the way home, if I do that.'

'Why?'

'I don't have enough fuel to fly all that way. I'll take

you to the coast, but then we have to go to Ottawa; it'll be the nearest place for a top-up.'

'Okay, that's great by me.'

Without further ado, we were off heading for the coast. Following the trail was not as simple as I had anticipated. Apparently, they don't use it much in the winter or the snow had blown over it. Either way, it mattered little as we knew roughly where we were going. Every now and again we spotted the correct route and eventually reached the coast. There were no visible buildings, but I could see a sort of jetty sticking out into the frozen water at the shoreline. Johnny landed.

'I'd like to keep the engines on idle,' he said. 'I'd hate them to freeze and strand us up here.'

'Okay.'

'Will you be long?'

'Maybe an hour or so.'

'Hmm, I'll shut down and start up again in thirty minutes. We don't want to run out of fuel and make an unexpected drop-off in the middle of nowhere.'

The going wasn't easy as the snow was quite deep. Dave and Paul went one way while Newf and I went the other. We couldn't see any buildings even from ground level, which I thought was rather unusual as in the summer I swear I saw some close to the waterline. Suddenly, I spotted it. There stood a standard Miskins aircraft hangar. It's not much more than an arch. They were especially designed to be camouflaged in the Second World War. The front was painted white to match the snow and the rest of it looked like a bump or hill.

''old me glove,' Newf said as we reached a human-sized door.

In moments he had the door open and we entered. Unfortunately, the lights didn't work and we hadn't brought any light with us. After a short time we were able to see enough the push a little deeper into the building. Newf jumped into a large 4 x 4 and turned the headlights on. Man! what a surprise. The hangar was filled with vehicles, equipment and stacks of boxed stores. There were snowmobiles, snowcats and even amphibious vehicles and one boat on a trailer. The stores were marked as canned food of various varieties.

'What you reckon, Bill?'

I shrugged my shoulders, as nothing seemed to make any sense and there was nothing I could see that was incriminating.

'Don't know. Maybe we should get the hell out of here. We'll come back another day with a flashlight and see if there's an office we can ransack.'

By the time we got back to the helicopter, Paul and Dave were already in the warm waiting for us.

'Okay, Johnny, let's make like a leaf in the breeze.'

'You what?'

'Let's go.'

The flight to Ottawa was eventless and totally boring. The scenery seemed hardly worth the watching with its endless expanse of snow and ice. At least landing a helicopter at an airport is so much easier than a regular aeroplane. We were able to settle down only a stone's throw from the refuelling depot, which happened to be just the other side of the main buildings.

'I'll fuel-up,' Johnny said. 'You guys may as well head over to the lounge. Better still, there's a good place to eat in the departures area.'

Having not eaten real food for almost two days, his suggestion made a lot of sense. Dave, Paul, Newf and I wandered over to the restaurant and ordered a slap-up meal.

'Is we going back to 'amilton today?' Newf asked.

'Are we going back,' I corrected.

'That's what I said. You's losin' it, Bill. So is we?'

I sighed. 'Your English deteriorates with your age. It's "are" we going back to Hamilton, you twit. And yes, of course we are.'

'I's didn't want to call you a twit, Bill.'

At that point in time a smartly dressed man in a navy-blue blazer uniform with captain's stripes walked up to our table.

'What are you lot doing here?' he asked and grinned from ear to ear.

Suddenly, I realised who it was.

'Josh, Josh Tyler? What the heck are you doing in that get-up? I didn't know you were a pilot.'

He grabbed a chair and spun it round then plonked his backside down onto it.

'I'm not, but as you're not taking any action, I thought I'd better do something.'

'Like what?'

He surreptitiously looked around then in a hushed voice, he said, 'I've clobbered the pilot of Quiberon's plane. He thinks he's going to the Institute, but I'll fly him to nowhere and torture him.'

'Can you fly a plane?' I asked.

'Can't be that hard, now can it.'

'You're crazy. You'll never get it off the ground and even if you do, you'll never land it. Man! you're a nutcase.'

He looked at me imploringly. 'You're a pilot, aren't you?'

'Yeah, so?'

'So, I got the pilot; he's locked up in my closet. You take him and keep him quiet until I've finished with Quiberon, then you can blow the whistle. Or if you like, you take the plane and I'll look after the pilot.'

I nibbled my fingernails and thought for a moment, then suddenly the light of day began showing through the clouds of confusion.

'I've got it,' I said. 'To save everyone! Yes, by heck, I've got it. Okay, this is how it will happen. I'll fly the minister to Lake Muswabik.' I rifled my pockets for my wallet, extracted the piece of paper with the coordinates on it and handed it to Newf. 'Here, take this to Johnny and tell him to meet me there.' Then I snatched it back, tore the paper in half and put the coordinates on my half as well.

Newf looked at me, dumbfounded. 'Then what?'

'I'll fly to Muswabik and grill the minister. One way or another, he'll cough up.'

'Yeah, then?'

'Well, you and the seventh cavalry will come to the rescue. I'll have all the information I need to fix the Institute's wagon.'

'What abart the real pilot?'

'Paul and Dave can keep him occupied till I give the word to release him.'

It was a crude plan, but in the time allotted, I rather thought it was brilliant. Josh and I were roughly the same size, so we swapped clothes and he showed me where the plane was and where to find Quiberon.

The man in question turned out to be a stuck-up twit with a little briefcase, little moustache and silly, small-brimmed homburg or trilby hat. He spoke with a thick Quebecois accent and stood bolt upright. We found him in the lounge and Josh pointed him out to me.

'I'm your pilot,' I said. 'The other guy's off sick.'

He stood up and glared at me. 'I have been waiting. You are late.'

'Yeah, sorry. Shall we go?'

The plane was a twin engine, low-wing Piper Chieftain fitted with skis on its wheels. According to the plate on the dash, she was a 1981 version. This in itself was no problem, but I'd never flown with skis. I figured it would be about the same as a floatplane. After we were settled in, I extracted my piece of paper and dialled the coordinates into the GPS. I felt both nervous and stupid. I fumbled with the controls and instruments for a moment and eventually figured out how to start the engines. My *Cloudier* had been a single engine, but the difference was little, just that this plane had two of everything.

When the tower gave me permission I just opened the throttles and took off in a straight line. Once we were airborne my nervousness seemed to fade. Flying was something I was born to do. Quiberon didn't seem to be very talkative; he merely sat there as if asleep. Little did he know that I was not flying to the Institute. The distance slowly clicked down as we flew over the boring countryside. Unfortunately, one pile of snow looks like any other pile of snow. At length, the GPS said we had arrived.

Oh, Man! I looked out of the window and all I could see was snow, snow and even more snow. I couldn't tell lake from land. I did a slow and low pass, hoping to at least distinguish lake from land. At low altitude things looked a little friendlier. The lake seemed to be piled with snowdrifts, but careful examination showed that the land was slightly higher and rougher. Trying to fix my sights on a nice clear space, I circled and levelled out for a landing.

'What are you doing?' Quiberon snapped.

'Landing, of course.'

'But dis is not Lak' Opinnagau. Are you lost?'

'Just hold your horses and let me put this thing down.'

I needed all my concentration, having never landed on skis before. We levelled out, flaps down, and then I dropped the tail a little and throttled back on both engines. I wanted to hit the snow as slowly as possible.

Gradually, she became unstable and the airspeed slowed. Then gently as a feather, the skis made contact with the snow and instantly there was a blizzard as the props and the skis stirred up the light snow.

At first I thought I'd made the perfect landing, then we hit some obstruction or other and the skis sheared off. The plane plunged nose down into the snow, sending cascades of the stuff over the plane like a wave in the ocean. The propellers made contact with solid ice and stalled the engines. After what seemed like an eternity, the noise and vibration stopped. The quiet was deafening.

'Well,' said Quiberon, 'you 'ave done it now. What kind of pilot lands in de wrong place and mak's a 'ash of it?'

'Shut up.'

'I beg your pardon. 'oo do you t'ink you are?'

'You're my prisoner.'

He laughed. 'I am *your* prisoner. What are you, some foolish and untrained terrorist?'

'No, now shut it and listen to me.'

'You are making a grave mistake, sir. Just 'oo are you?'

'Bill Reyner. You're the one who put the kibosh on my mining operation around Lake Opinnagau.'

He shook his head. 'Well I 'ope you are satisfied, for now we will both die in the frozen nord.'

'No. So you admit you stopped my mining operation?'

'A admit not'ing. 'oo do you t'ink you are, abducting a minister of your government?'

'Listen, you Froggy twerp. I want to know all about the Institute. You are going to tell me everything. Failing that, I'll kill you. I might just kill you anyway.'

He sighed as if I was boring him. 'I t'ink you 'ave the wrong end of de stick, my friend.'

'Wrong end of the stick? I know all about you and your visits to the Institute. You are in league with them. I want to know how they make their money, then I'm going to expose them and you.'

He blinked a few times and pulled a face.

'I 'ate to burst your *bulle*, but I t'ink we are bot' lookin' for de same ting.'

'Looking for the same thing? You are in league with them right up to your *derrière*.'

He shook his head again. 'You are mistaken. I 'ave been trying for over a year to find out 'ow dey operate.'

'What about the dead girls and the two doctors? If you really were on the side of the law, you'd raid the place and get the RCMP to lock the entire gang up.'

'Well, monsieur, I would love to lock de entire gang up, but I 'ave no evidence. I t'ort you were one of dem.'

Oh! crap. I scratched my forehead and needed to think, then I heard the seventh cavalry.

Chapter 21

Destruction in the Snow

I couldn't believe that Quiberon was telling the truth. As the sound of Johnny's helicopter approached, I continued to question my suspect.

'What about Joshua Tyler's sister?'

He looked at me with obvious curiosity showing on his face.

'One would presume 'er to be Mademoiselle Tyler, yes?'

'I don't know; maybe she's married. That's not the point. She's being held against her will. If you are on the good guy's side, why don't you allow her to go home?'

'I 'ave never 'eard of 'er, until this very moment. And if you 'aven't noticed, I seem to be engaged in a struggle for survival in a snowbound wilderness.'

Suddenly a great flurry of snow blew up outside, completely obscuring our view as the helicopter descended very close to us. The engines shut down and the snow began to settle. Someone banged on the side of our plane. I popped open the door.

'Ah, we fort yous was all dead in there,' Newf said, grinning from ear to ear.

'Our pilot seems to have made many mistakes,' said the minister.

'Yeah,' Newf answered. 'You're lucky, 'e usually flips 'em upside down, especially when I'm wiv 'im.'

We all made our way over to Johnny's helicopter. Neither Quiberon nor I had any arctic clothing. Stepping outside was like plunging into a freezer chest. Once inside Johnny's machine and with the door closed, I began to warm up again. Dave threw a blanket over my shoulders and Paul did the same for Quiberon.

'Well this is a fine mess,' I said. 'He says he's on our side and not the enemy.'

'What say we chuck 'im artside for ten minutes an' see if 'e changes 'is tune?'

'Please, gentlemen, I beg you to believe me – I am on your side. My only purpose 'ere is to discover the trut' about the Institute. Dar 'as been questions asked. De RCMP 'ave found not'ing. Let me 'elp you or conversely, why don't you 'elp me? If we can discover the trut' about dis place, we can all rest 'appier.'

I had to think about it. The implications were most serious and it's very hard to think clearly when your brain is frozen.

'Alright, alright,' I said. 'Whatever happens, we're in the shit. I've wrecked a perfectly good plane, kidnapped a Member of Parliament, abducted a pilot and probably broke at least nine of the Ten Commandments. By the way, what happened to the pilot?'

'Josh has him in his apartment,' Paul said.

'In Ottawa?'

'Yeah.'

'Okay, so I can pay for the plane and maybe I can bribe the pilot to keep quiet, but what are we going to do about him?' I said, pointing to Quiberon.

The minister smiled. 'You 'ave only two alternatives. You can give yourself up to de RCMP and spend a long time in de jail or you can believe I am on your side and we can solve dis mystery between us.'

'Why, what's in it for you?'

'I will show my people dat I am a good minister and dat I care for de people.'

'Like you're an altruist, what about the five hundred grand we taxpayers give you annually?'

'I don't get dat kind of money. What you t'ink? Maybe we work togeder, *oui*?'

For the first time, Johnny put in his two pennyworth.

'What's the difference? If we go along with the Frog and he's genuine, we all win. If he's a traitor we go to jail. I can't see the difference; either way, this has to end somehow. I can at least plead innocence, you lot led me into it.'

'Okay,' I said, looking at Quiberon, 'what do you suggest?'

'You are the detective. Let us finish dis inspection. You come as my assistant. Togeder we will infiltrate de enemy's 'ouse and discover dere real purpose.'

'I'd love to, but they already know me. And besides, they will be expecting you to arrive in a plane, not a helicopter.'

'You 'ave rescued me after a most misfortunate accident, no?'

'I could go as his assistant,' Dave said, grinning like the proverbial Cheshire cat. 'It'd be a lark. I think I could probably get the information you want, anyhow.'

'How?' I growled.

'Dongle,' he said and grinned.

'Up yours, too,' I replied.

'Nah, a dongle is a plug-in. Look at it this way, I have one that allows me to communicate with my large computer from up to about half a kilometre away. All I need to do is plug it in the USB port of a computer and I'll be able to take control of the machine from a distance.'

Not being a technical person, I have no idea what he was talking about.

'So how would you do this magic trick?'

'If Mr Quiberon can get me into the room where they have their main computer or one that's on a network, I can stick it in the rear USB port and no one will be any the wiser.'

I looked at the minister.

'If you are genuinely an honest man, which I find hard to believe of any parliamentarian, I might just trust you to get my man into that place, what do you say?'

For a man in his precarious position, he seemed very calm and with a smile he said, 'My friend, what 'ave you got to lose? You are already very deep in de doo-doo. You have only two alternatives. You can kill the pilot you 'ave abducted and kill me also, or you can come clean and tak' your punishment as it now stands.'

'What exactly do you mean?'

'It is obvious even to a *bouffon*. You 'ave committed serious crimes. 'ow will you emerge widout incurring the anger of de law?'

'So what do you propose?'

'I 'ave been trying to crack, as you say, dis ring of criminals for over a year. I 'ave 'ad no success. Dey always know when I am coming, in advance of my arrival. Dey are always prepared and not'ing unlawful is ever exposed. I suggest dat you and me togeder could melt this ice of conspiracy into a 'ot soup of disclosure.'

'Well, apart from your stinking English, you might have a good plan. So if I agree, what happens to my boys?'

'You 'elp me solve dis problem. We bot' can come out looking lily-white. *Avec carte blanche.*'

'Right,' I said, trying to show authority and determination. 'Looks to me as if there's no choice. Dave, do you have one of these dingle things with you?'

'Dongle. Yes, I never travel without my gear. We have a portable computer at the camp and I have a laptop with me.'

'I don't care how many computers you have, do you have the ability to get into an Institute computer without us going back home?'

'Yes, of course.'

'Okay, so this is how it's gonna be. Dave and the minister will enter the Institute. You are his assistant. The rest of us will wait for you in the hut. Mr Quiberon, you will mention nothing about the plane crash. Just say you arrived in a hire helicopter. Get my man into a room where he can infiltrate their computers and we'll have what we need.'

'Excellent, monsieur.'

'So didn't you find the butcher's shop a little suspicious on your inspection visits?'

The minister shook his head and after a moment said, 'I do not know of which you refer.'

'The theatre. It looks like an operating theatre but inside it's a butcher's shop.'

He laughed. 'Oh, I see. Where would you carve an animal? Perhaps you would do it in the kitchen?'

'What do you mean?'

'Dee old operation t'eatre is used as a meat processing plant. It is for when dey catch a moose or sometimes 'ole animals are brought dere.'

'What about operations, medical operations?'

'Udder dan obstetric operations, dey don't do any.'

'Okay, Johnny, let's get the hell out of here. Head for our camp.'

In moments, the whine of the turbines heralded our take-off. My mind was in a spin – what with the kidnapping of the minister and wrecking of an aeroplane. I looked at the minister as the thought fled through my head: is the man really honest? Does he have anything to do with the Institute? How the hell am I going to get out of this one? All the way to the camp my head throbbed with the thrashing of the blades, the roar of the engines and the fear of the future. Eventually, we landed on the frozen lake only a couple of hundred metres from the shack.

'I guess you want to go to the Institute?' I said as the engines whined down to a quiet whistle.

'Dey will be expecting me.'

'Do you call ahead?'

'No, dey 'ave a spy in de Parliament or de airfield.'

'Oh, really? You're not dressed for the weather, how you gonna get to the Institute without freezing to death?'

'De pilot call dem on the de radio.'

'Oh, yeah. What frequency?'

'He call on 101.5.'

'Johnny, can you tune into 101.5?'

He smiled and replied, 'Anything you like, why?'

'Call the Institute on 101.5 and tell them the minister is here. Dave, you ready?'

He nodded and while we waited for any action Newf, Paul and myself walked back to the hut. I didn't like this operation at all. It felt that everything was out of my control. Only minutes after we reached the hut a snowcat came ploughing down the road. It drove directly to the helicopter and didn't stop at our camp. Just to show my love for them, I gave them the one-finger salute as they passed our window.

'This is all going to end with a bang,' I said, turning to my friends. 'I can feel it in my bones. We should have sold the gold claim and left this Institute to whatever they do.'

'Yah knows yah can't do that, Bill. It ain't in your blood to let no bad guys get away wiv murder.'

I looked at Newf and stroked my chin in thought.

'I think we should go in there fists blazing. I reckon that Ms Morningblood would crack if I was to put some physical pressure on her.'

'Ain't that what I's bin sayin' all along, Bill?'

'Well before we let this minister go, we'll see just what Dave can rustle up on his dingle thing. In the meantime, have we got any beer? I'm freezing my ass off.'

Paul grinned. 'I've got the heat on – we'll probably need some fuel soon. Should I go check?'

'Sure; don't get lost in the snow.'

'What abart the 'elicopter?'

I glared at Newf. 'You ask the dumbest questions. 'What about the helicopter? Man, what do *you* think? Maybe we should fold it and press it.'

'Bill, sometimes I fink yous got nofin' in yours 'ead. Johnny can't stay long cuz 'is engine will freeze up and 'e won't get it to start again.'

I rubbed my eyes in order to think. This situation was gradually but surely getting worse.

'Is there any beer in the hut?'

'Nah.'

'Well he'll have to leave his engines running until the minister gets back.'

'What yah gonna do about the plane you crashed?'

'Pay for it, I guess.'

'What abart the pilot?'

'Shut up, Newf, you're getting on my tit.'

The door opened and in walked Johnny.

'Bloody cold, ain't it.'

'How long can we stay?' I asked as he closed the door.

'I left the generator running. It'll keep the engines warm for about four hours, then we're out of fuel. I have to leave. We don't have enough fuel to reach Ottawa, anyhow.'

'We don't?'

'No, we'll have to pop in at Moose Factory and take on some fuel or we'll finish up like that Piper Chieftain of yours out on Lake Muswabik.'

Newf glared at Johnny. 'If we's out of juice in four hours, 'ow you gonna fly to Mus-wab-whatever?'

Johnny chuckled. 'The generator has its own supply of fuel, but as I said, it'll only last about four hours. We're not going to Lake Muswabik – are we?'

I shook my head. 'No, as soon as we get a download from Dave's dingle thingy, we're off.'

'Maybe I should go fuel-up now and come back.'

'How long will that take?'

'I could be back in say, four or five hours.'

'Okay, call the Institute and tell Quiberon you're leaving.'

As Johnny left, Paul returned.

'We've got enough oil for about fifteen hours' heat, then we freeze. I put the last barrel on. We should get these drill samples to an assayer, like asap.'

'They won't go off, will they?'

'No, but the quicker we get results, the sooner we'll outwit anyone else trying to muscle in.'

'Okay, quick, run after Johnny. Go with him and get heating oil.'

After Paul had left, Newf looked at me and said, 'Well nah we's on our lonesome, what yah suggest?'

'Nothing, you twit. We'll wait for Paul to return.'

'So what we gonna do in the meantime?'

'I'm going to get some sleep as soon as you shut your gob.'

I pulled on one of the spare parkas and curled up on the cot. That cold weather seems to make me sleepy, or at least tired.

I woke up with a start as Johnny flew over the shack at low altitude; man, that machine is noisy. Using the little hand transmitter, he called us.

'I thought I'd wake you boys up,' he said. 'Got your oil and the minister is on his way back.'

'Roger that, Johnny. We'll hang tight in the hut till the minister is loaded and the Institute people have left.'

Only moments later we heard the snowcat trundling up the roadway. My plan was to act as if the helicopter was nothing to do with me. I wanted the Institute people to think it was Quiberon's hire and not mine.

After a while I heard the snowcat returning to the Institute – it passed very close to our hut. We waited five minutes then buttoning up our coats, we left for the helicopter. The engine was running and Johnny was ready to take off by the time I got there.

'Okay, Johnny, did you get me the heating oil?'

'Sure, it's in the main bay. You want I should lift-off and land close to the hut?'

'Great idea.' I climbed aboard.

A few moments later we lifted off the frozen lake and Johnny set a nice slow course for the shack. We were about 50 metres from landing again, when there was the biggest explosion I ever want to witness. The old hut vanished in a mass of flames and debris. The shockwave almost knocked us out of the sky. Johnny had difficulty bringing us in to a safe landing.

As soon as we were down, Johnny shut the engines off. He looked quite pale.

'I'll have to do a check to make sure we haven't got any damage,' he said.

'Bloody 'ell, Bill. Them buggers is playin' my game.'

'You're right, Newf. I think it's time to take the gloves off.'

'What about my dongle?' Dave asked.

'Okay, I'll see what's left of the shack and get the info from your dongle, then I think I'm going to kill someone.'

'Don't tak' chances, monsieur. We don't want any

274

dead 'eroes,' the minister said, looking quite ashen himself.

Newf of course lit up like a lighthouse. He loves nothing better than a good, honest fight and this was obviously a challenge we couldn't refuse. Quickly, we ran over to the still-burning hut. I looked round the back. The shed and generator were more or less intact and one snowmobile had survived, but the living quarters were totalled.

'Pity we ain't got no gun,' Newf said, staring at the burning wreckage.

'Why, what would you do with it?'

'Go freaten that Ms Morningblood and maybe see if she ain't got no afternoon blood.'

We hopped on the snowmobile and drove over to the helicopter. Johnny was up a ladder and had his head stuck out of the roof near the back rotor. After a while he came down and didn't look so happy.

'We got some damage to the swish-plate gear on the rear rotors.'

'Meaning?' I quizzed.

'I'm afraid to fly. If we should lose control of the rear lift, we'll flip over and finish up like your hut.'

'Are you trying to tell me that we are marooned here?'

He nodded in the affirmative. This of course put a whole new light on our situation. We stay and freeze to death or leave and possibly die in a crash.

'Well, what do you suggest?'

Quiberon stepped in. 'Maybe dey would believe the trut'. I could call the Institute an' say you people 'ave 'ad a accident an' you 'ave damage my 'elicopter.'

'Then what?' I asked.

'I could use dere phone an' call for 'elp.'

'Alright, alright, you lot,' I said, scratching my head in an attempt to think clearly. 'We have to organise. Mr

Quiberon, you and Dave will go back into the Institute where it's nice and warm. Dave, you take your laptop with you and sit somewhere nice and quiet playing with your electronic toy. In reality, you'll be downloading the Institute files. Mr Quiberon, you keep them talking. Talk about anything. Paul, you stay here with Johnny and the helicopter. Newf, you and I will take the snowmobile and the ladder.'

'What for?'

'Because we're going to break in.'

''at's dumb. Why don't we go in froo the front door wiv everyone else?'

'Because I said so. Now, has everyone got their parts clear?'

'What do we do when help arrives?' Johnny asked.

The question left me blank for a moment.

'Well you need a part for your machine, don't you?'

'Yeah.'

'Well, somehow you'll have to get it.'

'What about you and Mr East?'

I shook my head. 'Well if we were successful, we'll be going with the RCMP, and if we fail ...'

'We'll be going wiv the RCMP,' Newf added.

Newf and I headed out to hide in what was left of our camp. The idea being that we would wait until the snowcat had collected the others then we'd follow at a respectable distance. I had had enough of these people – they must be taught a lesson and Newf and I were excellent educators.

After only a short time, the snowcat came by and collected the minister and Dave. Somehow, I knew this adventure was going to turn sour. I could feel the hairs on the back of my neck begin to hackle.

Chapter 22

Surrender

The clouds of doom slowly seemed to settle over the countryside as Newf and I loaded the remaining snowmobile with the folding ladder.

'You's a bit on the quiet side, ain't yah, Bill?'

'I'm beginning to wonder. What if these geezers *are* honest and above board?'

'Oh, I can see that, Bill. Maybe the polar bears 'as learned 'ow to use dynamite.'

'You're right, let's go give these people hell.'

'Yous realise, Bill, them buggers will spot us on their radar.'

'So?'

'Well they will be expecting us.'

'So?'

'Well if *you* don't care, I guess that's good enough for me.'

We climbed on the snowmobile. To say the least it was not very comfortable – the ladder, although folded, stuck out either side like aluminium wings. As soon as we reached the crest of the rise we could assume the enemy would have us on their radar. I figured it didn't matter as when we got close, they would lose the image and wouldn't know exactly where we were. My plan was to drive around the wall a little and see if I could find the place where we entered before. The wind and the light, fluffy snow very quickly hid our tracks, making it difficult to follow the cat, never mind find our spot on the wall.

'This should work, Bill. It's like a triple attack.'

'Triple attack, what are you on about?'

'The French git, Dave, wiv 'is computer invasion, an' us shinnin' over the wall. If one of us don't 'it the jackpot, no one will.'

'Shut up and help me extend this ladder.'

With arctic gloves on and a heavy parka it makes even simple tasks difficult. Eventually, we got the ladder extended and leaned it against the wall. I went up first. At the top there was plenty of space to wait for my idiot companion to climb up. Together, we hauled the ladder up and over the wall then climbed down into the courtyard.

Thinking back on the event, it was one of the daftest ideas I ever had. We found a handy back door and it was not locked. As surreptitiously as possible, we slipped into the corridor beyond. I'd just got my heavy coat off, when two doors opened and at least three heavy and white-coated males leapt onto us. In seconds we were both restrained and sitting on the floor like a couple of naughty schoolboys. I had my hands tied behind my back. I could only assume Newf had been likewise treated.

Miss Ugly-as-Sin Morningblood waltzed from another door even farther up the corridor. She walked rather like a regimental sergeant major and had a particularly ugly smirk on her face as she glared at me.

'So, you didn't get enough the first time, Mr Reyner.'

'Enough what?' I growled.

'This time, Mr Reyner, I think we have you exactly where we want you.'

'I don't think so,' I said with a smirk as though I knew something she didn't know.

Her expression never changed and the two bullies holding us seemed immune to intimidation. Ms Morningblood glared at me all-knowingly as if she had God on her side, or maybe she was His right-hand man.

I use the term "man" because looking at her, the word "woman" just doesn't spring to mind.

The third tough guy had slapped something on my wrist and after a little while it was painful. I couldn't move my hands at all as they were pinioned firmly behind my back. I saw what it was as he did the same thing to Newf. He'd used a plastic cable tie as a handcuff.

We were marched unwillingly down the corridor and into another room. It looked like an office, having a desk and a couple of chairs.

'Kneel,' growled the thug holding my collar.

For a moment I thought this was it – execution Mafia style. Having no alternative, I found myself on the floor kneeling. The handyman with the cable ties slipped one round my ankles and pulled it tight. Newf was treated likewise.

'I shall return and deal with you when the minister has left,' said Ms Morningblood and then with a flourish, she left the room.

Uglies one, two and three followed. I never was one for much kneeling and the position began to pain my knees. With difficulty I managed to move, then fell over sideways. Still not a comfortable position, I sort of laid on my stomach with my hands pinioned behind and my legs out straight.

'Yah does it like this, Bill,' Newf said.

The man must be a contortionist, for somehow he leaned back and forced his toes between his wrists. In one quick movement, he stood up with his hands now in front of him.

'Holy shit, Newf, you must be made of rubber. I can't even reach my feet.'

'Nah, the trick is to get art o' these Jewish handcuffs.'

'And how do you intend to do that? They don't have

a lock to pick.'

Even under these circumstances he giggled at my poor joke.

'Them's is only plastic, Bill. 'as you got yours Swiss army knife wiv yah?'

'Yeah, I always carry one, but at the moment I don't seem to be able to move, you blithering idiot. How the hell do you expect me to cut my way out, when I can't move a muscle?'

In a sort of hop-scuffle motion he approached me and then crouching down, fell back onto his backside.

'Now I is at yours level, Bill. Which pocket 'as yous got the knife in?'

His hands, like mine, were tied back to back, which virtually rendered them unusable and very uncomfortable. He struggled for a moment, forcing his hands into my trouser pocket, and magically extracted the knife. But only able to hold it in one hand, there was no way he could open it.

'I told yah, Bill, yous should carry a flick knife. If I gives it to yah, don't drop it.'

Now that his hands were in front of him he could see what was happening, though I was effectively blind. I felt the knife and closed one hand over it.

'Great, Bill, now 'ang on tight an' I'll open the blade.'

After a while I felt him forcing against my strength. Somehow, he managed it.

'That's got it, Bill. Nah, 'ang on nice an' strong, like. I's gonna try to rub the plastic along that blade. If yous move, I'll slit me wrist an' you'll have to get yourself out this mess.'

I could feel the pressure as I hung on tightly. Suddenly, there was a click and Newf gasped.

'Got yah. I's free, Bill. Nah, give us the blade an' I'll finish the job.'

Quickly, he slit the plastic restraint on my wrist. Man! what a relief. I rolled over and by this time he had cut his feet free. He handed me the knife I released myself.

'So, nah I reckon we'll be bashing a few 'eads in.'

'In that respect, my friend, you are 100 per cent correct. Let's pretend we're still tied up and when uglies one through three put in an appearance, we'll test their skulls for density.'

'What abart Ms Nasty knickers?'

'For her, I have a special present. I'm longing to see just what colour and how much blood she has in that scrawny, witch-like body of hers. Shush! someone's coming.'

One of the big bruisers poked his head into the room. 'You lot still here?' He closed it and we heard him walking away.

'You know, Newf, that door isn't locked.'

'There ain't nowhere to go. Let's just relax an' fink abart the fun we's gonna 'ave.'

Again we heard footsteps close to the door. It opened and two of the heavies walked in and closed the door behind them. My heart began to race as one came close to me.

'You guys are for the chop,' he growled then leaned a little too close.

I punched him in the groin as hard as I could muster and while he did a little dance of agony, I leapt up and rearranged his face with a left hook. The other had turned and extracted a small revolver from his inner pocket. Before he could bring the weapon to bear, Newf smacked him one on the back of the neck. The blow seemed to have little effect, other than that he started to turn and ran into my right fist. He went down and the gun skidded across the floor.

'Two down and a whole bunch more to go,' I said,

feeling proud of the way we had quickly stopped our foe.

'I's got the shooter,' Newf reported. 'Nah what?'

'Good, we can use it to threaten Ms Morningblood.'

'Oh wow! Bill. This 'ere is a Para-Ordnance Warthog,' Newf said, smiling from ear to ear. He snapped the magazine and slipped it into his palm. 'Wow! She's fully loaded, Bill, ten rounds of .45. We can really do some damage wiv this little baby.'

I shook my head. 'So suddenly you're an arms expert.'

'I's always bin. Nah, I was in Smiffy's gun shop only a week ago lookin' for somefin' nice an' easy to carry. Para-Ordnance is Canadian.'

'Well whoop-de-do and you don't have a firearms licence.'

'I've applied.'

'Well reload that thing and keep an eye on these sleeping beauties.'

At that moment one of the uglies began to move. Newf gave him a kick and then cocked the automatic. For a moment or two it was a silent stand-off, then Ugly spoke.

'You morons won't get away with this. There's nowhere for you to go.'

'Really?' I replied. 'I'll tell you what, while you're still breathing, call Ms Morningblood.'

'No.'

'Well if you're feeling like that – Newf, shoot the bastard, we don't need him.'

Ugly climbed to his feet and put his hands out as if he could fend off a bullet.

'No, I'll tell you what. You guys surrender and you'll come to no harm.'

I thought for a minute he was going to grab Newf and I started in that direction when suddenly, bang. Oh boy, Newf fired and Ugly tumbled to the floor.

'Well you's did say shoot 'im.'

'Crap! Is he dead?'

'Not unless 'e he bleeds to deaf in a few moments; I only shot 'is arm.'

Ugly lay on the floor groaning and holding his wound.

'Newf, tie the other twit up while I look out for this thug. I would imagine everyone in the province heard that bang.' Somehow, I managed to drag Ugly to a chair near the desk. 'Now, my stupid friend, there's the phone, call Ms Morningblood or the next bullet will be the last one needed.'

He picked up the phone.

'Any tricks and you're horsemeat.'

With the same hand he held the receiver, he pushed a couple of buttons.

'This is Ellerton,' he said. 'Page Ms Morningblood. Tell her she's needed urgently in 107.' He put the receiver down. 'Is that okay?'

'Sure.'

'Well what about a doctor for my arm?'

'You're not bleeding too badly, you'll last. So how do they make a profit at this place?'

He shook his head. 'They look after wayward girls.'

'So where's the profit in that?'

'Government grants, Ontario Health and some public donations.'

Newf had finished tying up the unconscious heavy and was sitting on a chair next to the door when it opened. Ms Morningblood took two steps into the room and stopped. With her face aghast, she glanced around the room and then noticed Newf and his gun.

'Are you totally insane, Mr Reyner?' she said.

Newf slammed the door with his foot.

'I's surprised yah didn't 'ear the bang when I shot

your feller there,' he said, grinning.

She walked over to the bleeding muscleman and began examining his injury.

After a moment she looked at me and said, 'You will pay for this effrontery, Mr Reyner.'

'You've murdered at least two women and dumped one corpse in my lap, blown up my shack and generally pissed me off, and you think I'll do the paying.'

'You are insane.'

'So why dump a dead doc in my hut?'

'You were responsible. Miss Billings, poor girl, was having delusions and when our people left the premises to inspect your thing you had planted close by, she escaped. Seeing your post-like device, she extracted it to use as a weapon. When the good doctor and Trevor tried to arrest her frantic ravings, the thing she was holding exploded. The poor girl died, and both Trevor and the doctor were hurt. They managed to return to the building. The doctor died several days later.'

'So you just left the woman out in the snow?'

'She was your responsibility. You killed her, not me.'

'And the doctor?'

'He died. I thought you should see the result of your work. Now if you don't mind, the RCMP are on their way and the minister is still here.'

'Tough. I'm going to kill you slowly,' I said and grinned, trying to make her think I was psychotic. 'I want to know everything. Like what happened to Dr John Bromley and Jenny Stilton. They bit the dust even before I knew about you and this house of horrors.'

She glared at me for a few moments, trying to put her thoughts in order.

'Mr Reyner, you are insane. You insult my intelligence. We run a perfectly legal and proper establishment here. Ask the minister.'

'Should I shoot 'er, Bill? Like, I could blow a few of 'er fingers off – maybe she'd feel more like talkin'.'

'Believe me, that loony will do it,' said the ugly with the bullet hole in his arm.

She was solid and stalwart, but I think I got a glimpse of fear in her eyes – our play-acting was beginning to wear her assurance down.

'So why did you blow up my camp?'

She glared at me as though I had insulted her or something.

'Mr Reyner, I, that is we, know nothing about your petty explosions. If your camp has blown up, then I suggest you buy better heating equipment.'

'It weren't 'eatin' equipment,' Newf said. 'I could smell the cordite.'

'Shut up, everyone,' I said, raising my voice. 'Ms Morningblood, get on that phone and get someone to bring Delilah Tyler here, like now.'

'Delilah Tyler? Why should I do that?'

'Because I said so. Now, if you are ready for us to start reducing your living membership, I suggest you continue to play ignorant. But if you are feeling like staying alive, I suggest you do as I say and quickly. My patience is wearing thin. Oh yes, and any silly heroics and Newf here will be happy to create three corpses in this very room, if you get my drift.'

She stroked her chin thoughtfully and her eyes flashed with indignation. After a few moments of just standing there, she walked to the phone and picked it up.

'This is Dian Morningblood. I need patient Delilah Tyler here immediately in 107. Yes, immediately.' She listened for a few moments and then said, 'Exactly and as quickly as possible.'

There are times when you just know things are doomed not to work out and this was one of them. A banging came to our door, which startled me. Even before I could regain my composure, Ms Morningblood shouted, 'Enter.'

Oh crap, two of her heavies burst in and a fight started. I wasn't sure who was hitting who or why. As quickly as possible, I grabbed Ms Morningblood in the desperate hope I could use her as a lever against the invaders. Bang! Bang! And even a third bang. Apparently the scuffle was over, but the noise must have ricocheted throughout the entire Institute building. Ms Nasty went limp in my arms and one of the heavies fell to the floor – the other ran for his life. Newf slammed the door shut.

'Sorry, Bill, but I fink I's done the broad an injury.'

I looked at the woman.

'You alright?'

She struggled and I let go of her. In an instant she slithered to the floor. Blood fairly spurted from her upper thigh.

'You imbecilic morons,' she groaned, clutching the inside of her thigh. 'You've punctured the femoral artery. If you don't get help, I'll bleed to death.'

'What about Bonehead on the floor?' I said, pointing to the heavy who was taking a nap right in the centre of the floor.

Newf walked over to examine him just as the phone went. I snatched up the receiver.

'Yeah, what?'

'This is Inspector Morgan of the RCMP. Why don't you be a good fellow and put down the weapon and surrender.'

Holy crap! I slapped the receiver down and looked at Newf. 'The bloody Mounties are here already.'

'So what yah figure, Bill?'

'Is Pretty Boy dead?'

'Nah, 'e's just fakin'.'

I breathed deeply, trying to clear my head. This was not going according to plan.

'Okay, then,' I said. 'Maybe we'd better fess up before someone does get killed.'

'Yah mean like us?'

'Yeah, like us.'

'Well I ain't surrendering no gun to that broad. She'll blow us away an' tell the cops it were suicide.'

I picked up the phone. 'You still there?'

'Yes, Mr Reyner, I'm still here.'

'Okay. We'll surrender only to the RCMP, none of this hospital or Institute lot, is that clear?'

'Yes, Mr Reyner. I'll be there personally. Please open the door and toss the weapon out into the corridor. Then place your hands on your heads and kindly walk away from the door.'

'Well,' Newf said, handing me the weapon, 'I reckon we's buggered this one up real proper, like.'

'Not all our irons are running cold,' I said and tossed the weapon out into the corridor.

As soon as I stepped back the burly RCMP officer came in smiling. A couple of white coats rushed in and took charge of Ms Morningblood and her injured workers.

Chapter 23

Disaster Upon Disaster

After we were fully restrained and frogmarched to the lower reception area, it dawned on me that the RCMP officer was alone.

'Where's your men and transport?' I asked.

He glared at me. 'RCMP retired,' he replied.

My heart sank – oh boy, we had surrendered to the enemy.

'You mean you work here?'

'Of course.'

'I demand to see Minister Quiberon.'

'Do you? Well, I doubt he wants to see you idiots.'

'I guess we keep shtum about the bomb then, Bill?' Newf said just loud enough to be overheard.

Inspector Morgan grabbed Newf by the shoulder.

'What bomb?'

Newf grinned. 'That's for me to know and you to sit in fear of.'

'I could beat it out of you.'

'Not before it explodes. We planted it to give us a getaway. Looks like we'll 'ave to use it, don' it.'

'Tell me where it is and I'll take you to the minister.'

'Der! Like I was born yesterday. You RCMP wallahs must think everyone else only climbed art o' the trees yesterday.'

Morgan did not look very pleased – you could almost see the cogs turning in his head.

'Why the minister?' he demanded.

I chipped in, 'Because he's the only one around here we can trust.'

'Trust doesn't come into it,' Morgan said almost angrily. 'I shall report you for break and enter, sabotage, abduction, bodily injury, grievous bodily harm and threats and menaces.'

'Okay, why not throw in terrorism and conspiracy to commit honest acts.' For a moment I thought he was going to hit me, but he didn't. 'Shouldn't be long now and the fire alarm will be going off. I suppose you do have fire alarms here?'

Reluctantly, he ordered one of his minions to go and inform the minister. For me that was a relief – at least we would only land up in jail, not under the Institute's frozen courtyard.

'So where's this bomb?' he demanded.

'Not till the minister gets here. We'll probably have time to defuse it, if you speed things up a bit.'

An uneasy silence ensued and lasted for some five minutes, when at last we heard multiple footsteps in the corridor. The door opened and the minister entered with three of four of the Institute staff. The room was becoming quite crowded.

'So where's this bomb?' Morgan demanded.

'Minister,' I said. 'I'm Bill Reyner.' I thought it best to pretend I was not acquainted. 'These men have illegally arrested me and tied me up. I demand you intercede on our behalf.'

'If you are de law breaker an' I 'ear dat you are, den you'll 'ave to wait till the Royal Mounted arrive. What is dis I 'ear about a bomb?'

'There isn't one,' I admitted. 'I just didn't want Egore here to do his master's bidding and plant us under the roses. I thought you would give us safe passage to Ottawa and a nice cosy and warm jail cell.'

Quiberon looked at his watch. 'I should t'ink the representatives of the law should be 'ere in about fifteen minutes. I 'ave reported my plane troubles.'

I sighed with relief – for sure they wouldn't interfere with a government minister, but Newf and I were still in deep trouble. Ms Morningblood would obviously get her revenge and have me thrown into the ugliest jail available. Nonetheless we were all taken to a large reception room, where we could sit in comfort and await our fate.

We didn't have to wait long – I assumed they must have come by plane, for it would be a lot quicker. Man, did I ever feel relieved to see real RCMP; though, I wasn't looking forward to what they would do with us.

The cops certainly knew how to handle themselves and the weather. About an hour after the first ones arrived, three huge military helicopters turned up. I had no idea what had happened to Johnny, as we never saw him. I can only assume he was fixing his helicopter. We also never got to see Delilah Tyler. One thing that made me smile was Dave and his laptop. As he passed me, walking with the minister, he winked and grinned. It seemed that at least one part of our plan may have worked.

Needless to say, Newf and I were treated like common criminals. A military helicopter took us to Moose Factory and from there we were transferred to a ski plane and flown to Ottawa. A nice reception committee greeted us with weapons drawn and we were quickly transferred to a warm but inescapable jail, whereupon we were thrust into separate cells.

I expected we would, as usual, have to meet the magistrate in police court first thing in the morning, but a very strange thing happened. The chief of police himself suddenly appeared outside my cell. The jailer pulled the lever and the door unlocked. The big man walked in all grins.

'Good morning, Mr Reyner. I trust you had a comfortable night?'

I stood up slowly. 'Sure. So what happens now?'

'Well, I have to apologise for the mix-up, but all's well that ends well. Is there anything I can do for you?'

My head began to spin. 'Is Alice about?' I asked.

He looked puzzled. 'Alice who?'

'Don't know her other name; you know, the one with the big rabbit and the Mad Hatter.'

He glared at me for a few moments then a broad smile slowly spread across his face.

'Oh, I see. Please I must apologise for the unnecessary actions of my men. You must be a little confused. You see, Monsieur Quiberon explained the mix-up and when we checked with the Director of the Cormorant Institute, she begs your forgiveness for her hasty and inaccurate decisions.'

'Hasty decisions? You don't mean Ms Morningblood, do you?'

'Yes, that's the lady. Now, if we can be of any assistance to you ...'

It felt that I was on some fast-turning roundabout – nothing made sense. Newf shot at least two people and no one wants to mention it. I had to find Josh Tyler. Oh! and there was the small matter of a missing aeroplane. While my head was trying to get around the fog of confusion, we somehow had walked to the reception area and there standing in his best fur coat was old Purvis of Purvis & Pringle Law Partners.

'What are you doing here?' I asked as soon as we were in range.

The old fellow grinned. 'Can't let our CEO spend time in the clink, can we now, eh?'

Somehow I was pleased to see his cheery face, but my mind remained clogged with all the problems and puzzles yet to be solved.

'We can't talk here. Let's proceed to my aeroplane; at least it will be warm in there. Have you seen David

Carter anywhere?'

'It was Mr Carter who phoned me yesterday. He thought you might need some legal assistance.'

'So where is he now?'

'He's in the hotel with that young and foolish lad Tyler.'

'Oh, great, and where's Newf, I mean Mr East?'

'He, too, has departed for the hotel. Perhaps we should follow.'

'And Paul?'

'He's already there.'

'You seem to have all the answers, Mr Purvis. Do I pay you enough?'

'No. But I'm working on that. I have a very large bill to settle for Mr Cedric Corner.'

'Who's he?'

'Your stranded helicopter pilot.'

'Oh! crikey. Johnny, where is he?'

'He's at Sault Ste Marie. His helicopter is grounded on some lake up north.'

After the bitter cold, freezing uncertainty and miserable cops, the hotel room seemed overcrowded and definitely a whole load friendlier and warmer. Old Purvis had in fact taken three rooms. The only stranger was the captured pilot. He sat on one of the beds and grinned, with a glass of champagne in one hand and huge, fat cigar in the other.

'Who the hell are you?' I asked.

'Your saviour.'

'Really, and why would that be?'

'Josh wanted to take the Big Knob on his flight up north, so I thought it might just be a whole load of fun.'

'A whole load of fun? You mean you are in on it?'

'Sure, Josh is my cousin.'

'So why didn't you do the flying – you could enter the Institute?'

'Josh has a degree in several of the oriental martial arts; he could knock the shit out of any six men at the same time. Me – I'm a wimp who flies aeroplanes.'

'So who are you?'

'Glen Blanchard.'

'Well, Mr Glen Blanchard, I hope you realise you are now one of the many unemployed people in Canada.'

'Nah.'

'What do you mean, no?'

'Well, it's like this. You hijacked my plane, so I figure, well … yah see what I mean.'

'No, I don't.'

'Well … it's like this, see. I need a job and you need a pilot.'

'I do? Since when?'

'Since you kidnapped me.'

I shook my head in disgust. 'I don't remember advertising for a pilot. Can you fly jets?'

'If it flies, I can pilot it.'

'Like, do you have a licence?'

'Sure.'

'Okay, I know when I'm licked. What about the one I crashed in Lake Muswabik?'

He grinned, showing his many gold teeth. 'I've been in more unhappy landings than I can remember. I'll tell the boss I had engine trouble, the plane's crap and I quit. Just give me the coordinates and I'll pop round and settle the account – that is if I'm working for you?'

'Mr Purvis,' I yelled above the room noise. 'Write this man up an employment contract, we'll settle the wages later.'

Purvis seemed all bubbly and happy. 'Is that working for you or for us?'

'For us? What do you mean, for us?'

'Well, I've drawn up a limited company, a mining

293

and exploration company. I chose the name Magnuscarter. I thought that was rather clever, don't you? It's all legal and registered. We have the right to minerals in the northern area, as you requested.'

'We? Who's we?'

'Yes, indeed. In your absence, I negotiated with Mrs Magnus and we created a board of directors for the Magnuscarter Mineral Exploration Company. We have Mrs Magnus, John Magnus, David Carter, Paul Manningham, North East, yourself, of course, and myself.'

For a moment I was staggered.

'What? Like … You've done what? So who the hell's Mrs Magnus?'

'Your grandmother, dear boy.' I was about to explode, when he added, 'I've had a first offer from Northern Mining Inc. They have placed a reserve on the property of fifty million dollars. Of course, it is negotiable, depending on the assay. If the deal goes through, that's a little over seven million dollars each. I should think I could retire comfortably on a sum of that magnitude.'

Not only had I failed to solve a simple murder mystery, but I had also lost control of a company that I invented. I sank back and sat on the bed. The rest of the boys were sharing out the champagne and the stench of cigar smoke was overwhelming.

The following day and still nursing a hangover each, we all assembled at the airport. No way was I going to let Glen fly my new baby. Once everyone was aboard and the doors closed, I allowed Glen to co-pilot; I gave him the job of radio operator. I figured at this rate I would soon need a larger house. Josh tagged along, too – he said he would be my new bodyguard.

I decided to put Glen up in the garage with the three stooges. Deloris acted like Punch and I was the local bobby. I'm sure she would have beaten me with a baton if she had one handy. I was given strict instructions not to leave the house in the future without getting her express approval. Gran had a permanent grin waxed on her face and Edward Magnus followed her about like an expectant puppy. Talk about make a person sick.

At breakfast, when we were all assembled at the big table, I opened the morning conversation.

'Newf, did you know that Mrs H in now Mrs M?'

'Sure I did. It looks good on yah, Mrs M.'

Gran nodded her approval. 'Thank you, North. I think we are all entitled to a little happiness. Edward and I will be moving semi-permanently to Cromlet.'

I didn't say a word – what was the point, anyway? The world seemed to tick by all by itself and didn't require my assistance. After breakfast I retired to the garage to watch the Brains Trust do something interesting. That turned out to be the second most boring thing in my life. After almost an hour I'd had enough and was about to leave, when the gang exploded into peals of laughter.

'So what's going on?'

Dave grinned like an ape with a banana stuck sideways in his mouth. 'You gotta see this, Bill.'

'What?'

'Look on this rendering – I've blown it up. See, there is the courtyard or what Ms Morningblood calls the quadrangle.'

'Yeah, so?'

'So? Look, there are nine coffins as clear as the Empire State Building.'

'Marvellous,' I smirked. 'So we have nine coffins. I should imagine nine people have died.'

'That's the whole point, twenty-eight people, or should I say twenty-eight women, died.'

'So what did they do with the surplus, prop 'em up

as ornaments?'

Dave pouted. 'In the records it says nine women were buried in the quadrangle. Then they installed the crematorium and a total of eighteen were cremated.'

'Oh! So?'

'So that adds up to twenty-seven. What happened to the other one?'

I shook my head in disgust. 'So you found a discrepancy in the accounts, how does that help?'

'It means they have a body missing. That's a very important thing – you can't just lose people. We should tell LePort and see what he makes of it.'

'What we need is information on illegal operations, body parts, baby selling and stuff like that. Do you mean to tell me you downloaded all those accounts and all you can find is a missing corpse?'

The following day we got some really nasty news. The Cormorant Institute had initiated an injunction to prevent mining in the Lake Opinnagau area, effectively making our gold claim worthless. Purvis said it was nothing to worry about. It would only be a slight delay of the inevitable. I merely wondered what the inevitable would be.

By popular vote, we decided to give the Cormorant Institute a miss – that is to say, withdraw our efforts and let nature take its course. I did call LePort and report the missing body. We also got an official letter from François Quiberon thanking us for our assistance. Worst of all, I received a bill from Johnny for $76,548 for parts and service to his helicopter. Funny thing, we never heard anything from Warren Air – it was their plane I left on Lake Muswabik.

We passed the information about the coffins to LePort and the minister then tried to forget about institutes and other expensive distractions. The weeks quietly and boringly passed. The assayer reported that our drill cores were the richest they had ever seen. The mining company almost doubled their offer for our claim and the court threw out the Institute's injunction. Altogether, things seemed to be working out very favourably. Glen turned out to be an asset and a damned-good pilot. He was ex-military and could fly anything from helicopters to four engine jets.

Even though Gran had decided to go and live at Cromlet, there was still the small matter of a Viking boat in Norfolk. The big do was arranged for mid March. We, that is I, decided we would all go and have a slap-up time in good old Blighty.

Chapter 24

No Loose Ends

We were making the preparations for the entire entourage to move to Britain, when Joshua Tyler came to me and said, 'I'm your bodyguard.'

'Since when?'

'Since I decided you need my help. If I'd been with you in the Institute, you would never have been captured. I've decided you permanently need my assistance.'

I remember when he threw me around like a rag doll, but I surely did not need a bodyguard.

'Sorry, young man, but the position is not vacant.'

'Course not; I've already taken the post.'

'So what about your sister?'

'You will help me get her out, won't you?'

I sighed. Really there was nothing I could do.

'Okay, I'll tell you what, you can come with us to the UK and for the time being, yes, okay, you can be my bodyguard. When we get back we'll see what can be done about Delilah.'

Griffin came into the study and with a huge smile said, 'Excuse me, sir, there's a gentleman to see you.'

'Who?'

'He said not to report his name, sir.'

'Tell him to get lost.'

'I do believe this gentleman occasionally wears a bright red uniform, sir.'

'Oh, no, okay, you may as well send him in. Josh, you stay here.'

After a few moments Griffin returned with Inspector LePort.

'The inspector, sir.'

'Thank you, Griffin.'

With a face like a lemon tester, the inspector sort of sidled in, eyeing the room suspiciously.

'So what do you want?' I asked.

'A glass of whisky would be well appreciated.' He slid onto one of my chairs and glared at me with those piggy and penetrating eyes.

'Josh, would you oblige the inspector? There's makings in the cabinet over there.'

'I 'ave good news,' he said without a change in his expression. 'Your worries with the Institute are over, *finir.*'

'Oh, why's that?'

'The little cemetery. Yes, the little cemetery. You see, Minister Quiberon put some people to work analysing the data Mr David Carter kindly supplied. They found sufficient grounds to acquire a court order to search and seize.' His ugly face slowly encouraged a smile to show.

'And?'

'Three of the coffins contained more than one corpse. Interesting, no?'

'Yeah. So what's happened, like ... I mean, what happened to Ms Morningblood?'

Josh handed the inspector a glass of whisky.

'Once we were able to find due cause, we tore the place apart. The inmates quickly gave much verbal evidence and led us to uncover the entire network.'

'So what were they up to?'

'The innocent women who had answered their advertisements were taken and given all that was promised. You see, pregnant and poor or frightened girls fell for the confidence tricks of the Institute. Their pregnancy was taken care of, but then they were forced to produce more babies, if the woman was up to it.'

'Really, why?'

'There is a market for healthy babies and of course some were sold for spare parts. Some of the women were also used for spare-part surgery.'

'You're kidding!'

'What about my sister?' demanded Josh.

'The young lady in question is in Ottawa General Hospital. She is fine, but many young women were not so lucky.'

'So where's Ms Morningblood?'

'She has been arrested along with her husband. I should think they will spend a long time in the penitentiary.'

'And your job?'

'My job is over. I spent many years trying to penetrate this place and with your assistance, they finally became careless enough for you to place them in my hands.'

'I thought you were fired?'

'No, just a little ruse to convince you to assist me.'

'And Jenny Stilton?'

He pouted for a moment. 'Well, I think this must have been the beginning of the end. The O'Brien brothers, though criminals, were innocent concerning her demise. From what I gather, she escaped by swimming out to Dr John Bromley's aeroplane when she heard he was taking a heart to Owen Sound.'

'So how did she get on his boat?'

'Supposition only, but we think she hid there until the doctor was well clear, but the O'Brien brothers collected the boat and … well, you know the rest of the story.'

'So who killed the boaties?'

'Boaties?'

'The O'Brien brothers.'

'Oh, that's still under investigation, but my belief is

the Institute sent a few 'eavies to clean up any mess that Dr John Bromley may have left.'

'So am I off the hook?'

'Off the 'ook? My friend, you were never on it.'

'What about Ms Morningblood? Newf, I mean North shot the cow.'

'Oh, so that is 'ow she acquired that injury. Well, she 'as not made any complaints.'

'Really?'

I was happy to get rid of LePort, but nonetheless dissatisfied with the results. It really wasn't me who finished off the Institute. Monsieur François Quiberon was the one who had everyone arrested. Still, I guess that was his job.

'You look like something the cat mauled,' Newf said as he walked into my den.

'What?'

'If I didn't know better, I'd say you was finkin', but then again, you'd need a brain fer that.'

'I quit being a detective. I've had it up to here with bad guys.'

'Again, eh? I reckon if I 'ad a penny for every time yous quits, I'd be a millionaire.'

'You *are* a bloody millionaire.'

'See what I mean?'

'Oh, shut up, Newf. We'll get this Viking fiasco over and done with then, then …'

'Yeah? What?'

'I don't know. I think I'll give my new plane to Reggie and maybe settle down to be a regular businessman and father to my kids, what do you think?'

'Great, I'm wiv yah, as long as you don't go into that depression shit again.'

'Okay, it's a deal. We'll think of a business that maybe all of us can take part in.'

A couple of days later, Griffin came to me while I

was at lunch and handed me the mobile phone.

'I'm sorry, sir,' he said. 'But we have a most urgent phone call.'

'Hi, Reyner.'

'Ah, Mr Reyner. This is Mr Purvis of Purvis & Pringle Law Partners.'

'Oh, sure. What can I do for you?'

'I have received a most interesting offer for our mining company.'

'Yeah, like what?'

'Pembroke Mining and Explorations Company would like to purchase your gera device and the operating software to go with it.'

'Well I'm not so sure it's for sale. I'll have to talk to Dave Carter and see what he has to say.'

'The offer is most generous.'

'How generous?'

Purvis giggled for a moment. 'Well, they are offering ten million US dollars plus 5 per cent of anything they find in the first ten years.'

'Wow! I'll get back to you; keep them dangling.'

'Yes, I will. This has nothing to do with the claim we already have at Lake Opinnagau.'

'I'll check with Dave. See yah.'

I handed the phone back to Griffin and left the dining room immediately in search of Dave. I found him in the garage with the others.

'Dave,' I said, walking in unannounced.

He turned and grinned. 'We've nailed those Institute bastards.'

'Yeah, never mind that. Purvis phoned. He said he has a buyer for your gera and its software.'

'Okay, how much?'

'Ten mill, US, plus royalties.'

'So how much do I owe you?'

I shook my head. 'Considering all the fun we've had

together, let's say it's a company expense.'

'You're writing off what we owe you?'

'We're all part of one big, happy company.'

'Oh, wow! Okay, sell it. It's company property.'

I tried to make the arrangement to move all of us to the UK for the upcoming festivities, but … well, what with one thing and another, progress seemed impossible. I hate to sound miserable, but I felt as though I had lost control of my life. Gran seemed distant as now she had that twit with her all the time and he appeared to make most of the decisions for her. They wanted to get to Cromlet for another extended holiday and neither had any interest in the Viking project or, for that matter, the Institute. Edward had booked them both on a British Airways flight to Prestwick. Deloris decided she, the children and the nannies would fly first class to England by Air Canada and not in my plane.

At least it would seem I had a little control left, as I was still the commander of my own aeroplane. Newf, Glen, Josh, Dave and Paul would be coming with me and at the last minute Morag decided to come with us. Then of course we would meet up with John Magnus, my new grandfather's son, when we reached Norfolk. The plan was to fly to Gander, refuel and fly on to Ireland, then to Norwich Airport in England. Glen would be my co-pilot for the long flight. If all goes well, we should hook up with Reggie in Norwich.

The flight was long and tedious. I let Glen fly most of the way, as he seemed to enjoy it more than I did. Reggie was already at Norwich waiting for us when we eventually got through customs. I thought he would fly us, but instead he hailed a taxi and we were off to King's Lynn.

'So where's your chopper?'

'She's out on a run; my boy is taking her this

afternoon. We have a contract supplying oil rigs and it's keeping us quite busy.' He smiled at Glen. 'I hear you're a pilot.'

'Sure.'

'Do you fly windmills?'

'If it flies, I can handle it.'

'Yes, old bean, but are you qualified to fly?'

'Absolutely everything, from B-52s down to ultra-lights. Jets, props and even rockets.'

'Excellent, old bean. Would you be unemployed or looking for a good job?'

'I'm Bill's pilot. I guess you'd best ask him.'

I shook my head in surrender.

'So now you poach my pilots as well as my planes. Sure, you can have him. I had decided to lend you my new bird; you may as well have the driver to go with it.'

We arranged for Reggie to fly to Cromlet and collect the rest of the family for the ceremony at the Viking site. I thought William Tan might like to see some of the sights in Norfolk. Gran and my new granddad were only going to stay for the ceremony, then they were flying back to Cromlet. Deloris would stay with me and the children for a week or two; she wanted me to go to Cromlet before returning to Canada.

I phoned old Purvis to see what was happening on the home front. He was all bubbly and excited.

'There's excellent news, my boy,' he said, hardly able to get the words out for his excitement.

'So, what's the news?'

'They have done another drilling at the site up north and the assay was even higher than the first. The offer for the land and rights has been considerably increased. I have accepted it and now we are all very rich, or will be.'

'Will be?'

'Yes, as soon as the government approves. You see, I pushed them, leading them to think there were other offers. They have increased the bid to $100 million Canadian, for all rights.'

'Wow! Okay, you have my go-ahead.'

'There is one other piece of news.'

'Well don't keep me in the dark.'

'You reported to LePort that someone in Parliament was involved with the Cormorant Institute.'

'Yeah, so?'

'So, my dear boy, the mole has been uncovered. It turns out that an interoffice courier was reading and in some cases altering documents and communiqués.'

'Good, I hope they send him to a place well up north without an overcoat.'

After closing down the phone I couldn't help but grin. I could imagine the look on the gang's face when I tell them the good news.

Surprisingly, when I released the information it was received with a couple of grins and a slap on the back, then it was business as usual. So what's a few million dollars? I noticed that they had lost interest in King John's treasure hunt. Good, I'd had enough treasure hunting and detective work. I figured when I get back to Canada I'd start some non-dangerous business, one that excluded criminals, doctors, lawyers, government officials and anything that looks even slightly deadly.

The great day had arrived. Man! I really hate this kind of limelight. The excavation site was clearly roped off but you could see the boat, or at least what was left of it. Personally, I couldn't get excited over a load of old rotten wood, but apparently they had found ancient church artefacts, mostly in gold. It seemed such a shame that all that value was going to sit in the Norwich Museum. I really didn't need the fame but

Deloris, Morag and Newf thoroughly seemed to enjoy the attention and John Magnus, MA, BA, was at the height of his glory.

I asked, but the rest of the gang wanted to give King John's treasure a miss. Who cares? Personally I'd had enough with exploding fence posts. Besides, I don't think anyone or thing could find it after almost 1,000 years. There again, I really didn't want to spend all that money on another futile attempt and wind up looking stupid. Selling the device seemed the very best idea.

The mayor and his wife sat to the left of Deloris and I had the Bishop of Norwich to our right. These English people must be a very hardy bunch. The weather was cold and a brisk wind had its own mind. The outdoor proceedings were, to put it mildly, boring. The ITV cameras were everywhere and loads of newspaper people turned up.

His Grace, the bishop, gave a lengthy and boring speech about some geezer called King Edmund. Apparently, he was the king of Norfolk and was murdered by the Vikings over 1,000 years ago. Listening to him prattle on I began to have thoughts of murder about the bishop, but everyone else seemed to enjoy it. I kept smiling and nodding to the odd dignitary, and I do mean odd. Eventually, I had to give my rendering of how it all came about. I do so hate public speaking, but I did my best.

At the very end there was a shocker: I was presented with the keys to King's Lynn and John Magnus was presented with an honorary degree in archaeology from the University of Norwich. Thank goodness it didn't rain – that would really have made my day. With all the official proceedings over, we had a slap-up party out there in the field and eventually, after shaking hundreds of hands, I managed to get a lift back to the hotel.

The very next morning I met Newf in the foyer of

the hotel. He had a suitcase in each hand and was wearing his winter coat.

I stopped him and asked, 'So where the hell are you going?'

'I fort me an' Morag would take a cruise.'

'A cruise, are you crazy?'

'Well accordin' to you, yes. She wants to take the ferry to 'olland.'

I couldn't believe my ears. 'What's wrong with flying?'

'Your plane ain't 'ere, Reggie's busy an' Morag would like to see some of the country. Nah, if yah ain't got no objections, we'll be on our way.'

I shrugged and waved him on. Personally I wanted to get back to Canada, but Gran wanted me up at Cromlet and Reggie wanted me to give him a hand with planning the aerodrome he intended building.

About a week after the Viking fiasco Reggie popped into the office, where I was discussing the new runway with a building contractor.

He grinned all over his face and said, 'I'm doing a supply run this afternoon, would you like your first flying lesson in the big bird, old bean?'

'Sure, where we going.'

'I'm picking up supplies in Aberdeen then flying out to rig National North Sea Oil 308. I'll do all the landing, but I thought it just might be good practice for you flying out there and back.'

'Sure, great.' I told the builder I approved of what he had proposed and would get back to him tomorrow.

I can certainly see why Reggie likes his work. Landing on an oil rig in the middle of the ocean is quite exciting and the workers are most appreciative. I had no idea an oil rig was so big. It was like an island country unto itself. They had everything an ocean liner had, except the passengers. Apparently, the thing operated 24/7 and the dining room was always open. After a really nice tour of the rig by the captain himself, Reggie once again took to the sky.

'We'll head back to Aberdeen, via the Shetland Islands. Here, take the epi.'

Flying a helicopter is moderately easy as long as you are going in a straight line. I had tried to hover, but for some reason the thing wouldn't stand still for me. Reggie makes it all look so easy. Holding the controls and listening to the power of the mighty engines, I began to daydream about the future. No more detective work or even treasure hunting. I think I'd like to run a hovercraft business.

'Oh, look, there's someone in dire straits down there. Looks like they're shipwrecked or about to be.'

I looked where Reggie indicated and far below was a boat up against the cliffs on a small island. Immediately, Reggie took the controls and we rapidly descended almost directly over the boat in peril.

'I don't have a hoisting gear, but there's a beach just up the way. I'll put her down and we can go back and help those people, old bean.'

In moments, he accurately landed on a narrow beach and what I thought dangerously close to the cliffs. We left Sikorsky in charge and scrambled over the rocks to see if we could help the sailors struggling with the tide. When we got there the boat had broken up, but the two occupants of the small, doomed vessel had managed to offload several fairly large bundles.

'Need a hand?' yelled Reggie as we emerged over the rocks.

The two men did not seem overly surprised to see us. We helped them carry their rescued goods over the strewn rocks to the small beach where the helicopter was parked. Neither of the two characters could speak a word of English. Both looked quite shady in their dark, almost railway uniforms and little black peaked caps.

Sometime later, Jane Overland or to use her new name Jane Asquith, was sitting in her office at Reggie's little airport, when Reggie's son came rushing into the room.

'There's been a disaster,' he yelled breathlessly.

Jane looked up from her work.

'Why? What's happened?'

'The coastguard reported a helicopter hitting the cliffs up near the Shetland Islands.'

Jane turned pale. 'Oh my God. It's … it's not … it's not ours, is it?'

''fraid so. Looks like Dad didn't make it.'

Jane sank to the chair, her face ashen.

'They said there was two bodies.'

'Two? What about Sikorsky?'

Previous Bill Reyner stories

Fiend's Gold

On a remote island in the Canadian Georgian Bay there is much more than hidden gold. After inheriting a fortune, Bill finds himself stalked by the angel of death. Murder at every turn and no one to help. Discover how William Reyner earns his name and his fortune.

Mania

Cannibalism and carnage seem to be the order of the day. Joining a secret and unholy sect, Bill finds that he just might have feasted on the flesh of his latest girlfriend. How can he escape the clutches of these demonic characters?

Edinburgh Cuckoos

Lookout, rich people of the world, the cuckoos may already be in your nest. Bill's nose for gold leads him to Scotland and lots of trouble. Taking a holiday in the Highlands and at the same time trying to locate a missing person, Bill discovers a horror that has existed for centuries.

Damp Graves

What price second-hand bodies and parts thereof? Maintaining his Midas touch, Bill stumbles into a new horror and constantly remains one step behind the mastermind, while his friend Newf is one step ahead. Looking for a missing girl, Bill discovers a human spare-part market and becomes the quarry.

Lions and Christians

Bill discovers a remote hunting lodge in a northern Canadian lake, but what do they hunt? The horrors that await there grip William in a new and all-encompassing terror. It is so easy to get into the lodge but not so easy to get out alive.

The Canadian

Bill buys a hotel and gives up gold hunting, only to discover he has bought the ghosts of gold fever, which is infectious and dangerous. The hotel is the key to stolen bullion and the thieves want it all back.

The Dutchman

Buying a share in a helicopter company, Bill finds himself mixed up with an ancient cemetery and a Spanish galleon. A ruthless gang of gold thieves believe he is after them and take measures to prevent him from succeeding.

The Mermaid

Bill retires from gold and mystery hunting. Turning over a new leaf and along with his blushing bride, he is suddenly cast into an international smelting pot of secrecy, deceit and mutiny. Hounded by a motorcycle gang and the secret service, nowhere seems safe.

For details and insight into the William Reyner series visit www.billreyner.ca

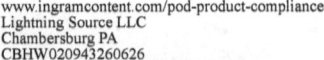